MAKE THE FIREFLIES DANCE

Make the FIREFLIES Dance

RACHEL
BATEMAN

RP | TEENS
PHILADELPHIA

Running Press Teens
Hachette Book Group
1290 Avenue of the Americas, New York, NY 10104
www.runningpress.com/rpkids
@runningpresskids

Printed in the United States of America

First Edition: May 2023

Published by Running Press Teens, an imprint of Perseus Books, LLC, a subsidiary of Hachette Book Group, Inc. The Running Press Teens name and logo are trademarks of the Hachette Book Group.

The Hachette Speakers Bureau provides a wide range of authors for speaking events. To find out more, go to www.hachettespeakersbureau.com or email HachetteSpeakers@hbgusa.com.

Running Press books may be purchased in bulk for business, educational, or promotional use. For more information, please contact your local bookseller or the Hachette Book Group Special Markets Department at Special.Markets@hbgusa.com.

The publisher is not responsible for websites (or their content) that are not owned by the publisher.

Print book cover and interior design by Frances J. Soo Ping Chow.

Library of Congress Control Number: 2023930531

ISBNs: 978-0-7624-7891-0 (hardcover), 978-0-7624-7893-4 (ebook)

LSC-C

Printing 1, 2023

For Holden Rhys, the best back roads companion
I could've asked for while plotting this book . . .
even if you did sleep the entire time.

I love you, Rooster.

PREFACE

PEOPLE SAY MEMORIES AREN'T RELIABLE. WELL, I REMEM-ber it like this: me and my mom cuddled up in a nest of blankets and pillows in the back of her rusty old Ford, the faint sounds of a bluegrass festival carrying to our ears on the warm twilight breeze. When the fireflies blinked to life around us, pinpricks of light flashing in the darkness, she pulled me closer.

I knew that, in the movie of my life, this night would forever be one of the standout scenes.

With the fireflies overhead, I told Mom about the game, the closet, my friends teasing me for not wanting to play. *It's just kissing*, they'd said. *It's not like you have to marry him.*

"I want it to be like the movies," I confessed. "I want butter-flies in my stomach and a love song playing in the background."

Mom squeezed me tight. "You'll get your perfect first kiss when you're ready, my girl. And it will be amazing and magical and everything you've ever wanted." She lowered her voice so it was barely more than air, "But don't wish for butterflies."

"Why not?" I twisted around so I could see her face in the quickly fading light. "I thought butterflies in the stomach . . ."

Mom let go of the hug, and we sat cross-legged, knee-to-knee. "Butterflies are flighty and nervous. You feel butterflies before you do something that scares you, right?"

I nodded.

"Butterflies are great if you're only having fun," Mom said, turning her face to the sky, a wistful smile spreading across her perfectly red lips. "But you want *love*, and love isn't butterflies."

She gestured me back to her, and I tucked myself under her arm. We lay back together, the soft pillows and blankets keeping us from feeling the cool metal of the truck bed. I fit perfectly against her side; it was my favorite place in the world.

"Fireflies are one of my favorite things about early summer," she said after a long moment. "See how gentle and warm and calm they are?"

"Um, yeah."

"That's what love is, Quincy," Mom said softly. "Love is the calming warmth of a firefly in your chest, the beauty of nights like this and the wonder of two people finding each other in the darkness of the world." She pointed across my body, and I followed her gaze. In the sky just beyond the end of the truck bed, two beads of light flashed at each other—a subtle Morse code in the dark. They came closer and closer, their patterns repeating one after another, until they met in the air and spiraled around each other to the ground.

"Don't go looking for someone whose kisses will set butter-flies loose in your belly," she said. "You want someone whose kisses make the fireflies dance."

"Did the fireflies dance when Daddy kissed you the first time?"

Her cheeks contracted into a smile against the top of my head. "Your daddy still gives me fireflies every time we kiss," she whispered. "And someday, you'll find someone who does the same for you."

chapter
ONE

"YOU'RE PUTTING THAT ONE UPSIDE DOWN." SHYLA'S VOICE echoes across the empty lobby. A quick glance at the poster in my hand—an old one-sheet for *The Long, Long Trailer*—confirms she's right. I quickly flip the poster paper around and drop it into the case.

"Thanks," I say over my shoulder.

"Where do you want this one?" Shyla's sister, Naoise, asks. She's holding my favorite poster. It's the one for *Too Many Girls*, the movie where Lucille Ball and Desi Arnaz first met. I gesture to the case at the end of the line, and she moves to insert it.

"How about Old Hollywood as our prom theme?" I ask as I attach a photo of my grandma on the set of *Mother of Stardust* between two posters. Naoise was elected to head the Prom Committee this year, and her first order of business was recruiting me, Shyla, and our other best friend, Hadley, to help.

I can practically see what Naoise is imagining as I tell them my idea: the red carpet leading into the prom, vintage film reels on the tables as centerpieces. We could rent the old Rialto Theater. It's even more gorgeous than the Orpheum, where we are now. The Rialto isn't a working theater anymore, and the open events center would be perfect for the dance.

Naoise nods slowly like she's considering as I finish with, "We could run a loop of scenes from famous old movies on a projector as a backdrop."

"Movies at the prom?" I jump at the sound of Tyler's voice. I didn't know he'd been listening. He had his earbuds in the last I noticed, bobbing his head to music as he prepped the concessions counter for the party. My face warms.

"Well, not with sound on," I stammer. "We'd play them silently for ambience. Like part of the decorations, you know?" I offer a small smile and mentally beg him to ask me to prom already.

"I like that idea," Shyla says. She's busy setting out gift bags on a table at the ticket booth. The bags are filled with mini bottles of bubbles, cardboard confetti poppers, and cheap noisemakers. Each guest will get one, so when we bring out Nana's cake, everyone is set to fully celebrate her eightieth birthday.

I turn to Naoise. "It could be fun, right? Can you imagine the outfits everyone would wear with a theme like that?" Appealing to Naoise's sense of fashion is the quickest way to get her on board. I already know what dress I want: a fluffy white tulle one Lucy and Ethel both wore to sing "Friendship" in a Season Three episode of *I Love Lucy*. Just without all the flowers and leaves. I've been begging Naoise for months to sew it for me, but she's so busy working on her portfolio for Lipscomb—not to mention her own prom dress, which she's already designed but refuses to show me until prom night—that she's not agreed. Yet.

Hadley rushes through the front doors, her breathing heavy and face flushed. "Sorry I'm late," she says. "Rehearsal went way over today." Hadley's dad, Pastor Starr, runs one of the biggest churches in Wilmington, and she plays guitar and sings for the church band.

"No worries," I say. "There's really not much left to do. You're still free to help with auditions tomorrow, though, right?"

"Yep! Wouldn't miss it."

"Auditions?" Tyler asks, and I jump at his voice again. We've worked together at the Orpheum for more than a year now, and I've had a crush on him practically since day one. So why am I suddenly so jittery around him? Maybe it's because of prom. He asked if I had any prom plans on our last shift together, and I got the distinct impression he was trying to feel things out.

He's staring at me, waiting for an answer, but for some reason I can't get my brain and mouth to work together. Thankfully, Shyla jumps to my rescue. "Our girl Q is holding auditions for her movie tomorrow afternoon," she says. "You should come. You're totally leading-man material. Don't you think, Q?" She smirks at me, one eyebrow cocked sky high.

"Yeah," I manage. "I mean, if you can act at all, that'd be awesome. I'm kinda nervous that not enough people will audition for me to fill all the roles."

"Cool," he says. It's not exactly an answer. He rounds the counter to join us in the main lobby. Standing close, it's easy to see how much taller than my five feet, two inches he is. I look up at him, and he tilts his head down, a smile crossing his face. I know my friends are all watching, but they fade from my mind along with the rest of the lobby. In this moment, there's nobody here besides me and Tyler.

His gaze flicks to my mouth, and I can't help but lick my lips. Holy cow, is he going to kiss me? I mean, he wouldn't, would he? Right here in the middle of the theater as we set up for my nana's birthday party? I feel like we've been getting closer to this for months, but it all seems so sudden and out of the blue.

He reaches a hand toward me, and I involuntarily lean closer. Then he pats me on the shoulder like I'm his little sister and says, "Thanks, Quin. I'm gonna run upstairs and make sure the projector is ready," before loping off toward the stairwell door marked Employees Only.

As soon as the door clicks shut, Shyla dissolves into a fit of laughter. "Oh . . . my . . . gosh," she manages between giggles. "You looked like you were going to swoon right onto the floor. Should we find you a fainting couch so you can lie with one hand on your forehead for a while?"

"Ugh," I groan. "Why am I such a doof?"

Hadley hops up to sit on top of the counter and grabs a handful of caramel corn from the display Tyler just filled. Swinging her legs in front of the candy case, she pops a piece into her mouth and says, "Because if you weren't, you wouldn't be you, and we love you."

"Thanks for that," I say. "Anyway, changing the subject. What do *you* think about Old Hollywood as the prom theme, Hads?"

She looks quickly toward Naoise and then back at me. "I like it. How about you, Neesh?"

Naoise steals a piece of Hadley's popcorn before answering. "I dunno. I mean, it's better than anything I've thought of so far. Which is exactly nothing. But I'm not totally sold on it."

"Come on, Neesh. You know you love it," I plead. "Plus, it'll be perfect. You'll see. Tyler will finally ask me in some amazingly adorable way. My dress will be perfect"—I tilt my head down to look over my glasses at her—"hint, hint. And we can all go in a big group with our dates and take pictures. It'll be like a movie premiere. We'll set up a red carpet with velvet ropes and everything. Dinner will be delicious, and then we'll dance the night away. And when he takes me home at the end of the night, he can finally give me my first kiss." My stomach flitters just thinking about it.

"Not your *first* kiss," Shyla interjects.

"First," I repeat, throwing her a cutting look. I never should've told her about Ezra and the closet. Everyone at that party back in eighth grade assumed I'd chickened out and didn't go through with it, and I'd let them believe it. Because my first kiss wasn't supposed to be like that. It was supposed to be perfect, incredible, magical.

Only recently had I told Shyla the truth. Me and Ezra, in Hannah Metcalf's closet, for the longest seven minutes of my life.

"We don't have to," Ezra had said, softly.

"I know," I snapped. He didn't seem to want to be in the closet any more than I did. We were practically brother and sister at that point. Our mothers had been close since even before we were born, and we'd always been a part of each other's lives. I'd seen him barf. He used to think it was funny to sit on me and fart—and I'd done the same to him. We were way too close for anything romantic. So when the girls wanted to play this game at the party, of course *his* would be the name I pulled from the bowl.

We sat on the small closet floor facing each other and played Rock Paper Scissors for a few rounds. I could hear sounds from the party on the other side of the door. Girls laughed, and one of the boys yelled, "Dude!" incredulously.

Someone called out, "One minute left, lovebirds. Better start putting your clothes back on," and the room exploded in laughter. My cheeks flamed, and I stared at the diamond-shaped space between our crossed legs. I noticed Ezra's deep olive skin standing in stark contrast to my pale, freckled knees.

"Hey," Ezra said. He pushed my hair back behind my ear. "Forget them."

Then he kissed me, the softest flutter of his lips across my own. My eyes drifted shut, and I leaned toward him without a thought.

But before the kiss could turn into anything more than a whisper of a touch, he jumped to his feet and covered his lips with his fingers.

"Hey, what's—" I started, but then the door swung open and the light from the main room flooded in. I squinted against the brightness.

"Y'all having a good time in here?" Hannah asked with a smirk.

"Fine," Ezra said, pushing past her and going to sit between two guys on the futon. I stared after him, and when he didn't even glance in my direction, I stood and ran from the closet and up the stairs. I hid in Hannah's kitchen for as long as I could before slinking back down to the party, curling up in the corner of the giant sectional sofa.

Ezra didn't look at me for the rest of the night.

chapter TWO

"QUINCY," HADLEY SAYS, "HAVE YOU BEEN KISSED? I CAN'T believe you didn't tell us!"

"No," I say firmly and cut my gaze to Shyla, swearing her to secrecy with a look. "Shy's just . . . being weird."

"Whatever," Shyla says.

"Anyway," I insist, "it'll be perfect, don't you think?"

Naoise looks at me, a weird expression I can't identify on her face. "What if it doesn't go like that?" she asks. "What if Tyler doesn't ask you or it turns out that dinner sucks? What if at the end of the night he drops you in front of your house and drives away? You can't storyboard the perfect prom night, Q. Not when other people are involved."

"Ladies and gentlemen, I give you my sister, Naoise, supreme cynic." Shyla sweeps her arms in an arc as if she's introducing Naoise as a pageant contestant.

"Not cynical," Naoise says. "Realistic. Love isn't something you can plan for or control every aspect of. Sometimes love just happens. Maybe instead of planning your entire prom night, Q, you should wait and see how things unfold on their own."

I shrug noncommittally. "Yeah. Maybe."

Shyla smirks at me, and I'm sure she's about to tell every-one about *the* kiss. There's no reason to keep it from them, but I've built up this idea of what a first kiss should be like, aided by watching dozens of romantic comedies. And the one thing I know a first kiss *isn't* is a barely-there brush of lips on the floor of a smelly closet. If I pretend like it never happened, then when I get my *real* first kiss, it can be the perfect rom-com moment I know it will be.

The door to the stairwell swings open with a groan, and Tyler saunters back out. "All right," he says. "Everything is good to go here. When's this shindig starting?"

I pull my phone from my dress pocket and check the clock. 6:38 p.m. "People should start showing up in about twenty," I tell him.

At that moment, I hear the theater's main door open behind me, and Shyla says, a bit too enthusiastically, "Oh, hey, Ezra! What are you doing here?" She looks at me with barely contained glee, and I groan softly. What *is* he doing here?

"Oh, um . . ." He shuffles his feet a bit. "I'm helping my mom?" He says it like a question.

"Oh, right." Of course. His mom runs Sage & Zest Catering. When I called to see if she would be interested in doing the food for Nana's eightieth birthday, she was more than happy to help. She even insisted that I only pay for ingredients and not her time on the condition that I could provide wait staff. That's why I had roped my group from film class into helping. I bet she asked Ezra to come so at least one of the servers would have experience.

"I'll show you where she's set up," I tell him, and he follows me through a door opposite the stairwell.

Inside the small kitchen, I'm hit with the most amazing smells. The countertops are covered with trays of Nana's favorite foods: lobster rolls and cucumber sandwiches; mini key lime pies; berries and cream with a tiny sprig of fresh mint on top placed in little crystal bowls. Trays of meatballs and stuffed mushrooms sit on the counter, ready to go into the oven. A long table holds flutes of sparkling cider. I didn't even think about appropriate drinks, and I'm touched that Ezra's mom remembered Nana is a recovering alcoholic and brought cider rather than champagne.

A petite woman with a mess of wild curls piled on her head squats in front of the oven. When she hears the door close, she turns around, and her face lights up, her teeth bright in contrast to the dark olive skin she shares with her son.

"Oh, Quincy, you look beautiful!" She rushes across the room and pulls me into a bone-crushing hug. I feel a tug of something deep in my stomach as I melt into her. Her hug is almost as familiar to me as if she were my own mother.

"Thanks so much for doing this, Lylah," I say into her curls. "Everything looks and smells amazing."

She lets go of me, holding me back at arm's length. "Not a worry at all, baby girl. I'm so happy you asked me."

Guilt. That's the feeling gnawing at my stomach. Lylah's been like a second mother to me my entire life. My mom's best friend, she was always around while I was growing up, her and Ezra joining our family for all our important moments. She's tried to recreate that since Mom's accident. She reaches out, invites me to dinner, to a movie, just to talk. I know she and Dad still see each other often and that Dad goes to Ezra's lacrosse games and orchestra concerts. Ezra's dad left his family when Ezra and I were so young—I don't even remember him—and Dad happily stepped in to be a father figure to Ezra in his place.

But it's too hard for me. The few times I've joined them, the two families spending time together like we used to, all I can see—all I can feel—is the gaping hole where my mom should be.

"What do you need me to do?" Ezra suddenly blurts out, and Lylah startles like she'd forgotten he was there. She glances at him and then back at me, the surprise at seeing us together showing on her face for only a moment before it's replaced by complete elation. I guess I'd never thought about how me and Ezra drifting apart affected her too.

In an instant, Lylah shifts into efficiency mode, directing her son to get the food onto the proper serving trays. I used to love hanging out at events she was catering, watching as she led her full crew.

When Ezra's dad left them, Lylah was a stay-at-home mom with no way to support her small family. It was my mom who suggested she start Sage & Zest Catering, pushing Lylah to come up with a business plan and recipes and then paying for the equipment and start-up supplies to get the company going. That's how my mom was—always encouraging and generous. She believed it was a waste for her to make so much money if she wasn't using it to help others. Now, fifteen years later, Sage & Zest Catering is one of the most popular companies in Wilmington, North Carolina.

Once I've been assured, twice, that Lylah and Ezra have everything under control, I push the door open to the lobby— and run directly into a body.

"Oh my gosh, I'm so sorry," I say, taking a step back. Looking up, I see who I collided with and freeze when I see Kenyon, a guy from school. "What are you doing here?"

"Wow," he says. "Nice to see you too, Walker."

Kenyon moved here in October, partway into senior year, and suddenly he was the new golden boy in Mr. Welles's class. The rest of us had to work our way up, starting with Basic Video Production to prove our skills before we were allowed into Advanced Film. I was already halfway through writing *Maybe, Probably* for my senior project when he showed up in class. I put in the hours, and I did the work, and he was able to drop right into class like he'd been there from the start.

"Seriously," I say, glaring at him, "this is a private event. You can't be here."

He grabs his chest dramatically like he's been shot. "You wound me, Q."

"Don't call me Q."

"Apologies, Miss Walker."

"Oh, shut up." I lean around him and see that a couple of early guests have arrived. I don't have time to deal with Kenyon's crap. I move to sidestep him, but he shifts to block my way.

"What is your deal? Move!"

He holds his hands up to his shoulders. "Relax. I'm here to help."

"Right. *You* want to help."

"*Want* isn't exactly the word I'd use. I was under the impression this was a mandatory event." At my bewildered expression, he says, "In class today? You told us we all needed to come help since your dad and grandma got us the camera to use for the movie."

I groan. He's right. Dad and Nana used their connections at the University to get us a loaned Blackmagic camera for filming, and I used *that* to rope everyone into coming to help tonight so we didn't have to pay Lylah's serving crew.

"Okay, fine, whatever. Go wait for the food to be ready. Ezra can show you what to do." I gesture to the kitchen door then move around him and back into the lobby.

Hadley chats with some guests while leading them over to the donation table. When I told Nana I wanted to plan her big birthday party, she was adamant about not wanting any gifts. Instead, I put a request on the invitations for donations to the scholarship Nana and Dad set up in Mom's name. The Desiree Hunt Foundation scholarship pays full tuition to UNCW for a deserving student of Film Studies. I hope to raise enough this year to add a film festival prize that will cover the entry fee for students who can't afford it.

"Thanks for coming," I say as I cross the lobby toward a couple. I recognize them from Sunday breakfast with Nana a few weeks back. They live in her condo complex. "My nana will be here soon, and the caterers have appetizers coming out any minute now. We also have popcorn, drinks, and candy over at the concession counter. Feel free to look around"—I gesture at the lobby where, interspersed between the movie posters, we've put pictures of Nana's life—"or if you want to sit and relax, you can head into the theater, where we'll be showing *Beloved of the River* at about eight o'clock."

"Thank you, dear," the woman says.

"Was your grandmother really in the movie?" her husband asks.

I beam and nod. "She was! It's not a big role, but it was her first, and it's what made her fall in love with film."

The man looks pleased and seems ready to speak again, but then Ezra breezes into the room with a tray of steaming mushrooms on a platter.

"Heard we have guests already," he says with a smile, crossing to us and offering the tray. "Would you like a stuffed mushroom? They're hot and delicious." His eyes flick to me before returning to the couple.

The man declines, but his wife grabs a mushroom, along with the small napkin Ezra offers. Before Ezra walks away, I snag a mushroom for myself and then survey the room. My eyes find Naoise, and I'm about to head her way when I see the door opening for Dad and Nana.

"Happy birthday!" I call and rush over to engulf Nana in a huge hug. Nana is my hero. She's a cold, sassy old broad, but beneath it all, she has one of the softest, kindest hearts I've ever known. She's always made time for me, even when I was younger and she was still working regularly. When my parents got married, she totally embraced my mom, helping to fill the hole left behind by her own parents, who disowned her when she chased her dream of becoming an actress. She's the one who helped me convince Mom and Dad to get a cat when I was five . . . and then kept it herself when it turned out I was allergic. Huge softy.

When Nana was seventeen, she lied about her age so she could get a job at an eighteen-and-over revue, and before long, she was taking on more stage shows. She started out only sing-ing and dancing as part of the chorus, but the more she went on, the more she knew she wanted to act. One night, the producer for *Beloved of the River* came to the revue looking for girls for some smaller roles, and she insisted he give her a shot. He did, and the rest, as they say, is history.

"Quincy, this is amazing," Nana says. "Thank you so much."

I give Dad a quick hug and kiss on the cheek before saying, "There's a couple people here already, and I'm sure everyone else will show up soon. Ezra and Lylah already have food com-ing out. The mushrooms are amazing." I look back at the door, realizing no one else is with them. "Where's Clark? I thought he was coming with you."

Dad shrugs. "I thought so too. But he never came by the house." Sensing my growing annoyance, he quickly adds, "I'm sure he got caught up with his classes and work and will be here in a minute. You know Clark isn't one to show up early."

More like he isn't one to show up at all. Over the past few months, my brother has been coming to family events less and less, but he promised me he'd be here tonight. Whether he fol-lows through remains to be seen.

Before I let my annoyance with Clark ruin my mood, I give Nana another quick hug and direct her and Dad to go look at the pictures we set up. By now, a steady stream of people has arrived to celebrate. I recognize more people from Nana's condo complex along with several of her colleagues from the UNCW film school. I stand a little straighter and smile welcomingly at them. It never hurts to mingle for a bit. These will be my professors starting in the fall, and I want to make a good impression.

An hour later, I excuse myself from a conversation with Nana's embroidery circle—the Stitch and Bitch group, as Dad calls them—and make my way to my friends, who stand in a loose circle. "Have y'all seen Clark yet? I want to make sure he's ready for the family toast and stuff."

Naoise grimaces. "He's not here."

"What? The party started almost an hour ago. Are you sure?"

She nods. "I've been watching for him. Ezra told me his mom wants to talk to Clark when he gets here. But he hasn't come in yet."

Anger ignites inside me, hot, fast, and intense. This is just like my brother, to skip an important family function. I don't know what's up with him these days, but I'm sick of him missing family dinners and failing to visit Dad and me. It's not like he lives far—he shares an apartment downtown with his friend Eric. It takes barely fifteen minutes to get to our house from his place and less than that to get to the theater. He should be here. He *promised* he would be here.

"That little—"

"Maybe he's running late?" Shyla says.

"He said he'd be here before it started. This is more than a little late." My knuckles whiten around my phone. "I'm calling him."

I storm off, already pulling up Clark's name on my phone. It's too loud in here with all of Nana's friends talking, and a bunch of people are already mingling in Theater One, waiting for the movie to start, so I head to the opposite side of the lobby toward Theater Two. I pass Tyler talking to Marcus and Donovan, two guys from film class, and I force a tight smile onto my face as I rush by the group and push my way through the door into the quiet theater.

The room is almost entirely black, my phone screen a beacon in the dark. I mash my thumb against the call icon and hold the phone to my ear. Irritation brews with each unanswered ring. Right before the voicemail picks up, filling my ear with Clark's annoying voice, someone grabs my hand.

I drop my phone with a yelp, watching as it bounces off a theater seat then lands face down on the ground. What little light the screen gave to the dark room is snuffed out.

"Hey, it's okay," a soft voice says, and my rapidly beating heart calms with the words. The hand surrounding mine squeezes gently. "Sorry. It's me."

Who is *me*? I dig into the recesses of my mind, trying to place the voice with someone I know, but it's impossible to connect this deep, soft whisper to anyone familiar. The guy's thumb slides softly over my inner wrist, sending a ripple of goose bumps up my arm and across my neck.

Tyler? I ask. Or I try to ask. It's the only thing that makes sense, the lone name my confused brain can conjure up. But all I get out is "Ty—"

Because then the hand pulls gently, urging me a step closer, and the other slides to the back of my neck and tangles in my hair at the same time as lips press to my own, warm and soft.

I open my mouth in surprise, and he pulls back for the briefest moment before kissing me again. The kiss is gentle and slow, the softness of his mouth at odds with the strong passion of the embrace. What. Is. Happening?

The guy lifts me to my toes as he deepens the kiss. When his tongue slides across my lips and explores my own, my heart trills in excitement. Without thinking, I raise my hands and cup one around the back of his neck, my pinky finger feeling soft hair. My other hand flattens onto his chest.

I don't totally know why but I kiss him back, pulling his lower lip into my mouth and gently nibbling. I saw that in a movie once, and I'm suddenly ridiculously happy I watch so many romantic comedies. Those things are like kissing lessons rolled into ninety minutes of swooning and laughter.

My body is electric with excitement, and my pulse pounds beneath his touch on my back. This is what I've been missing. It feels freaking amazing. I could keep kissing forever.

He moves his lips from my mouth and trails them along my jawline to my neck. I let my head fall back, the movement coming naturally as if I'd done this a thousand times before. In this moment, it feels like I have—like this guy and his kisses are as familiar to me as my own reflection in the mirror.

Gentle lips press against my collarbone, and a soft, deep moan rises in my throat. He stills. His lips are on my skin, but he doesn't move.

"Um," I say, but no words follow. I mean, what do you say when someone kisses you senseless with no warning, then freezes statue-still? Nothing, that's what.

He pulls his hand out of my hair and lowers me so I'm standing flat on the ground. Then he lets go of me completely.

"What—" I start at the same time as he says, "I'm sorry," his voice a choked whisper. He rushes past me, his arm lightly grazing my shoulder as he goes. I hear the theater door whoosh open, light from the lobby spilling in, then fall back, blanketing me in darkness again. I'm all alone.

What on earth just happened?

chapter
THREE

"WHERE DID YOU GO?" HADLEY ASKS WHEN I EMERGE FROM the theater a few minutes later. "We've been looking everywhere for you."

I hold a hand to my lips, which are still tingling from the kiss. Even after standing in the dark room trying to compose myself, I can't quite process what happened in there.

"Yo," Shyla says, snapping her fingers. "Earth to Quincy."

"Were you able to get a hold of Clark?" Naoise asks. Her question snaps me back to reality as I remember how mad I am at him. I look around the lobby, where only a handful of people now mingle, and shake my head.

"Where is everyone?" I ask.

Hadley cocks her head like she knows I'm holding something back, but she doesn't press the issue. I've been friends with Hadley longer than anyone else—ever since we met in first grade—and she can easily read my *later* look.

"They all headed to the theater," Had says. "The movie's going to start in a bit. That's why we were looking for you. Your dad said something about toasts?"

"Right," I say. "Shoot. Yeah, I need to do that. I can't believe Clark couldn't even be bothered to—"

Before I can finish my thought, the front door swings open and my older brother strolls in like he doesn't have a care in the world.

"Where have you been?" I shriek. I cross the lobby to him, and through gritted teeth I say, "The party started an hour ago. Where the *hell* have you been?"

"Relax, Q," Clark says, completely unrepentant. My anger spikes even higher. "I'm here now. You said the toasts would be right before the movie, so I came for that."

"Classic Clark," I spit out. "Showing up for the bare minimum. Heaven forbid you be with your family for a second longer than you absolutely have to."

Hurt flashes across his features, but it's gone almost before I see it. His jaw tightens, the muscles jutting out on the sides of his face.

"Are we going to go wish Nana happy birthday, or are we going to stay out here so you can lecture me all night?" His words roil with sarcasm when he adds, "I'm good either way, but if you're going to keep on with this tirade, can I at least grab a chair? I'm exhausted."

I don't answer but spin around and march toward Theater One. His footsteps sound behind me. My friends stare at me, and I shake my head, silently stopping any questions. Together, we enter the theater, and I do my best to put on a happy, normal expression. Nana hates when we fight, and I don't want her to know we got into it at her party.

When Nana sees Clark, she pulls him into a tight hug, and he winces a bit at her touch. Jerk. She doesn't seem to notice, though. I glance around the room, taking in all the guests, wondering if I'll be able to tell who kissed me with only a look. Kenyon and Donovan lean against the side wall, talking in hushed voices, while Ezra and Marcus huddle in the back row, heads bent together so they can see whatever's on Marcus's phone screen. I scan the room for Tyler but can't find him anywhere.

Dad calls for the guests to settle into their seats, and we give our toasts. Dad talks about how lucky he was as a child, saying people think it's unfair to be raised without a father, but he never noticed because his mom was so incredible that he never felt the hole his dad left behind.

I can't help but watch Ezra's reaction to Dad's speech. I knew Nana was a single parent and that Dad never knew his father, but I never made the connection between his childhood and Ezra's until now. I wonder if Dad has always taken such an active part in Ezra's life because he knows what it's like to be a kid without a father.

Clark is, as always, incredibly charming. He jokes and teases, making cracks about Nana's age and her stubbornness. At the end, though, he grows somber.

"She's my biggest supporter," he says, "my secret keeper, my advice-giver. Nana, you're my best friend. Happy birthday."

A lump rises in my throat, and I'm afraid I won't be able to speak for my own turn. I can't believe it. Clark—my big brother, my protector, my onetime best friend—is back with us in this moment. Not the hard, cynical Clark-clone who skips family functions and doesn't care who he hurts. The Clark who spoke so passionately and kindly about Nana is the brother I admired fiercely growing up. My heart twists with how much I miss that version of him.

I peer up to find Dad gesturing to me with a *Come on, Quincy* look on his face. I swallow hard and clear my throat with a nervous chuckle.

"Hi," I say. "First, I want to thank you all for coming to help celebrate Nana's birthday with us. You all know how amazing Vivian Walker is. You wouldn't be here if you didn't." My eyes catch Nana's, and she smiles.

"Nana, you gave me my love of movies. People always think because Mom was an actor"—I choke up unexpectedly, and I have to take a moment to swallow back my tears—"Sorry. People think I love film so much because of who Mom was, but it was you, Nana. All those weekend mornings curled up with you watching old Lucille Ball movies made me the person I am today. I fell in love with Lucy, and I fell in love with movies, all because of you. You also taught me to be brave. You taught me to stand up for myself. You taught me that my size doesn't have anything to do with the amount of power I have, that I am as strong as anyone. You taught me that we short women are simply more concentrated awesome than the rest of the world."

A few chuckles sound around the room. "You taught me to never be embarrassed or ashamed for what I want, to never apologize for my ambition, and to always, always follow my dreams. Thank you, Nana. I want to be just like you when I grow up."

There's applause, and Nana stands to pull me into a bone-crushing hug. Over her shoulder, I see Clark. His face is soft and unguarded as he watches us. This is the brother I've missed, and I hope this glimpse of the old Clark is the beginning of him coming back to us.

"I'm exhausted," I say as Shyla and I both dump the contents of our dustpans into the trash. Cleanup is finally done. After the movie—the theater erupted in wild applause when a young Nana first walked on screen—we had cake and sparkling cider, then people stayed to chat and mingle. I barely had a moment to breathe as I was swept from group to group to hear stories about Nana and her wild antics. The last of the guests left shortly before midnight, and I shooed Nana and Dad out the door when they offered to help clean. Clark surprised me by volunteering to stay too.

He pulls the bag from the trash can and ties it up quickly. "I'll drop this in the dumpster on my way out," he says. "Need anything else, Q?"

"No, I think we're done. Thanks so much for staying to help."

He grunts something that I think may be "You're welcome" or "No problem" before shooting me a quick smile and pushing his back against the glass door. I watch him disappear into the night.

As soon as he's gone, Naoise says, "How do I always forget how unbelievably hot your brother is?"

"Ew," I say.

"I thought you didn't care about guys like that?" Hadley says.

"I'm asexual, not blind," Naoise replies, not unkindly. "I can tell he's super hot. I'm just not attracted to him. Or, well, anyone."

Shyla nudges her sister with a hip. "Well, if you don't want him, then I can—"

"Shyla," I interrupt, "for the love of Lucille Ball, don't you dare finish that sentence."

She laughs her deep Shyla laugh, and her face tells me she was only teasing.

I check to make sure all the lights are off, then we walk to the front door and step outside. I'm locking up when Naoise says, "So are you going to tell us what happened tonight, or are we going to have to use our imaginations?"

"I'll tell," I say, "but not here. Tara's Diner?"

"I'll drive," Hadley offers, and we follow her to the Bronco and climb in. It wheezes to life, and the speakers blare The Levity Inn's newest album as we ride to our favorite all-night diner.

When we get there, we head straight to our usual booth. The overnight server waves at us from behind the counter, signaling that she'll be with us as soon as she's off the phone.

"Okay, spill," Shyla says. "What went on tonight?"

Before I can reply, the server's at our table with a tray of mugs filled with hot cocoa. She sets one in front of each of us and says, "Hey, girls. You need menus tonight?"

"Just the cocoa for me, thanks," I say. Shyla and Hadley skip food but Naoise orders chicken strips and French fries. She's basically a bottomless pit.

As soon as the server is out of earshot, my friends lean in, anticipation clear on their faces.

"Well?" Naoise prompts.

My cheeks heat up, and my stomach does this weird little flip-dip. It's like I can feel him with me still, his hand in my hair, arm wrapped tight around my waist. His lips soft but eager on my own. I can still taste him.

"Ohhhh, it's gotta be something good," Shyla says. "Look how red she's turning!"

"Okay," I say, and I take a deep drink of my hot cocoa before telling them about my first *real* kiss.

chapter
FOUR

WHEN I FINISH MY STORY A FEW MINUTES LATER, MY FRIENDS
stare at me, dumbfounded. Naoise holds a chicken strip halfway
to her mouth, apparently forgotten after my revelation.

"So, yeah," I say. "That was my night."

"Wait," Naoise says. "So, this random dude just, like, attacked
you?"

"No," I say. "It wasn't like that at all."

"Kinda sounds like it was," Shyla says.

I sigh. "Really, I promise. He didn't *attack* me. He just—this
isn't coming out right. But it was . . . I dunno. Nice? I felt safe."
I shrug, looking around at my friends, who all watch me with
varying levels of belief on their faces.

"Who do you think it was?" Hadley asks.

"I'm not sure." I twirl a spoon around on the table in front of
me. "It was too dark to see anything."

"Okay, but what did it feel like? What did you hear and smell?"

Shyla snorts. "She's not a bloodhound, Hads."

"Shut up, I know! But, like, when you lose one sense, don't
the others get stronger or something?"

"Yeah," Naoise cuts in. "I'm not sure that's a thing that happens in only five minutes."

"Well, I don't know. It could!"

"It all happened too fast for me to really pay attention to anything like that," I explain. "I mean, one minute I was preparing to tear Clark a new one, and the next, he was . . . there."

"Kissing you silly," Shyla interjects.

I touch a hand to my lips and nod.

"Okay, let's think about this rationally," Naoise says. She pushes her empty plate away and grabs a napkin. She rummages through her bag for a moment before emerging with a purple glitter pen. "Who all was at the party? I bet we can figure it out."

"There were, like, 150 people there tonight," I say. "No way we can name them all. Even if I go back to the guest list, I don't know who all was actually—"

"Slow down, turbo," she says. "I'm assuming it wasn't one of your grandma's old-man friends, right? I mean, he didn't seem old, did he?"

"Ew. Gross, Neesh!" A shiver runs up my back and *not* the good kind.

I think back, remembering the strong arm holding me up on my toes, the firmness of his chest under my hand. The softness of his lips and the tiniest bit of stubble that left the most deliciously chafed sensation in its wake.

"No," I say firmly. "He definitely felt younger."

"See, I told you that you could notice things without sight!" Hadley says triumphantly.

Naoise is scribbling on the napkin. "Tyler was there, obviously. And Ezra, Marcus, and Donovan were helping with the food."

"And that Kenyon guy," Shyla adds. "He was doing food too."

"Right." Naoise adds Kenyon's name to the list. "Okay . . . am I missing anyone?"

"Clark," Hadley says. "He was there."

"He's my brother! That's even worse than some old dude." I pretend to vomit into Shyla's lap, and she pushes me away with a laugh.

Naoise taps her pen in a rapid staccato. It leaves a tiny speck of glittery purple on the napkin each time it touches the paper. "So that's five guys. Do you remember anything specific at all? Maybe we can narrow this down a bit and figure out who your mystery kisser is."

She is living for this, I can tell. Other than fashion design and sewing, there are two things Naoise loves more than anything: mystery and romance. She practically has hearts in her eyes and a magnifying glass in one hand. It confuses a lot of people because they can't seem to compute how she can be both asexual and incredibly romantic, but I've never understood what they don't get. That's just Naoise. She's always been like this.

I register after a beat too long that she asked me a question. I think back, trying to recall anything specific. How tall was he? No idea. Was he wearing cologne? Um, maybe, but not anything I'd ever be able to place. Hair? Shortish, I think, based on what my fingers brushed at the nape of his neck. The only things I know for sure are that he seems strong and that he kisses like his life depends on it.

I tell my friends this and suddenly a thought occurs to me. "But, well . . . I couldn't find Tyler afterward."

"He was probably upstairs getting things ready," Shyla says. "Didn't this happen right before the movie started?"

"Yeah, but . . ."

"And it's not like he really wanted to hang out with your family and your grandma's friends. He was there to work, right?" Naoise adds.

My friends all know about my crush. It's not like I've exactly kept it quiet. I've basically fantasized about dating Tyler since we first started working together. Hadley thinks it's cute, but Naoise and Shyla have always been weirdly opposed to the idea. I don't get it—they have exactly zero reasons to *not* like him.

"That's the thing," I say, trying to figure out how best to explain this thought that's been brewing. "All the other guys *were* hanging out in the theater with the rest of the party when I came in."

"So?" Hadley looks genuinely confused.

"So . . . they were all in there acting totally normal. They were hanging out and talking and stuff. None of them looked flustered or embarrassed or . . . or . . ."

"Or like they just had a mind-blowing make-out session in a dark theater?" Naoise supplies.

"Exactly! Like, wouldn't whoever it was look awkward or nervous, or something? And none of them did. But maybe Tyler was. I dunno. I didn't see him again until the movie was over, and then it was only for a few seconds. Maybe he was embarrassed and avoiding me?"

"Maybe," Naoise concedes, but I can tell by her tone that she's not convinced.

Across the booth from me, Hadley leans her head against the wall, her eyes drifting closed. I watch as she fights it for a minute before calling it a night. We thank the server and pay our bill, then we help Hadley from the booth and lead her out to the car. Shyla digs the keys from Hadley's bag and tosses them to me before climbing into the back seat and pulling a seatbelt around an already snoozing Hadley. I coax the Bronco to life and drive us home.

Dad's still up when we get to the house, perched in his recliner in front of the TV watching some late-night documentary he's probably seen at least twice before. Dad's even more of a night owl than I am. I help get Hadley to my room then leave my friends to find pajamas and get ready for bed while I go back to the living room.

I squish into the recliner next to Dad and tuck under his left arm like always. It's an extra wide one, but even so, if I were much bigger, I wouldn't be able to fit on here with him.

I can still remember Mom's tinkling bell laugh when he brought it home.

"What is that thing?" she'd asked him, looking at it like she wasn't sure if she should laugh again or cry.

"It's a chair-and-a-half!"

"A chair-and-a-half," she repeated, deadpan. I looked up from my movie and watched her scrutinize it.

"Yeah," Dad said, red blotches creeping up his neck the way they did when he was embarrassed. "It's bigger than a normal chair but not quite big enough to be a love seat. It's a chair-and-a-half."

"You can't be serious."

"Really," he insisted. "That's what the tag read at the store."

"Okay, so it's a chair-and-a-half," Mom said. "But what is it doing in the middle of my living room?"

The thing about our house is, it's small—barely 1,200 square feet with three bedrooms and one bathroom, so the common areas like the living room didn't have the space to add a bulky leather chair-and-a-half.

Nana bought the house when she and Dad first moved to Wilmington. She was asked to come teach at UNCW in the brand new film school when it opened, and she jumped at the opportunity to have a permanent position that would allow her to be home with her son more often than she could as a working actor.

At the time, all the houses on the street were small like ours. But our yard backs up to the Intracoastal Waterway, so over time, the neighbors tore down their old houses to build newer, bigger mansions—the kind you see along the water all over Wilmington. Nana thought she would do the same some-day, but she actually liked her little house. Then, when Mom got pregnant with me, Nana bought her condo and gave this place to my parents. They moved in with Clark, and I was born here. It may be tiny compared to all the other houses around, but it's all I've ever known, and I love it.

In the end, Dad convinced Mom to try out the recliner, and she snuggled up next to him to watch a movie. By the end of the night, she'd agreed it could stay. It's been in the same place ever since.

Dad wraps one arm around my shoulders and pulls me to his side. "Good night," he says. "You did a beautiful job with the party, John." Dad thinks it's hilarious to call me John—as in John *Quincy* Adams? When Mom agreed to name me after his favorite president, I don't think she realized what she was getting into.

"Thanks, Dad." I love this spot next to him. We've spent countless hours curled up here watching documentaries together. Mom always made him put on something else, saying that if she was going to watch TV, she wanted to be transported to new worlds and take part in daydreams unfolding—not learning about history. But I love documentaries. I've watched them with Dad for as long as I can remember.

"What are we learning about tonight?" I ask, trying to make out the chaos on the screen.

"Peter the Great."

"Oh, is this the one where you learn that his court was basically like a nonstop bachelor party for years?" I knew it looked familiar.

"One and the same," Dad says. Dad's forte is US history, but he'll watch documentaries about anything.

We watch for a few minutes before I move to leave. "Are we still good to use the rehearsal space tomorrow?" I ask him. Dad reserved a space on campus for me to use for auditions rather than the high school auditorium. He also posted fliers around the film school buildings. I'm hoping it'll bring in some college students to audition and give me the best chance of finding the perfect cast for my film.

"Everything is set," he says. "Jerry is working the morning shift, so he'll be there to open the building and get things set up for you, okay?"

"Sounds perfect. Thanks so much for doing this."

Dad waves off my thanks. He's been my biggest supporter since day one, encouraging me to follow my dreams and paying for classes and books and more movie tickets than I could possibly count. He's cheered me on and watched every short film I've ever made—even the terrible early ones. Tomorrow's auditions are for my first full-length feature, a romantic comedy I'm submitting to the Cape Fear Student Film Festival in August. The winner of the festival gets $10,000 for their next project and an internship slot at Screen Gems Studios. I'd be the youngest winner ever, and I want it so bad I can taste it.

"I better get to bed," I say, working my way out from under Dad's arm.

"Are you sure you don't want to see how it ends?" he asks, a joke in his voice.

"Don't say up too late." I kiss the top of his head, where his hair is starting to thin, and head to my room.

chapter FIVE

THE NEXT THING I KNOW, I'M JOLTED AWAKE BY HADLEY trying to climb over me and out of bed.

"Sorry," she whisper-laughs. "I'm gonna pee my pants." She makes it off the bed and rushes from the room.

"What time is it?" Shyla croaks from her spot on the floor. Her eyes are barely open. Sunlight cuts across her face from the window opposite her.

I reach my hand under my pillow and pull my phone out.

"Holy crap!" I yell and scramble to get out of bed. A muffled "Wha . . . ?" sounds from the top bunk. It's 10:36 a.m. I have twenty minutes to get ready and get to campus. This is so not how I wanted to start this day.

"Get up, get up, get up!" I yell to Shyla and Naoise. "We gotta go, like, now!"

I start to pull on the same dress from last night, thankful that it still looks fresh, not crumpled, but then I remember Marcus is helping with auditions today. What if he was the one in the theater? I can't show up wearing my clothes from the party. I throw open my closet doors.

Hadley comes back into the room at the exact moment I find the perfect dress: long and flowy, it falls mid-calf and has tiny buttons all the way up the front and an oversized sunflower pattern. It was my mom's when she was my age, and it's one of my favorites. I pull a fitted short-sleeve crop top on, then slip the spaghetti-strap dress over it. I dig to the back of the closet and throw another dress to Hadley and shirts to Naoise and Shyla.

"We don't have time for y'all to go home, so you can wear these. Get dressed. We gotta go."

I twist my hair back into submission and poke some bobby pins in to hold it in place. It looks like a messier version of the updo I wore last night, and that works for me.

By the time I've got Mom's old Doc Martens on and finish brushing my teeth, everyone is ready to go, if still a bit bleary-eyed. It's ten minutes to eleven when we pile into Hadley's car and head toward campus.

The next hour passes in a blur. We rush to set sign-up sheets and scene copies on tables outside the Black Box Studio in Kenan Hall. I'm setting up my camera in the corner to record the auditions when Hadley breezes in with coffees for us. Her boyfriend, Tanner, trails behind with a box of pastries, which I take gratefully before they head back to the hallway to wait for the actors. Hadley and Shyla, my producers, will make sure things run smoothly today. I couldn't do this without them.

The first actors show up at 11:45 a.m., and nerves flutter in my stomach. I watch as the hallway fills with people. Giddy excitement bubbles up. I can't believe this is finally happening.

I started writing this movie script at the beginning of last summer. When school started, I convinced Mr. Welles to let me use it as my senior thesis—he agreed to let me make it a solo project if my group wanted to film something else, but thankfully everyone was more than happy to work on a script I'd already written. This is the most ambitious project I've done by far.

Promptly at noon, Shyla leads the first hopeful actor in to start the auditions for the role of Sebastian. I recognize Shane McAdams immediately; we've been in classes together since sixth grade. He was in the drama club's production of *My Fair Lady* last year and did a remarkable job playing Henry Higgins. He'd make a great Sebastian.

I check over Shane's audition profile briefly before setting it aside and saying, "Go ahead whenever you're ready, Shane."

Naoise steps forward to stand in for the Adalyn role so Shane can have a scene partner. She's been my audition stand-in since I cast my first short film after eighth grade. She's incredible, but she always refuses to be on camera in an actual film.

It's almost an hour before we get to the last of the Sebastian hopefuls, a guy who's apparently in one of my dad's classes at the

University. I have pages full of notes on my yellow legal pad, and Naoise's voice is hoarse from repeating her lines so often.

"Why don't we take a quick break before moving on to casting Adalyn." I stand and stretch, twisting my back until it makes a popping noise.

"Oh my gosh, thank you so much," Naoise says, bouncing on her toes. "I have to pee so bad."

"Neesh! We could've taken a break so you could go to the bathroom."

She shrugs and rushes to the door, calling over her shoulder, "It's all good. I just gotta go now!"

She pushes through the door, and I glance into the hallway. It's jam-packed with people. Some stand in small clumps talking and laughing, but I notice several holding script pages and mumbling lines under their breath.

Before the door swings shut again, I catch a glimpse of Hadley, a look of panic on her face. We stare at each other for less than a second before the door clicks softly into place. It's probably not a big deal—Hadley stresses easily. Still, I should check.

But before I make it to the door, it swings open, and Hadley slips through. She pushes the door shut behind her, leans against it, and sighs. "We have a problem," she says.

"Okay," I say, stretching the second syllable out way too long. "Like a *real* problem, or like a we-need-to-make-more-copies problem?"

"More like a we-don't-have-a-male-lead problem."

"Of course we don't," I say. "That's why we're doing this, Had. We just had auditions for that role. I'll figure out who to cast later." Maybe we should have gone straight home after the party last night instead of spending time at the diner. Hadley obviously needed the extra sleep.

"No, not that," she groans. "I mean Marcus. He was supposed to come stand in for the Adalyn auditions, right?" I nod. "He's not here. Shyla texted him, and I guess he's sick? I don't really know."

"Why didn't he tell me?" I say, pulling my phone from my back pocket to text him. I see a message on the screen.

MARCUS: Hey, Q. I'm not gonna be able to make it today. Sick. I'm so sorry!

The message was sent right before we started auditions, and I clearly hadn't felt my phone buzz. If I'd seen it then, I would've called one of the other guys. Donovan could've easily filled in. Even Kenyon if it came to that.

"What about Tanner?" I ask.

Hadley shakes her head. "He stopped by for a bit, but he had to go run some errands for his mom and won't be back for at least an hour."

I pull a deep, slow breath through my nose, trying to refocus. This isn't the end of the world. It's a setback for sure, but not one I need to let derail the day. "Okay," I say. "I guess we'll have Neesh read for Sebastian too. It's not ideal, but it's—"

The door flies open, interrupting my train of thought. This time, Shyla bursts in. "Ladies, I've solved all our problems. I present to you your lead actor." She flourishes grandly toward the door. "At least for today."

When nobody comes through, she reaches back into the hallway and grabs a forest green sleeve in her fist, tugging it and the guy wearing it into the room.

chapter

Six

"EZRA?" I SAY. "WHAT ARE YOU DOING HERE?"

He looks uncomfortable, a blotchy blush rising on his neck and cheeks. "Well, I was trying to take a shortcut back to my car, but apparently I'm needed in some sort of life-and-death situation here. You can let go now," he tells Shyla. She loosens her grip and steps back. Ezra's sleeve stays crumpled where she had it in her fist.

"Oh my gosh I almost wet my pants." Naoise runs into the room and slams the door behind her. "There are so many people here!" She stops short when she sees Ezra standing next to her sister. "Hey, what's he doing here? I thought we were done with Sebastian auditions."

"We are," Shyla says. "He's our stand-in for the Adalyn auditions."

"What happened to Marcus?" Naoise asks as Ezra simultaneously says, "What? No, I'm not."

I look around the room at my friends. Hadley stares at Ezra with a quizzical look on her face. She seems to have calmed. Naoise shrugs and crosses the room back to her seat

43

behind the table. Shyla beams at me, and Ezra stands at her side, confused.

"Could you?" I ask.

"Could I what? I'm not even sure what's going on here." Ezra looks sideways at Shyla, one eyebrow cocked.

I take a quick moment to explain the situation, then say, "So?"

"So what?"

"Can you stand in for Marcus so the Adalyn hopefuls have someone to run the scene with?"

"I don't—"

"I'll buy you dinner when we're done," I blurt out. "Please help us out."

Ezra sighs. "Fine. I'll do it. But I expect a PT's burger for this."

Shyla hugs Ezra tight, surprising him, and I bring him a scene printout. "Thank you for this. Seriously—you're saving us here."

He shrugs and reads over his part. "It really was life and death then, huh?"

Hadley and Shyla head back to the hallway to organize the next auditions, and after I guide Ezra to where he needs to stand, I join Naoise behind the desk.

Now that we're all set and waiting for the first actor to come in, what I just did starts to sink in. Dinner with Ezra? That's going to be weird. I can't imagine it being any other way. He wasn't only my first pseudo-kiss—he was my first best friend, my other half for so long. We did everything together as kids. Even though we went to different elementary schools, we saw each other almost every day when we went to his grandma's house in the afternoons until our parents got off work. He ate dinner at our house at least twice a week.

I mean, we slept in each other's *beds*. All. The. Time.

But since high school started, it's not been like that at all. I couldn't handle being around him anymore. Not after my mom. He tried for a while, calling me after school, approaching me in the halls, but I became great at avoiding him. And after a while, he stopped trying. I had Hadley, Naoise, and Shyla. Now, in the last semester of senior year, it's almost like we never knew each other at all.

So, yeah. Dinner is going to be awkward.

Our first Adalyn hopeful comes in and takes her place by Ezra. Naoise passes me the headshot and resume. Wow. This girl has some serious roles under her belt. Most people don't have much experience when they audition for a student film; she's the first one we've seen today who brought a resume on an actual honest-to-goodness headshot.

"Whenever you're ready," I say, setting the headshot on the table in front of me.

The girl reaches out and grabs Ezra's hand. He jumps a bit but relaxes quickly. "Sebastian, wait!" she cries. "Please, let me explain."

She's good. After one line, I can see her as Adalyn. I sit up straighter, eager to watch the rest of the scene.

Ezra stands, frozen to the spot, his hand clenched in his scene partner's as he stares at the sheet of paper in his hand. For a moment, I think he won't say his lines, that she'll have to act the scene alone, but then he looks up and it's like his whole demeanor has changed.

"Explain what, Addie?" he spits out. "Explain why I'm the only one who's ever actually been in this relationship? Or maybe you can, can"—his gaze drops to the script—"explain how you're embarrassed to be with me? Or, and this is the explanation I'd really like . . ." He takes a deep breath, and I swear his eyes flick to mine for a second. "Why don't you explain what twisted part of you got off on making me fall for you just so you could stomp on my heart?" He laughs, derisive, exactly how I'd imagine Sebastian in this part. "Because unless you're going to explain all that, Adalyn, I don't want to hear it."

The girl playing Adalyn has tears running down her face. Her voice breaks on her next line. I sit back in my chair and stare at the two of them, completely transfixed as I watch the rest of the scene unfold.

Too soon, it's over. I have goose bumps. Like, actual, literal goose bumps on my arms. I stare at them, slack-jawed. Beside me, Naoise does the same.

"Um," the girl says, "was that okay?"

I shake myself from my trance and check her headshot to remind myself of her name. "Yeah, um, Kira. That was . . . great. We'll be in touch."

"Thank you so much," she says and glides out of the room.

As soon as she's gone, Naoise and I explode in excitement, talking over the top of each other. Finally, I hold up a hand to silence Naoise and turn to Ezra.

"What was that?" I ask.

He twists his hands in his pants pockets. "Sorry. I knew it wouldn't be good. Does it work for auditions, at least?" The blush, which had managed to recede during the scene, is back full force now.

"Are you kidding?" I say. "That was . . ."

"Incredible," Naoise finishes for me. "Better than anyone we saw during auditions."

Ezra stares like he doesn't believe us. His mouth opens twice, but he says nothing. Then the door opens, and the next Adalyn hopeful enters.

Twenty-two girls read for the role of Adalyn, and Ezra's performance blows me away every single time. Even when he's paired with actors who flub their lines and have the stage presence of a soggy turnip, he embodies the Sebastian character one hundred percent.

After the last audition is over, I thank him for taking time to do this, and then I say, "We still have some smaller roles to cast, so I can pick you up for PT's when I'm done? Or just bring a burger to you?"

He shrugs. "I have some homework to finish anyway. I'll hang out and wait for you if you don't mind."

"Oh," I say, looking around the small room. "In here?"

He laughs, and it's the same laugh he's had his entire life. I wonder if I'm just as different and the same to him as he is to me. "Nah, I'll find a spot outside. See ya in a bit."

As soon as he's gone, Naoise spins toward me. "Oh my god, Q, did you know he could act?"

I shake my head. "I had no idea. I mean, we used to make movies as kids and stuff, but . . . not like that."

"He *has* to be your Sebastian!"

"He wasn't even auditioning. I'm pretty sure he only did it because Shyla scared him."

She grabs my legal pad from the table and fans through the pages before dropping it back down with a thud. "He was the best we saw."

She's not wrong. We had several promising auditions for Sebastian—at least three guys I would be happy to give the role to—but none of them held a candle to what we saw from Ezra. After seeing his performance, I'm struggling to remember what I saw in those other auditions.

"I think you should offer him the part," she says. "He's perfect."

"I dunno," I say. "What if he doesn't want it?"

"Make him want it," Naoise says. "You're taking him to dinner tonight, right? Convince him."

I sigh. "I suppose I can try."

Hadley pokes her head in. "Y'all ready for the next wave?"

I nod, and we take our seats again.

An exhausting two hours later, we've seen every person who came to audition. While finishing up, Hadley and Shyla clean the hallway, and we stash the chairs and tables back where they belong and head toward the parking lot.

"So, do you know who got parts?" Hadley asks as we walk out of Kenan Hall.

"I'm not totally sure yet," I say. "I have some ideas, but I need to go over my notes."

Ezra meets up with us about halfway to Hadley's Bronco. His overladen backpack is hiked up on one shoulder, and his hair sticks up on the side like he's been lying down.

"Hey," he says, looking awkwardly around at our group.

Oh, yeah, dinner. I totally forgot I'd promised to take him out. I look at him and then at the Bronco. "Hey. I, uh, don't have my car?" Why did that come out like a question? "So maybe we can, um . . ."

"I can drive," he says with a shrug. "I don't mind at all."

"Okay. I kinda have a lot of stuff though."

"No worries," he says. "The trunk is totally clear."

I hug my friends goodbye, thanking them for their help and pointedly ignoring their questioning looks between me and Ezra. "I'll text y'all later," I whisper before turning around and following him to his car.

The ride to PT's is maybe the most awkward seven minutes I've ever spent. Ezra and I both sit stiffly in our seats, neither of us sure what to say to the other. It'd be funny how little two people who used to share everything have to say to each other if it wasn't so painfully uncomfortable.

At the restaurant, we place our orders, and I wave off his offer to pay. "My treat, remember? You really helped me out today."

I slip the script I brought with me under my arm and press it to my side as I grab our drinks—sweat tea for me and lemonade for him—and then we make our way to the far end of the deck where there's a lone empty table. I put a cup in front of each of the chairs and then drop the script onto the middle of the table. It's dog-eared and obviously well-used. I've made directorial notes all over the pages until I had a clear visual of every beat, every scene, every movement the actors will make. This movie is as much a part of me as my skin and hair. My heart.

"It was actually pretty fun," he says as he sits. His back is to the railing, and I look past him for a second, watching the cars drive by as I gather the courage to say my next line.

"I'm glad you had fun because I want to offer you the part of Sebastian."

He stares at me for a moment that stretches into forever. "You're joking."

"Not at all," I insist. "Look, Ezra, you were amazing in there. We had a lot of good auditions for Sebastian, and you blew them all away with your performance."

He chuckles uncomfortably and takes a deep drink from his lemonade. "Okay, so I did decent with that one scene, but how do you know I won't completely fall apart with a full movie?"

"I don't know," I say, "but I also don't know that about any of the guys who auditioned today."

The man at the window calls my name, and I head up to grab our burgers. When I return, it's to find Ezra hunched over my beat-up copy of the script, brow furrowed as he reads.

I set his food to his right side before slipping back onto my chair with my own burger. He turns a page, eyes darting back and forth as he takes in the dialogue. I watch as he cocks his head to read a note I scribbled sideways in the margin.

When he turns another page, I can't stand waiting anymore. "Well?"

He raises a finger to silence me and keeps reading, his concentration intense. After a moment, he flips the script shut and leans back in his seat.

"It's a romance?"

I nod. "Romantic comedy, actually."

He's nodding with me, slowly. "So basically: boy meets girl, boy and girl fall in love, boy loses girl, boy pulls off some over-the-top gesture and wins girl back? Does that about cover it?"

The muscles in my shoulders and neck tighten as he speaks. I take a deep breath so my irritation doesn't show. "Actually," I say, "I like to think it has a bit more to it than that. And there's no big romantic gesture at the end of this one."

"But, basically, I'm right?"

I huff. "Yeah, basically."

Ezra holds up his hands, palms facing me in surrender. "Hey, I'm not knocking. You know I love a good rom-com."

Without warning, I'm overwhelmed with memories of the two of us, sometimes with our parents and sometimes without, curled up on the couch watching movies. One summer we discovered my mom's collection of romantic comedies and spent nearly every afternoon watching them. *13 Going on 30, Notting*

Hill, and *Never Been Kissed* were our favorites. We watched those three so many times I could probably still recite them.

"So, what's the meet-cute?" Ezra asks, bringing me back to the present.

"What?"

He looks at me like I've sprouted a third arm. "You know, the meet-cute. The moment when your girl and your boy"—he looks back at the script briefly—"Sebastian and Adalyn meet in some ridiculously cute way. You can't seriously have written a rom-com without a meet-cute!"

I roll my eyes. "Of course I didn't. I know what a meet-cute is. I was just surprised that *you* did. They meet when Sebastian's house-sitting for Adalyn's neighbor. The pet parrot gets out, and he's trying to catch it when Adalyn comes to see what's going on."

"And she helps him get the bird?"

"Naturally." I may have stolen the story directly from how we met Hadley's neighbor once. We came outside to find her standing on top of her Honda waving a piece of watermelon around at the tree branches.

"I like it," Ezra says. "It's weird."

"Gee, thanks," I say, but I smile to let him know I'm teasing. "Will you do it?"

He takes a huge bite of his burger—his first, I notice, while mine is almost gone already—and chews slowly. Then he takes a *long* drink of lemonade. He's doing this to taunt me, isn't he?

"Can I take this?" He picks the script up off the table and waves it in between us. "Maybe read the whole thing before I make a decision?"

"Yeah, sure, but can"—I wince when the corner of one of the pages gets dangerously close to the pile of pepper-laden ketchup Ezra has in front of him, and he laughs quietly—"oh my gosh, give that to me. I'll email you a copy, okay?"

"Good to see some things never change," he says. "You still can't stand not being in control of things, can you?"

"Shut up," I mutter. I slide the script safely to the edge of the table farthest from the food.

We finish our meals and I grab Ezra's cell number and email address to send the script his way. When we leave, I have him drive me back to the Orpheum so I can finally pick up my car, still left from last night.

Hours later, I'm lying in bed, replaying the auditions in my head, when my phone beeps.

EZRA: fine. I'll do it.

chapter
SEVEN

I WAKE UP SUNDAY MORNING TO A FLURRY OF TEXT MES-
sages. The first is from Nana, confirming our 9:00 a.m.
breakfast, as if I'd ever miss. We've been having breakfast every
week since Mom died.

The rest of the messages are part of an epic group text with
Hadley, Naoise, and Shyla. They've sent an ungodly number
already this morning. Hadley's up for church, I'm sure, but I'm
surprised the twins aren't still drooling on their pillows. I open
the thread and scroll to the top.

> **HADLEY:** So I was thinking and what if Ezra is your
> mystery kisser?
>
> **SHYLA:** Ohhhh that's very Dawson and Joey of them.
>
> **NAOISE:** Yeah. I'd ship that.
>
> **HADLEY:** Who are Dawson and Joey?
>
> **NAOISE:** Are you serious? Don't you ever Netflix?
>
> **HADLEY:** It's not like I've seen every show on there!
>
> **SHYLA:** Anyway. Was he flirty at auditions Neesh?
>
> **HADLEY:** Aren't you two together? Why don't you just
> ask her?
>
> **SHYLA:** Um that would mean I have to get out of bed and
> no thanks.

NAOISE: Plus then you and Q wouldn't get this awesome play-by-play of our convo.

NAOISE: Anyway he wasn't flirty. Like not at all that I saw.

SHYLA: Bummer.

They've been quiet for a few minutes, so I tap out a quick message telling them what's been in the back of my mind since Friday night.

ME: I really think it was Tyler y'all.

SHYLA: That's your massive crush speaking.

ME: No really. It makes sense. Nobody else makes sense.

NAOISE: I don't know. There were a lot of other guys there.

HADLEY: Maybe it was Marcus and he got embarrassed and that's why he didn't come to auditions.

She has a point. I hadn't even considered that maybe he bailed because he didn't want to see me after Friday night. But he seemed totally normal when I saw him later on Friday. Didn't he?

SHYLA: But isn't Marcus asexual? He wouldn't go kissing random girls, right?

HADLEY: He is?! I had no idea. Is he Neesh?

NAOISE: It's not like we have a club where we learn the secret handshake. How would I know?

HADLEY: Sorry. I wasn't thinking.

I set my phone on my bed and pad down the hallway to the bathroom. This chain will be going back and forth for a while and won't miss me while I shower.

It's almost time to leave when I get back to my room, so I get dressed and set to work doing my hair and makeup as fast as I can. Breakfast at Nana's really means breakfast at the café in her condo complex, where the residents are always dressed to the nines and tend to ask me if I'm feeling well if I don't have on a full face of makeup.

I scrunch some gel into my hair and twist it up in a loose French roll, letting a few curls fall free. I'm stabbing bobby pins in when my phone trills with an incoming video chat.

When I answer, it's to a split screen, Naoise and Shyla sharing one view with Hadley in the other. I recognize Hadley's dad's office at the church behind her.

"Hey," Shyla says, "you stopped texting."

"Yeah, sorry," I say around the bobby pin I'm holding between my lips. I move the phone to lean against the wall by my floor-to-ceiling mirror. There isn't room in here for a vanity, so I do my makeup sitting cross-legged on the floor.

"You'll have to watch me do my makeup. I gotta leave for Nana's in ten."

"What color today?" Naoise asks, and I know she's asking about my glasses. My collection of colored acrylic frames is legendary. Okay, maybe not legendary, but it is impressive.

"I was thinking of going simple and sticking with clear," I say. I set to work filling my brows. "So to what do I owe this privilege of a video call?" I let sarcasm lace my words. There's no way they would all three call me if they weren't cooking up some scheme I'm not going to like.

"Well, we were thinking," Hadley begins.

"That we are gonna set you up on a date!" Naoise yells over her.

"A date?"

Shyla leans closer to the camera, blocking Naoise's face from view. "More like five dates, actually."

I drop my mascara onto my lap, where it leaves a black streak across my bare inner thigh. "Five dates?! With who?"

"Whom," Shyla says.

I laugh, one short sound. "Yeah because that's the important part here. Who am I going on all these dates with exactly?"

Naoise elbows Shyla out of the way. Their screen shakes and spins as she grabs the phone and pulls it to her. She takes up the whole screen and is so close I can't even see to the top of her forehead.

"Here's the thing," she says. "I've been thinking. There's only one way to figure out who kissed you Friday night, and that's to get you out on dates with all the possible guys so you can find out. Genius, right?"

I'm not sure genius is the word I would use. "Well, I went to dinner with Ezra last night, and I'm pretty sure it's not him."

"But how can you know," Hadley asks, "if you didn't kiss him? You didn't kiss him last night, did you?"

"No!" I yell, probably too fast. Listening to make sure Dad isn't coming to check on me, I lower my voice and say, "I didn't kiss him. But I didn't get that vibe from him at all."

"Of course you didn't," Naoise says. "It wasn't a date. That's why you need to go on dates with them, so you can feel them out—"

"And kiss them! You gotta kiss them!" Shyla yells from somewhere in the background.

"I dunno, y'all," I say.

"Don't you want to find out who it was?" Hadley asks.

Immediately, I'm transported back to the dark theater. Hand in my hair, arm around my waist. Lips on my mouth, my neck, my shoulder. My stomach flutters, warmth filling my chest. I get a jolt just remembering. Hadley's right. I need to know who it was.

"Yeah, I do, but I'm not sure letting y'all set me up on a bunch of dates is the best way to find out."

"That's because you don't want to let someone else take control," Shyla says. She's wrestling the phone back from Naoise, so I can see her again. She's not wrong. I like having a plan and knowing I can control a situation. Letting my three best friends plan not just one, but five dates for me seems like a quick way to lose control of my life completely.

When I don't answer for a beat too long, Naoise sighs loudly. "Okay," she says. "I'll make the dress."

"What?"

"The dress," she repeats. "That one from *I Love Lucy* that you want so bad? Let us set you up on these dates, and I'll make you the dress for prom."

"Really?" I squeak, excitement raising my voice about two octaves.

"Really," she says seriously.

"Okay," I agree. Anything for that dress, I swear. "I'll do it."

What did I get myself into?

chapter
EIGHT

THE WEEK PASSES IN A BLUR, AND FRIDAY IS HERE BEFORE I
know it. When film class ends, I move to a table at the back of
the room. I'm supposed to have study hall in the library last
period, but Mr. Welles lets me stay in his room to work as long
as he doesn't need the extra space for his Intro to Video Production class. I settle in with my printed copy of the *Maybe, Probably*
script and a shiny pink pen. It's what I've used to make notes for
as long as I can remember—a habit I picked up from Mom.

Now that we have the cast set, I've been combing through
the screenplay and tweaking it to make it work better with the
actors' strengths. I'm reading over the notes I made on my last
read-through when a shadow falls across the page. I look up to
find Kenyon standing over me.

"Want some help with that?" he asks.

"I'm fine," I snap. It's bad enough he's in my group, but I don't
need his help on my own script.

"Whoa," he says, taking a step back. "Stand down, soldier. I
was simply wondering if you wanted to go over it together. Get
ready for Monday and all that."

Suppressing a groan, I push the chair next to me away from the workbench. He's right; we need to get ready to start filming next week. We may as well go over this now rather than later. We have a very short filming window, so we need to be efficient with our time. The more prep work we do up front, the more ready we'll be for the first day of shooting.

Kenyon accepts my silent invitation and sits next to me.

We jump right in, going over his notes on the script, as well as the ones I made for myself. It's hard, but I've tried to leave final camera decisions up to Kenyon. He's acting as director of photography, and as much as he irritates me, I know he's talented enough to make this film gorgeous. Plus, Mr. Welles was very clear that this needed to be a full group effort if I was going to give up doing this as a solo project.

As Kenyon talks, I can see his excitement build as he describes the shots he plans to catch with the Blackmagic. We'll use my Canon as our secondary camera so each scene can have two angles to work with. The Canon was a seventeenth birthday present to me from Nana, and I've filmed everything I possibly could on it for the past year. The Blackmagic will be a huge step up for us. Having it also means we won't have to check out a school camera, so we don't have to worry about the other groups' schedules when we plan our shoots.

"When do you think you'll have rewrites done?" Kenyon asks.

"In a couple of days," I say. "I've already sent changes to the actors as I've written them, and I only have a few scenes left to tweak. We're shooting only Adalyn and Sebastian first anyway, so everyone else will have time to learn their new lines." I've been working nonstop on rewrites and edits ever since the auditions, and now I'm wondering if I should've looped in the rest of my team beforehand. This has been so firmly *my* movie from the start that I often forget I have three other people whose grades also depend on this project.

"Cool, cool." He leans back in his chair. "Any big plans for the weekend?"

"Nah," I say. "Just work tomorrow and writing. Exciting life, I know." It's strange, this easiness between us. All our animosity seems to melt away as we talk about filming locations and camera angles, and now we're chatting easily, almost like friends. I start to pack my stuff into my backpack when I feel my phone buzz in the outer pocket. I reach in and bring the screen to life, careful to keep it out of view. Mr. Welles hates phones in class—even if I'm not actually part of the class. It's a message from Naoise.

"Um, how about you?" I ask as I tap the message open.

NAOISE: You have a date tonight! Operation Mystery Kisser is officially underway.

"You okay?" Kenyon asks, startling me. I've been staring into my bag at my phone for an impossibly long time.

"Oh, yeah, sorry! What did you say?"

He looks at me like he can't quite figure me out and then chuckles. "I said Tanner is hellbent on setting me up, so I guess I'm going on a blind date tonight. Should be interesting." His cheeks flush deep, and he flips his hair off his forehead.

I freeze, my bag's zipper pulled halfway closed. My fingertips are turning white with the pressure of squeezing them around the zipper pull. Kenyon has a blind date tonight, and Naoise just messaged saying I have a date too. There's no way this is a coincidence.

Kenyon was at Nana's party, after all. Could it have been him in the theater? I'm not sure how I feel about that. Kenyon's been little more than an annoyance to me since he moved here. Can I even *imagine* kissing him? Oh, wait. Yup, I can. Flutters well up in my stomach at the idea, and suddenly I kind of want to run my hands through his unruly hair.

My goodness, what did that kiss do to me?

I manage to gather myself, and we finish packing up before walking out together. Kenyon follows me all the way to my locker before peeling off and heading to his own.

"See ya later, Quincy," he says, and I wave.

I have a feeling we'll be seeing each other much sooner than he thinks.

chapter
NINE

I STARE ACROSS THE PARKING LOT TOWARD THE RESTAU-rant. It looks nice. I'd never even heard of Pier 23 before Naoise's text telling me to meet my date there at 5:30 p.m. The restaurant is in a gorgeous old building, obviously a converted house, overlooking the ICW. Twinkle lights spiral around the pillars on the front porch, and from my angle at the side of the building, I can see strings of swooping lights crisscrossing the patio out back. I wish Mom were here to see this. She would've loved this place.

I wish my mom were here for a lot of reasons tonight.

When I feel like I've sat in the car long enough to calm my nerves (they haven't calmed at all), I climb out and smooth my dress with my hands, working the seatbelt lines from the fabric. I put on one of my favorites tonight. It's another from my mom's collection: flirty with a swishy mid-thigh skirt and spaghetti straps. The fabric has the tiniest multicolored floral pattern, and I wear it over a fitted white T-shirt. I've paired it with my favorite Doc Martens, and I have a jean jacket in case I get cold later.

There's a picture in Dad's office of Mom wearing this exact outfit. The photo was taken by one of her friends in high school. In it, Mom's sitting on the top of a picnic table, her legs stretched out in front of her. One foot is propped up on the bench, her knee bent, and the other hangs off the edge. She's leaning back on her elbows, and she has her head thrown back in laughter, her wavy hair spilling onto the table.

It's my favorite picture of her.

A sudden burst of sound draws my attention back to the restaurant as a middle-aged couple makes their way out the front door. I can't put this off any longer. It's time.

Inside, the restaurant is every bit as charming. Tables are scattered throughout the rooms, which are still separated from when the building was a house, with glass French doors opening from section to section. No two tables are the same. They are all different colors, expertly painted and distressed, and none has a matching set of chairs. The place looks like it was furnished at the chicest flea market imaginable. I've never been any place like this, and I love it already.

Behind an antique drafting table, a pretty girl with wild blonde curls piled on the top of her head smiles at me.

"How many tonight?" she asks.

"Oh, um . . ." I twist my fingers in the fabric of my dress. "I'm actually meeting someone. Except, I'm not sure—"

"Oh! You're here for a blind date? That is the cutest thing. He's already waiting out back. Come on, I'll take you."

I follow her toward the rear of the house. The back wall isn't a wall so much as a series of French doors overlooking the patio and the ICW beyond. Thanks to the still-warm weather tonight, the doors are thrown open so I can smell the salt air. I slow my step.

"He's out here," the girl says. Then she turns to face me, lowering her voice and leaning in conspiratorially. "And he is cute." She says it like *ca-yute*, as though one syllable isn't quite enough to get her point across.

Even though it's exactly what I've been expecting since school got out, I still stop short for a moment when I see Kenyon sitting alone at a table for two at the very edge of the patio. He looks handsome in jeans and a button-down, the sleeves pushed up his forearms to his elbows. I think he even combed his hair—the normally wild shag looks like it's been beaten into submission. Somewhat.

"Oh," I say to the host and she beams at me. "I can make it from here."

"Okey dokey. I'll let your server know you're both here now. What can we get you to drink?"

"Sweet tea, please."

She bounces back into the house, and I take a deep breath and head over to the table.

He's looking down, twisting a cloth napkin between his fingers when I approach. I grab the back of the chair across from him. "Hey, Kenyon."

He looks up, and the shock on his face is clear, mixed with confusion. "Quincy, what are you doing here?"

"It seems that I'm your date," I say as I lower myself into the seat.

"You"—he shakes his head and swallows deeply—"why didn't you say anything? This afternoon when I told you I had a blind date. And you did too? Didn't you think that was a bit more than a coincidence?"

I shrug. "I didn't know." Not totally anyway. "My friends didn't even tell me about this until after school." Or, at least, *almost* after school.

I can tell by his expression that he doesn't entirely believe me. "I've known since Tuesday," he says.

"Tuesday?" I'd assumed this date was something Naoise and Tanner had only worked out earlier today. "My friends probably thought I'd bail if they gave me that much notice. I couldn't back out if they waited to tell me the day of, especially since they knew my only other plans were hanging out with them all night."

"Would you have?"

"Bailed?" I think about it for a minute. "Yeah, probably. I would've picked up an extra shift at work or something."

A server comes by with my sweet tea and a plate of hush puppies that he sets on the table between us. He places a simple one-page menu next to each of us and tells us to take our time figuring out what to eat.

"But," Kenyon says, "aren't you like this big romantic?"

I stare at him, unsure where he's going with this. It's not exactly like it's a secret—I mean, we are filming a romantic comedy together, after all. But I can't quite tell if he's making fun of me or not. I shrug. "I mean, yeah. I guess."

"You guess?" he deadpans.

"Okay, fine," I say. "You've got me. I'm a grade A, one hundred percent, hopeless romantic. Are you happy?"

"Thrilled," he says. He doesn't roll his eyes, but his voice tells me he wants to.

"Why?"

"Why what?"

"Why does it matter that I'm a hopeless romantic?"

Kenyon goes back to rolling the napkin between his fingers. "It doesn't, really. I just find it funny."

Oh my gosh, this is going to be the longest date in the history of all dates. Is he always this irritating? We've never really talked outside of film class, and most of the talking we do there is arguing, which is infuriating in its own way, but not like this. This thing he's doing—dragging out his point and not finishing his thoughts—is maybe the most annoying thing he's ever done.

It's becoming obvious that he's not going to continue without prompting. I should leave it alone, let him know I'm not going to play this game. But, well . . . not knowing what he's getting at is going to bother me all night.

"Okay, I'll bite," I say. "What's so funny about it?"

"You're a hopeless romantic who doesn't like blind dates." He chuckles to himself. When I don't laugh with him, he balls up his napkin and throws it across the table. It hits my chest and then clings there, hanging on like a bib. "Come on, Quin. It's funny."

"If you say so," I grumble.

Kenyon holds up his hands, palms out in mock surrender. "Okay, okay. Totally not funny. You're right." His lips press into a flat line, and I can see his chest shudder with the laughter he's fighting to keep in.

Sighing, I throw the napkin back. Kenyon catches it and smooths it over his pants like it's the most natural thing in the world.

"It's not that I don't like blind dates *in theory*," I say. "It's that I don't like not being in control." It's not like I can pretend to be somebody else around him. "So, yeah. Blind dates kinda give me the heebie-jeebies."

He laughs, and a bit of his hair falls back to where it normally is in front of one eye. "Did you really just say heebie-jeebies? That's great." He picks up his menu and starts reading. I follow his lead and do the same. "Why'd you agree to a blind date in the first place if you hate them so much?"

For a second, I consider telling him the whole story. It would be easy and could take away all the guesswork. Either he was in the theater with me a week ago or he wasn't. But I know Naoise. She'd never finish my dress if she knew I took the easy way out instead of following through with our deal. So I tell him a version of the truth instead. "Naoise bribed me. She's going to make me this dress I want super bad if I let her set me up on some dates. She lives for this stuff, setting people up and seeing romance blossom."

"Cool," he says, looking back to the menu. "I think we're gonna have fun tonight, Quin."

"What are we doing after this?"

He doesn't look up when he says, "You really think I'm going to tell you? And miss the opportunity to keep you guessing and"— he fake gasps—"not in control? Trust me. You're gonna love it."

"You're impossible," I say, and I pull my menu up to hide the smile breaking across my face.

The server comes back for our orders, and when he leaves, the awkward blind date chatter is over. We jump right back into our conversation from Mr. Welles's class as if the hours between then and now never even happened. We talk camera angles and locations and features of the Blackmagic we're excited to try out. Before we know it, the server's back with our food.

71

"We totally broke the first rule of dating," Kenyon says between bites.

My hand stills, a fork raised halfway to my mouth. "What's that?"

"Shop talk. It's like when two coworkers date, but all they can talk about is work. Or when parents go on dates, but the only topic of conversation is the kids they left at home."

I shrug. "It's kinda nice, though, isn't it?"

"Nice . . . how?"

My fork is still raised awkwardly, so I push the bite into my mouth and take my time chewing. The food is heavenly. "You know," I say after I've swallowed, "you and me talking about film without being at each other's throats." I lean in close and whisper, "If I'm not mistaken, we've actually agreed tonight. A lot."

Kenyon laughs. "I won't tell anyone if you don't." He winks and turns back to his own food.

We fall into comfortable conversation as we eat. While we wait for the checks—I insist on paying for my own meal—I can't help but think maybe Naoise knew what she was doing pairing me up with Kenyon first. We may be sparring partners in class, but I'm comfortable around him, so it makes the first-date jitters more bearable. By the time we leave the table and follow the small path around the side of the restaurant back to the parking lot, I'm actively looking forward to whatever he's planned next for us.

chapter
TEN

"WHERE ARE WE GOING NOW?" I ASK AS I CLIMB INTO KEN-
yon's Jeep. He's holding the door open, watching me as I twist
around to grab the seatbelt. I do my best to ignore his chuckle
as I fumble behind me, coming up empty.

"You'll see," he says. There's a tap on the side of my thigh,
and I look down to see Kenyon holding the end of the seatbelt
there. "It doesn't have shoulder belts."

"How does it not have shoulder belts?" I grab the strap and
pull it across my lap, pushing it into the other end with a satis-
fying *click*. "I thought cars had to have them."

"They do now, but this is an old beast. Nothing but lap
belts." With a smile, he pushes the door shut and circles around
the front of the car.

Suddenly, I'm more nervous than I've been all night. I'd
thought my nerves in the parking lot before going into the
restaurant would be the worst of it, but the twisting and fluttering in my stomach now tell me otherwise. Somehow it seemed
easier in the restaurant, but now that we have the rest of the
date ahead of us, I'm not sure what to think. As I watch Kenyon

walk to the driver's-side door, it hits me that this is going to be our first time truly alone together.

Unless we were alone in the theater at Nana's party?

"You okay?" Kenyon asks a couple minutes later while we idle at a red light.

I startle, sitting straighter in the seat. Adrenaline courses through my veins. This is ridiculous. There's no way people are normally this nervous on dates. Nobody would ever go on a second one. Kenyon's waiting for an answer, so I lie. "I'm totally fine."

He gives me a pointed look then continues driving. The light switches to green, and he eases into traffic. "You're about to snap your seatbelt in half," he says.

My hands freeze in my lap. Sure enough, I've been working the belt between my fingers, twisting and bunching the stiff strap into my fists. I force my fingers straight and press the belt flat across my hips with my palms.

Now I don't know what to do with my hands. I drop them into my lap, then I shove them under the sides of my thighs and sit on them.

"What?" I say defensively when I notice Kenyon smirking at me.

"Nothing," he says. "I've never had anyone so fidgety in my car before. Do I make you nervous, Quincy?"

Yes. "No."

"There's nothing to be nervous about. It's only a date." He gives me a sidelong look. "I promise I'm not a closet serial killer."

"Very funny," I mutter.

We pull up to another red light, and Kenyon eases the Jeep to a stop behind a beat-up old Cadillac. He pops the gearshift into neutral and turns in his seat to face me.

"Hey," he says, his voice soft. All traces of his earlier humor are gone. "Seriously, what's up?"

I shrug. "It's nothing."

Kenyon tilts his head and gives a half-smile. "How about you tell me, and I'll let you know if it's nothing. Sound fair?"

I can't help but roll my eyes at him, and as I do, I feel some of the tension leave my shoulders. There's no reason for me to be this jittery. It's *Kenyon*. It's not like it really matters if this date goes well or not. Unless—

"What if this doesn't go well?" I ask, voicing my thoughts aloud as fast as they come to me. "And then we have to spend all this time working on *Maybe, Probably* together, and it gets super awkward, and then the movie sucks, and—"

"Quin!" Kenyon snaps me out of my spiral. The light's changed, so he rotates back to face the road. "Calm down. It's just a date. It's going to be fun."

"Okay, but what if—"

"If it's not," he says before I can work myself into a panic, "then we'll go home at the end of the night and that's that. It won't ruin the movie. It won't even ruin our—dare I call it a friendship?"

"Very funny," I say again.

"Relax, okay? This doesn't have to be a big deal."

"Easy for you to say," I quip.

He looks at me quickly, an expression I can't quite read on his face, before shifting his eyes back to the road. "What's that mean?"

It means he doesn't have nearly as much riding on this date as I do. For Kenyon, this is a fun night out with his film class nemesis. A favor he's doing for a friend. But for me? If he was the guy at Nana's party, then this date is so much more than just a Friday night. I can't bring myself to tell him the truth about Operation Mystery Kisser, though. What would I even say? *I'm totally infatuated with someone, but I don't know who, and maybe it's you?*

Instead, I go with the only slightly less embarrassing truth: "I've never actually been on a date before."

My cheeks flush, and I squeeze my eyes shut, wishing I could take the words back. They sound so ridiculous now that they're out in the open, hanging between us in the sudden silence of the Jeep. I could've gone through this whole evening without opening my big mouth, and it would've been fine.

"Really?" he says. "This is your first date?"

Here it comes. This is going to be too much for Kenyon to resist. Tonight's been fine—better than fine, actually—but I know he can't withstand the urge to tease me for this.

"Yeah," I mumble. Heat floods my face. Turns out I was wrong. This is definitely not the less embarrassing option.

"Huh," he says.

Is that it? I watch him out the side of my eye, trying—and probably failing—to be nonchalant. His eyes are on the road, focused as he flicks on the blinker and takes a left turn. We ride in silence for a few minutes until I can't take it anymore.

"Huh what?" I snap. Kenyon looks at me. "You said 'huh.' What's that supposed to mean?"

He lowers his eyebrows then turns back to the road. "It doesn't really mean anything. I guess I'm surprised is all."

I'm not sure how to handle this version of Kenyon. Snarky, competitive Kenyon from class I can do. Even focused and driven Kenyon, setting aside all our petty differences to work on a movie together—I can work with that. But this third version, the one who is kind and softer-spoken; who I ate a full meal with without any biting, sarcastic comments; the one who can hear I'm almost eighteen years old and have never been on a date and not tease me at all . . . who *is* this person?

"Seriously," he says. "I didn't mean anything by it."

"Okay . . . wait. We're going to the mall?" I may not have gone on any dates myself, but I've watched a *lot* of romantic comedies, and if I've learned one thing from them, it's that the mall is not where you go on a date. Unless you're in sixth grade.

He parks and cuts the engine. Without bothering to answer, he slides out of the Jeep and crosses to my side, opening my door just as I'm reaching for the handle myself.

"It's going to be fun, promise," he says.

"Oh, come on!" Kenyon spins to face me, his teeth glowing under the black lights that surround us. "You cheated," he says, but he's laughing.

I laugh with him. "How on earth could I cheat? You were right there watching me the whole time!"

"I don't know, but you did." He nudges my Docs with his putter. "Nobody gets three holes-in-one on their first time mini golfing."

"Beginner's luck," I reply with a shrug.

"If you actually *are* a beginner. I'm still not sure you're not hustling me."

We move to the next hole and Kenyon lines up his shot. He swings, and we both watch as his neon green ball bounces off the wall and loops around a glowing palm tree. It rolls right to the edge of the hole, and Kenyon tenses with excitement beside me. Then, when I think it's going to drop, it hooks around the rim and shoots off to the side, finally coming to a stop only inches from the edge of the green.

"Not a word," he says as I line up my shot.

"Wasn't even thinking it." Truthfully, I was thinking it. We've fallen into a comfortable rhythm during our game, teasing and ribbing each other, but not in a mean way.

We finish the game—I get three free game coupons thanks to my excellent playing—and head back into the main mall.

"That was fun," I say as we walk the halls toward the exit.

"Yeah?" he says. "You didn't think it was dorky?"

"Oh, it was one hundred percent dorky, but I like dorky sometimes."

Kenyon smiles at me. "That works out nicely for me, then."

Heat rises in my cheeks, and I turn away from him, focusing all my energy on keeping my breathing steady. It surprises me how much I've enjoyed this date with Kenyon. In class he's arrogant and irritating, constantly pushing my buttons and contradicting my opinions. When it dawned on me that he was going to be my date tonight, I'd braced myself to put up with the same battle we've been in ever since he moved here. The night has been nice, though, and I find myself not wanting it to end.

When we reach his Jeep, Kenyon unlocks my door and pulls it open for me. I've concluded that there's no graceful way to climb into a vehicle this tall and not look like a clumsy toddler. Maybe if I were tall and willowy like Naoise, but my legs can barely reach the floorboards. After way too much struggling, I settle into the seat and turn to grab the lap belt.

Kenyon's already there, holding it out to me. When I take it from him, our fingers brush, and the contact jolts me. Whoa. Where did that come from? We're both still holding the buckle, my thumb resting against the side of his hand, the heat building there becoming almost unbearable. I glance up at Kenyon—is this affecting him so strongly too?

He's staring straight at me, an openness on his face I'm not used to seeing. I can't quite read his expression; it's some strange combination of desire and confusion. Or maybe I'm projecting my own feelings onto him.

"I, um . . . I've got it. Thanks," I say.

"Oh, yeah. Right." He lets go of the buckle and steps back, bumping into the door. His cheeks darken. "I guess I'll just . . ."

He shuts the door, and I smile inwardly as he crosses to his own side. It's not only me; he was absolutely affected by that moment. He's cute when he's flustered.

"What now?" I ask once he's buckled in. I'm afraid things will get weird between us now, and I don't want that to happen. If we jump right into the next thing without dwelling on this, we'll be fine.

"Um . . ." He twists in his seat and backs out of our spot. "This was all I had planned."

Inside, the excitement that's started to build deflates. I try not to show my disappointment, but I can feel it taking over my features. I'm not ready for this night to end.

"But"—hope blooms back in my chest at his word—"maybe we could . . . you wanna go get some ice cream?"

"Yes," I say immediately. "Ice cream. I approve."

chapter
ELEVEN

"ANY PREFERENCES?" KENYON ASKS AS HE PULLS UP TO A red light at the edge of the parking lot.

I shake my head. "Nope. Any ice cream is good in my book."

The light changes, and he eases the Jeep onto the road, heading east. "You good on time?"

"Totally fine." I didn't tell Dad when I'd be home, but as far as he's concerned, I'm out with my friends. He won't expect me back anytime soon.

"Okay, great." He switches lanes, twisting in his seat to check behind us as he does. "Donovan took me to this amazing place last month out in Carolina Beach. I can't remember the name. Sweet—Sweet . . . something."

"Sweet Aggie's," I say softly, a lifetime of memories rushing over me.

"Yes!" Kenyon drums a little victory cadence out on the steering wheel. "You know the place, then. Isn't it great?"

"I used to go with my mom," I say, the memory bittersweet. It was her favorite ice cream, and Mom didn't care how far away it was, so we drove down there whenever either of us wanted a cone, even though there were a half dozen closer scoop shops along the way. Sometimes we'd bring Clark and Dad with us, but it was mostly our thing. Just us girls.

"Used to?" Kenyon asks, and I startle with the realization that he doesn't know about my mom. Why would he? He's not from Wilmington, and he didn't go to school here when it happened. And it's not like I advertise about her accident.

"Yeah." It takes me a couple breaths to detach myself enough to talk about it without crying, but when I feel like I can, I say, "She died four years ago." Four years next week, actually.

"I'm sorry, Quin."

I shrug. "Thanks, but it was a long time ago."

"Why do you do that?"

"Do what?"

"Try to dismiss something that's obviously important to you?"

I look out the window so he can't see my face. My mom's death has been this heavy weight on me for the past four years, and I hate to bring people down with my own sadness. It *has* been a long time, but sometimes it feels like it happened yesterday, the pain is still so raw. And it's not that I'm dismissing what happened—I could never do that—but it's easier to deflect than to face my own emotions.

I wipe a stray tear from my eyelashes before it has a chance to escape, and I say, "My mom was Desiree Hunt."

It takes a moment for my words to register, but it's clear when they do. Kenyon's eyebrows shoot up in surprise, and he glances at me for a second before returning his attention to the road. "Like, *the* Desiree Hunt?"

My mom wasn't the biggest movie star, but she was a working actor since she was in her late teens. Her death was national news; of course he'd heard about it. I bite the inside of my cheek, hard, and inhale long and slow through my nose. I will not cry on this date.

"Yeah," I say, vocalizing the nod he didn't see. "So you know what happened."

Kenyon makes a small grunt of acknowledgment as we cross the bridge over the ICW and enter Carolina Beach. Already, my chest is bubbling with a strange mix of anticipation and dread.

"What was she like?" Kenyon asks, clearing his throat. "I mean, if you want to talk about her."

"You know," I say to the window, "she was a great actor. Her range was incredible. People always said that if she really put herself into her work, she could be the next—"

"That's not what I mean," Kenyon interrupts. "I can read her IMDb page if I want to know that stuff."

I pull in a sharp breath and hold it until I'm reasonably sure I'm able to control my emotions. Turning in my seat, I watch Kenyon as he pulls to the curb a block from the ice cream shop. He cuts the engine then unbuckles his seatbelt and turns to face me, his expression unguarded, making it clear that not only is he willing to talk about my mom, but he *wants* to hear about her.

"My mom was my best friend," I start, hesitant at first, but it's as if saying the words aloud shifts something in me. I'm not sad to talk about her. Instead, I'm filled with this incredible warmth at the idea of sharing the best parts of my mother with someone who wants to know about *Mom*, not just Desiree Hunt, the movie star.

"She was goofy and unpredictable. Sometimes she'd wake me in the middle of the night to make cookies and watch old movies together." Tears push at the back of my eyes, and I don't bother trying to stop them. Not anymore. "She loved Lucille Ball almost as much as Nana and I do. She made me and my brother special pancakes every year for our birthdays, but other than that, she couldn't cook to save her life. My mom burned more dinners than I can even count."

Suddenly, I'm laughing, remembering all the times Mom tried to surprise Dad by making dinner while he was teaching. She was hopeless in the kitchen; even when we made our middle-of-the-night cookies, I was the one in charge of getting them out of the oven before they burned. She always had good intentions, but she never quite got down the follow-through part of cooking. She'd put dinner on the stove, and the next thing you'd know, she'd be at the table pouring over a script, pen in her mouth and a highlighter stuck securely in her messy bun—all while pots boiled over and the smoke detector blared.

"When she went to work, she was *Desiree Hunt,* but as soon as she walked through our front door, she was simply Mom. We played Farkle a lot. She liked to eat edamame with parmesan cheese while we watched movies. And no matter how busy she was or how badly she needed to study her lines, whenever I needed her, she'd drop everything and take me to Sweet Aggie's for ice cream and girl talk." I swallow against the hard lump that's forming in my throat. "Tomorrow's the four-year anniversary of the accident," I whisper.

He doesn't respond, instead sitting in silence as the weight of my words settles around us. I'm grateful for his stillness. It's exactly what I need. Maybe I should feel weird about dumping that much information on Kenyon, but I don't. Instead, I feel lighter than I have in a long time.

Finally, Kenyon says, "My dad's in Afghanistan." His voice is so quiet I almost don't hear him.

It takes me a moment to shift gears. "Military?" I ask.

He nods, and I can see his Adam's apple bob with a slow swallow. "He got deployed right after school started. That's why I moved here, to stay with my mom and stepdad."

"I didn't know that," I say, unsure how else to respond.

"It's not even like he's in real danger, you know? He's in a relatively safe area, and he's well protected. But still"—

he shrugs—"it scares me. I don't know what I'd do if I lost my dad."

Silence falls over the Jeep. I don't know how to respond to his revelation, so I say nothing. It seems to be the right choice. Maybe, like me, he doesn't need a response. He needs someone to listen.

"Okay, enough of that," he says suddenly, and he flashes a quick smile. My stomach dips and flips. "I'm ready for some mint chip."

After we get our ice cream, we walk to the beach rather than stay at Sweet Aggie's. It's a beautiful evening—warm, with a light breeze coming off the ocean keeping the air fresh. The sun has already set behind us, and as we walk toward the ocean, the last lingering glimmers of twilight play across the surface of the waves. After a couple minutes, we step off the paved street and into soft sand.

We walk in silence, and I let the evening play back in my head. When I got to the restaurant, my only goal was to make it to the end of the night. Get through this date; find out if Kenyon was my mystery kisser. That's all. I didn't expect to have as much fun as I'm having. This has been one of the best nights I've had in a long time, and I'm surprised by how much I've enjoyed spending it with Kenyon.

His hand brushes across the back of my own, and my heart leaps into my throat. It was so subtle, so soft, that I can't tell if it was intentional or not. I glance at him to see if he's giving any indication, but his gaze is focused on the beach ahead of us. I watch as he takes a bite from his waffle cone. A piece breaks off and sticks to the light stubble on his chin. Without a thought, I reach up and brush it away.

Kenyon startles when I touch him, turning to face me with surprise in his eyes. And, holy cow, I didn't notice how close together we were walking until this very moment. His gaze burns into me, and my finger still lingers on his face.

Why is my finger still on his face?

I jerk my whole hand back, wrapping my fingers tightly around the paper cup that holds my ice cream.

"Sorry," I say, "there was—you had a bit of cone . . ."

Kenyon's mouth quirks into a half-smile. "Well, thanks then."

Turning from him, I focus on my ice cream and finally ask, "How long is your dad, um, deployed for?"

He's silent for a beat, and I start to wonder if the topic's closed for the night. I get it. As much as I love and miss my mom, I don't always want to talk about her. It was nice tonight, though, telling Kenyon about her, and I hoped I could give him the same opportunity. But maybe that was the wrong thing to ask.

Finally, he sighs and says, "I don't really know. They said a year, but I don't trust the timeline they give."

"Has he gone before?"

"Yeah." He takes another bite of his cone, and I follow suit, scooping the last spoonful of my ice cream from my cup. "He went out twice when I was little. I wasn't old enough to remember the first time, but the second felt like he was gone forever. They told him he wouldn't deploy again after the last time, but . . ."

"They made him go anyway?"

"Yeah." His voice is so soft now that I find myself leaning closer to him, trying to catch his words before they're snatched away by the ocean breeze. "You're never really done. So long as you're in, they can deploy you. It doesn't matter what they've said in the past."

"Wow." I can't imagine growing up with my dad gone like that for long stretches of my life. So much of who I am is because of my time spent with him that I don't know what life would even look like if he weren't around. Who would I be? These past four years, I've been so wrapped up in my mom's death that I forgot how incredibly lucky I am to have my dad.

Kenyon's fingers brush the back of mine again, the gentlest touch across my knuckles. This time, I don't let myself overthink things; I push my own hand lightly against his, just enough to let him know I'm interested. Smoothly, he runs his fingers down the side of my hand and then slides them around mine so our hands are palm to palm. My heart thrums in my throat, my whole body warming with his touch as we intertwine our fingers.

We walk for nearly an hour, falling into easy conversation. I learn that his parents divorced when he was ten and he's lived with his dad ever since. Now that his dad's deployed, he's back with his mom.

I tell him more about my mom—about growing up with her and Dad and Clark, how close we all used to be. My chest aches with the memories, but I find that talking to him helps take away some of the intensity of the pain. He laughs when I tell him about Sunday breakfasts with Nana until he sees I'm being serious about how much I enjoy spending time with her.

When the conversation shifts to my friends, he interrupts: "Why does everyone call Naoise and Shyla twins?" He looks down at me, twisting his mouth to one side in a puzzled expression. "They're not really twins, right? Like, there's no way."

I laugh, picturing Naoise's clear, pale skin and light hazel eyes alongside Shyla's deep Indian complexion, her eyes so dark brown that the pupils disappear. "No, they're not actually twins. They do have the same birthday, though. Shyla's dad and Naoise's mom met when they were in preschool together."

"Wow," he says. "What are the odds?"

"They actually met because they both brought birthday treats to their school that day." I shrug. "So odds were pretty good, I think."

We're nearing the public access point to the beach, almost ready to step back onto pavement and head toward the car, and a wave of disappointment washes over me. I don't want the night to be over. But even as I think it, a giant yawn overcomes me. I turn my head, trying to hide my face in my shoulder, but it's no use. Kenyon sees.

"All right," he says, squeezing my fingers between his. "Let's get you home."

chapter
TWELVE

"GIVE IT TO ME STRAIGHT. HOW WAS THE DATE?" KENYON cuts the engine and turns to face me. We're back at the restaurant, and he's pulled his car into a spot next to mine.

"It was great," I say. "I had so much fun. Thank you."

"I'm glad," he says. "I would hate for your first date to have been boring."

My cheeks heat up. I cannot believe I told him I'd never been on a date before. I mean, it's the truth, but I'm pretty sure you're not supposed to lead with something like that.

"Definitely not boring." I unbuckle and match his pose, turning toward him so our knees nearly touch between the seats.

"So," he says.

"So," I reply. "I guess, um, good night?" For most of the date, I successfully managed to ignore the end-of-date kiss hanging over my head, but now that we're back in the parking lot, it's nagging at me. I can't know if it was Kenyon that night without kissing him per Naoise's deal. This needs to happen.

I have only one problem: I have no idea how to get him to kiss me.

"Hold on, I'll get that," Kenyon says when I reach for the door handle. He hops out of the driver's side and jogs around the front of the Jeep to open my door. He offers his hand and helps me from my seat.

We walk the few steps to my car together. Kenyon chuckles and runs a hand through his wild hair. "Since I can't exactly walk you to your door, I guess this will have to do."

"Thanks," I say, looking down at the ground between our feet then back up at him. I have no idea what I'm doing, but I've seen this same move enough times in films that I figure there must be something to it. "I had a really fun time tonight."

I try to lean against my car casually, but it's farther back than I thought, and before I know it, I'm falling backward. A shriek escapes my lips, and I scramble to right myself, eventually grabbing the front of Kenyon's shirt to stop my fall.

Once I'm stable, I pry my fingers away from the fabric. It's bunched up and wrinkled where I was holding on, so I smooth it down with my palm. I'm basically petting his chest. Could I possibly make this more awkward?

"Sorry," I mutter. I stare at the ground behind him, my face burning. The whole ordeal took less than five seconds, but it feels like the longest part of the night. "I should probably go."

"Don't." Kenyon grabs my hand to stop me from turning away. I can't look at him, so I fix my gaze on the back tire of his Jeep. His other hand reaches for my jaw, and he gently tilts my face toward his. "Hi," he says when I finally look at him.

"Hi," I say back, and suddenly I'm overcome with laughter. When I calm myself down, I say, "Wow. That was super slick, huh?"

"If you wanted to touch my chest, you could've said so." Kenyon smirks and takes a step closer. I tilt my head back so I can still see his face.

"Well, if I'd known that . . ." I say in an attempt at flirtation. Maybe I can still pull this off. I stretch my hand forward like I'm going to touch his chest again, looking at him with what I hope is a flirty-slash-teasing expression.

Kenyon catches my hand in his, then presses it flat to his chest, holding it there with his fingers curled around the edge of mine, squeezing them gently. Under my open palm, his heart beats hard and fast, matching the wild thrumming of my own.

"This was really great," I say, my voice soft in my throat.

"A worthy first date?" Is he even closer now? Suddenly, his knuckles are a breath away from me, our hands sandwiched between our bodies. When did that happen?

"Definitely," I breathe, my voice barely more than a whisper.

He leans down, and holy cow this is really happening, isn't it? I tilt my head back, and my eyes drift closed. My heart stutters, excitement mixed with nervousness climbing into my throat. My hand on Kenyon's chest anchors me as I push up onto my toes, helping to close the gap between us.

Kenyon's lips are warm and soft as they press—to my cheek? My eyes fly open in surprise. How did I read this so wrong? I was certain he was going to kiss me for real. Now his lips linger on the skin just to the right of my mouth. Which, I'm rapidly realizing, is kind of hot. My breath hitches in my throat, and I let my eyes close again.

He pulls back, and my cheek is suddenly cold in the absence of his touch. That was . . . *wow*. Heat sparks in my chest and rushes to my face. I can feel a goofy grin overtake me. I had no idea something so simple could be so incredible.

"Have a good weekend, Quincy," he whispers, his breath warm on my skin.

"Yeah," I say with a sigh. "Um, you too. Thanks for tonight." My cheeks flush when I remember I said this same thing less than a minute ago.

Kenyon doesn't notice. He squeezes my hand, still held against his chest. "Anytime," he says. He takes a step back but doesn't drop my hand yet. Instead, he holds it a beat longer, giving it one more gentle squeeze before finally letting go.

I climb into my car, buckling my seatbelt and starting the engine before Kenyon finally walks back to the Jeep and does the same. When we leave the parking lot, we head in opposite directions, and I watch in my rearview mirror until he turns down another street. As soon as the taillights are out of sight, I pull over and throw the car into park.

"Oh my gosh," I say, my voice loud in the empty car. My fingers brush the place where his lips had been, and my head fills with memories of the night. My heart still dances an excited rhythm in my chest, and I can't help but shimmy in my seat. I'm filled with intense energy, and I don't know how else to disperse it.

Is this what dating's always like? If so, maybe Operation Mystery Kisser isn't such a bad idea. A girl could get used to this.

It's not until I'm lying in bed, my face washed and teeth brushed, that I realize I never got what I was after tonight. I'm no closer to knowing if Kenyon was with me in the theater or not. But as the night replays in my mind for the hundredth time since I left Pier 23, warmth growing deep inside me at the fresh memories, I can't bring myself to feel disappointed. I guess I'll have to try again with Kenyon another night.

There are worse things.

chapter
THIRTEEN

I WAKE UP THE NEXT MORNING TO A WHIRLWIND OF MES-sages from Shyla in our group thread, my phone's constant vibration pulling me from a fitful sleep. I squint at the screen, scanning the messages with still-bleary eyes. As I read, my stomach flits with memories of last night.

I scroll to the end of the thread and type a quick reply.

ME: Sorry y'all. No kiss last night.

Shyla's name pops up immediately, the bubble telling me she's typing. I wait until her words appear.

SHYLA: What?! That was the whole point!

I groan. Somehow, when they told me their plan for Operation Mystery Kisser, I didn't realize how difficult it would be. The idea of so many blind dates was hard enough to stomach that I wasn't even considering the actual kissing part. I guess I thought it would simply *happen*.

My chest flutters with the memory of Kenyon lowering his face to mine. I was so sure he was about to kiss me. My cheeks heat up, and it's almost like I can still feel his lips on the soft skin next to my mouth. I pull the phone closer to my face.

ME: I think he wanted to.
SHYLA: So what happened?

If only I knew.

I send a series of rapid-fire texts, telling her all about my night with Kenyon. Before long, Hadley and Naoise jump into the thread, probably pulled from sleep the way I was minutes ago. My phone blows up again, another burst of messages lighting the screen.

I'm typing out my work schedule for the week—requested somewhat forcefully by Naoise so she could plan my next date— when the doorbell rings. Through my closed bedroom door, I can hear Dad answer, then his muffled words carry down the hall- way. He's talking with a woman whose voice I can't quite place. I strain to hear what they're saying but am unable to make out the words.

A few minutes later, there's a soft knock on my bedroom door.

"John, you up?" Dad asks.

"Yeah. Come in." He steps into the room holding a small box.

"What's that?" I ask.

He looks at it with a quick shrug. "No idea. It's for you. A woman from Pastor Starr's church just dropped it off."

I gasp, realization washing over me, and tears spring to my eyes. I reach for the box. "I can't believe . . ." My words trail away, my brain unable to form a complete thought.

Dad rubs a hand over the back of his neck. "I, uh, was going to head out for a ride. You okay?" He hesitates, like he has something else to say. I can tell he wants to know what's in the box, but he won't press. He'll give me my space so I can take my time before opening it. He's always been able to tell exactly what I need.

I hide in my room and listen to Dad rustle around in the living room. It's not until I hear the familiar *snick* of the front door shutting that I crawl out of bed and make my way into the kitchen. I set the box on the table, and it stays there, taunting me as I make breakfast.

It's directly in front of me as I eat, delaying the inevitable. I push my plate away after I've eaten barely half of my eggs. It's time.

The box is wrapped in plain brown paper with a neat twine bow tied around it. I reach to untie it but pull my hand back and grab my phone. My thumb slips across the smooth glass as I scroll for my brother's name.

ME: You up?

The message jumps into the sent thread, the newest in a long string of unanswered texts. Before he's able to respond—not that I expect he will—I tap out another.

ME: I really need you today. Please.

I squeeze the phone until my fingers hurt, staring at the screen and willing Clark to reply. For the telltale dots to let me know he's there. That we still have some kind of connection.

They don't come.

With nothing else to delay me, I grab the twine and tug, releasing the knot in one swift movement. I slide my thumbnail under a strip of tape and pull away the paper. In the box, there's a small figurine nestled on a bed of crinkle paper.

It's a firefly, made from wire twisted around a chunk of raw peridot. When I found the stone in a booth at the Christmas Market in December, I knew immediately what it needed to be. It took a while to find someone to do it, but Hadley's dad knows a woman in his congregation who does custom wire work, so I brought it to her.

She's had it so long that I almost forgot about it. The fact that it showed up today, of all days, seems like a sign somehow. I pull the firefly from the box and give it a closer look. It's gorgeous, a work of art like I've never seen before. It's delicate but strong, exactly like she was. My heart twists, the familiar ache of missing her intensifying.

I call Clark, but his phone kicks to voicemail after only two rings. He knows how hard this day is. He was there to pick up the pieces for me the past three years. Where is he now? When I call again, it doesn't ring at all.

Suddenly, I can't stand being in this empty house anymore. I lace up my boots and head out to my car. I don't know where I'm going; I only know I can't be inside anymore.

I drive aimlessly, barely recognizing the scenery around me until it's too late. The curve is up ahead, coming at me fast. Before I get there, I slam on my breaks, my car skipping across the gravel and skidding to a stop. Dust rises around me in a hazy cloud, so much like that night, it makes my breath freeze in my chest, paralyzed by the memory.

Grief crashes over me, and I scream into the emptiness of my car, again and again and again, hitting the steering wheel with each yell that tears free from my chest. I relish the pain as my screams rip across my throat—crave it, even, because physical pain is so much better than the emotional pain battering me. Tears flow freely, dripping off my face and leaving dark spots down the front of the chambray romper I'm wearing.

When a knock sounds on the passenger window, I shriek, my heart leaping into my throat. I turn toward the sound, but it takes a moment to make sense of what I'm seeing.

I push the button to roll down the window. "What are you doing here?" I try to discreetly wipe away the snot that's dripping from my nose.

Ezra leans into the car a bit. "You okay?"

I stare ahead, unable to look at him.

"I was on my way home from a class, and I saw you driving out this way. You looked upset. It wasn't hard to figure out where you were going." He shrugs. "Can I hop in?"

I push the unlock button, and Ezra climbs into the passenger seat, pulling the door shut behind him.

"You all right?" he asks after a moment.

I shake my head.

"Wanna talk about it?"

Another shake.

"Okay," he says. He leans back in his seat and stares out the windshield. I wonder if he's imagining the same thing I am, seeing the truck come around that curve, the other car drifting across the center line.

"It's been four years," I say. My voice echoes in my head, the congestion my tears brought amplifying my own words.

Ezra nods and says nothing.

"How can it still hurt so much?" I cry. "When does this stop?" My heart is breaking all over again, and I struggle to gulp in air past my tightening throat.

Ezra reaches toward me, hesitating for a moment with his hand hovering over the center console before grabbing my hand and wrapping it tightly in his own. He squeezes. I squeeze back, hard, and use his hand as an anchor to help bring me back. He doesn't ask questions or push me to talk. He sits there in the passenger seat, holding my hand while I cry.

"How did you know I was coming here?" I ask once my sobs have been reduced to a few hiccups.

"There's not a lot out this way," he says. "Where else would you be going? Especially today."

"You know what today is?" I ask, surprised.

"Of course. Desiree was like a second mom to me, Quin. I'll never forget that day."

"Everyone else does," I say. "They only remember the day she died. They don't remember the accident. Not like I do."

"I don't think that's—"

I cut a glare at him, and his mouth snaps shut. "It's business as usual today for everyone else. Dad is on a bike ride like every other Saturday. Clark used to remember with me. Every year, he'd be by my side. But he won't even answer the phone today."

"Do you two come out here every year?" he asks.

I shake my head. "This is the first time I've been here since . . . since . . ." I can't say it aloud, and I don't need to. Ezra knows. He and his mom were there for the whole thing. When Mom's headache turned into vomiting and dizziness, Dad had Lylah come stay with me while he took Mom to the ER. I hid in my room, too embarrassed to face Ezra after Hannah's party, and I was lying on my bed when Dad called from the hospital.

Lylah's soft voice carried down our short hallway and into my bedroom, no trace of panic in her words.

A gentle knock sounded at my bedroom door after she hung up. "Quincy? Can I come in?"

"Yeah," I said.

Lylah slipped into my room, and I caught a quick glimpse of Ezra standing at the end of the hall with a confused look on his face before she pulled the door shut with a soft click. "That was your dad," she said as she crossed the room and lowered herself to sit on the edge of my bed.

"What'd he say? Is Mom okay?"

She nodded, slowly. "It sounds like it. They want to do some tests to see what's going on, and she'll stay overnight, but it sounds like everything will be okay."

With her words, I could feel the invisible fist that had been tightening around my chest for the past two hours loosen enough for me to breathe again. Mom was going to be okay. This was just one awful night, and then things would go back to normal.

"Do you need anything?" Lylah laid her hand across my bare shin, squeezing it in that familiar way of hers. I was glad she was there, even if I couldn't face her son. She was normalcy, nearly as close to me as my own mom, and her hand on my skin grounded me in that moment.

Now, Ezra's hand in mine does the same thing. I grip him tighter, calming myself through our connection. It may have been stretched over the past four years, but it's not broken.

"Wanna go somewhere?" he asks.

"Where?" I sniff and wipe the back of my hand across my nose. There's no hiding how gross I'm being at this point, but I don't mind Ezra seeing me like this. He's seen worse.

"Just someplace I like to go when I need to think," he says. "We don't have to if you don't want, but I thought maybe you wouldn't want to be here anymore."

"You're right," I say. "I don't know why I came here in the first place. Should I follow you?"

"Why don't we park your car, and I'll give you a ride. I can bring you back after." He nods across the street, where there's a turnoff for a fishing access.

I pull the car into a spot and lock it up, then we walk together across the street to where his car is parked.

"You okay?" he asks as he pulls open the passenger door for me. "Or okay-ish, at least?"

"Okay-ish."

chapter FOURTEEN

WE DRIVE IN SILENCE, AND IT STRIKES ME THAT THIS IS THE second time I've been alone with Ezra in the past week. We used to see each other almost every day, but this is the most time I've spent with him in years. It's nice, somehow, spending today with someone who also loved my mom.

As soon as we cross the bridge to Carolina Beach, I know where we're going. Ezra and I used to beg our parents to take us to the Kure Beach Pier. We'd sit for hours watching the people lined up fishing, concocting backstories about their lives. Once, an old man let Ezra help him reel in a shark. It was a super small shark, but still, it was the highlight of our summer.

We sit midway down the pier on a bench facing the ocean. A pelican perches on the railing in front of us, immune to the presence of humans. The pier is busy, people around us casting their lines into the water and posing for pictures against the railing, the ocean wide open behind them. But even with all the noise and bustle, it's peaceful.

"What class?" I ask.

"Huh?" Ezra doesn't look at me. We both keep our eyes on the ocean.

"You said you were coming home from a class when you saw me. What kind of class were you taking on a Saturday morning?"

"EMT training," he says. "It's every Saturday and Sunday for a few weeks."

"Oh, is that why you were on campus last Sunday?"

"Yep. I was finishing up and heading home when Shyla snagged me."

"Well, I'm glad she did." I lean and bump him with my shoulder. "You're going to make a great Sebastian. Ready to start shooting?"

"No," he says and laughs. "I have no idea what I'm doing. I've never acted before."

"First of all, that's not true. We made so many movies together, and don't even try to say those don't count."

He holds up his hands in front of him. "I would never. *Night of the Killer Cat* was a masterpiece."

"And you were marvelous in it," I add. It was our first movie together, and it's comically bad. Dad has a copy of it saved somewhere, I'm sure. "Besides, if you do all your scenes the way you did at auditions, you'll be just fine."

The pelican stretches up, beak high in the air and wings spread to its sides, then plummets toward the ocean. We watch as it glides over the gentle waves and dips its beak into the water, snatching a fish for lunch.

"Can I ask you something?" Ezra says.

"Yeah." I'm suddenly nervous. People only ask if they can ask a question if it's going to be a difficult one.

Ezra rotates in his seat, angling his body toward me. "Why did we stop being friends?"

"I dunno. I guess we grew apart when we hit high school. That happens sometimes."

"Except that's not what happened," he says. "We didn't drift apart. Middle school ended, and it's like you wanted nothing to do with me. I called you all the time that summer. And any time Mom and I came over, you'd shut yourself in your room. Then when high school started, you acted like you didn't even know me. Why?"

"I don't know, Ezra. My mom had just died. Did you seriously expect me to go back to normal? Pretend like nothing ever happened? Sorry, but no. I couldn't do it. I can't do it."

He suddenly takes my hand in his again, squeezing it gently. I refuse to look at him. I'm afraid that if I do, I'll break down, and I'm tired of crying. His thumb runs across the side of my hand, rubbing the scar I got on the Fourth of July when we were ten. It was the first year we had more freedom with fireworks, and we went way overboard. About halfway through the night, we found the bigger ones my dad had stashed away for the grand finale and decided to try some of those out. We were lighting a particularly stubborn fountain when a piece of the burning fuse broke off and fell onto my hand, burning me. Ezra and I snuck into the house to bandage it, and we never told our parents what happened.

"I don't want you to pretend like nothing happened. I was hurting too, Quin."

I glare at him. "You have no idea—"

"I'm not saying it was the same as what you were feeling. But I loved Desiree too, and then you shut me out and I lost my best friend in the world. I want to know why."

"Right. I lost my mom, and I was supposed to worry about how *you* were feeling?" I snap.

He lets go of my hand. "This isn't coming out right." Ezra takes a deep breath. "I'm not blaming you for how you handled things, Quin. I can't even imagine how you felt. But now that we're going to be seeing each other more, I thought maybe we could . . . I was just wondering what happened to us?"

"It was my fault," I say. My voice is carried away on the breeze, and I'm not sure he even hears me.

"What was?"

I turn to face him, our knees nearly touching on the bench between us. I've never told anyone this before, and I need to see his face when I say the words.

"Her accident," I say. "It was my fault."

Confusion morphs his features. "That doesn't make sense," he says. "I thought she slipped and fell?"

The scene unfolds in my memory as I tell him about that day. I remember it vividly: Mom and I were driving back from watching the fireflies, singing at the top of our lungs to compensate for the nonworking radio in her truck. As we came around the curve, a dark blue car drifted into our lane. My eyes connected with the driver's face, and I saw his own eyes staring at the glowing screen of his phone. I screamed.

Mom's arm shot out, slamming into my chest and pushing me back against the seat. The truck fishtailed with the pressure of the brakes, and she jerked the wheel to the side. When we hit the gravel shoulder, we skidded and bounced until the back end of the Ford smashed the guard rail with an ear-splitting screech. Finally, we stopped, a cloud of dust around us.

"Are you okay?" Mom asked, barely audible over the thundering of my heart in my ears.

My breath was coming too fast, but it was like I wasn't breathing at all, the air not making it to my lungs. I tried to nod, to let her know I'd be okay as soon as I calmed down—as soon as the intensity of the moment had passed—but something in my expression alarmed her. Pulling her arm from my chest, she leaped out of the truck and rushed around to my side.

"Come here," she said as she pulled open my door. She reached across my lap to release the seatbelt then helped me climb down from the cab.

My legs were shaky at first, but Mom looped her arm through mine and walked down the shoulder of the road, dragging me with her. By the time we'd gone thirty yards, my breathing was normal, and my legs were strong beneath me.

"Better?" she asked, and I nodded.

We walked a while longer before turning and heading back toward the truck. It was fully dark now, the road in this area lit only by the silver glow of the moon. Stars twinkled overhead, and the rhythmic crash of the ocean onto the beach down the hill kept us company as we walked. When we reached the truck, Mom checked the back bumper, shrugged, and pulled open her door.

When I opened my own door, a breeze rushed through the cab of the truck, rustling a stack of papers on the dashboard. I watched in the dim light as one of the papers broke free of the rest and blew out the driver's-side door, past my mom.

She spun, reaching out to catch it, but it flitted out of her grasp.

"Hold on a sec," she said before turning to chase after it.

I didn't see what happened next, but what she told me was she chased after the paper, which eventually settled onto the ground right beyond the end of the guard rail. She ran to it, reaching her foot to trap it before it could blow any farther away. Something about the way her stride hit the paper, or the way the paper was laying on the ground . . . I don't know what it was. All I know is that when she stepped on the sheet of paper, her foot slid across the gravelly shoulder of the road, and she fell, hitting her head on the guard rail on her way down.

I was at her side as soon as I registered that she'd fallen, but she was already waving me away, laughing at herself. She said she was fine, and she *seemed* totally normal. We climbed back into the truck and drove home.

It was after midnight when the commotion in the living room pulled me out of my sleep. I shuffled out of my bedroom, bleary-eyed and squinting against the light to see Dad draping a coat around Mom's shoulders as she hunched forward, wrapping her arms tight around her middle.

"What's going on?" I asked. I noticed Mom straighten at my words, but she immediately bent over again.

"Go back to bed, sweet girl," she said. Her voice sounded weird and distant, and fear prickled at the back of my neck.

"Dad?"

He left Mom by the door and made his way to me, crossing the room in three long strides. "Your mom's had a headache for a while, and now she's feeling sick. I'm taking her in to get checked, to make sure everything's okay. There's nothing you need to worry about."

I stared numbly past him to where Mom stood, her shoulders shaking ever so slightly.

Dad shifted to block my view. "Hey," he said, gently turning my face to his. "It's going to be fine, okay? I need you to get some sleep. Go back to bed, and don't you worry. Promise?"

He hugged me fiercely then nudged me back toward my bedroom. In the dark, I lay flat on my bed and listened to the sound of Dad's car pulling out of the driveway. Lylah and Ezra showed up only minutes after my parents left, but their presence in the house did nothing to fill the hole left behind. After Lylah left me in my room, I promised myself I would stay awake until my dad got home, but the next thing I knew, it was morning, and I was still lying on top of the bed covers.

Mom never came back home after that night. She spent three days in the hospital before she died, and in that time, she only woke up once. She seemed like her old self for a few hours, and we thought she was coming back to us. It was the last time I ever talked to her.

"We wouldn't have even been there if it weren't for me, Ezra. She wouldn't have gotten out of the truck if I hadn't freaked out. She drove me out to see the fireflies because I was upset. It was the night after that party at Hannah's house. She and the other girls were teasing me because of . . ."

I trail off, and one look at the blush rising in Ezra's face tells me he knows the rest. They were taunting me mercilessly about our time in the closet. As soon as the boys left for the night, Hannah and her friends bombarded me with questions. I'd told them nothing happened, but they still wouldn't let up.

"Anyway, I was upset, and Mom dropped everything to take me out on a drive. And then she died."

Ezra's face softens. "Quin, you can't blame yourself for this. It was an accident."

I shrug. "An accident that wouldn't have happened if not for me."

"You don't know that," he says. "Your mom loved fireflies. Maybe she would've gone out there that night anyway."

I don't answer, and after a while, Ezra says, "Want to hear something foolish?"

"What's that?"

"I thought it was because of me."

"The accident? That makes no sense."

He laughs, sounding nervous. "No, not that. I thought you didn't want to be friends anymore because"—his eyes flick to my mouth—"because I kissed you. I thought I freaked you out, so when you wouldn't talk to me anymore, I thought that was why."

"Not at all," I say. "I couldn't deal with everything. I didn't know how to live without my mom. I still don't, not really. You and your mom reminded me so much of her, so I avoided y'all when you came over. It was easier that way. I'm truly sorry."

He waves off my apology, and we turn toward the water. At the end of the pier, a man lets out a whoop, and a bunch of people rush to him. He must've caught something big.

chapter
FIFTEEN

IT'S A BUSY NIGHT AT THE ORPHEUM. WE MANAGED TO snag opening weekend for the newest installment in the Red Heart franchise, and the theater is packed. I can't remember the last time we had a sold-out show. People tend to flock to the bigger multiplexes, and historic theaters like the Orpheum get left behind. We do okay and stay afloat, mostly thanks to the occasional weekend like this.

When the last moviegoers file into the theater, arms full of popcorn and drinks, I lean back against the concessions counter and take the first full breath I've had in almost an hour. I've been running nonstop since the moment I walked through the door for my shift, and I'm grateful for it. Keeping busy has kept my mind off the sadness of the day.

Ezra and I sat on the pier for nearly two hours until it was time for him to take me back to my car so I could get ready for work. I didn't know until he was there how much his company would help me, but I'm not sure I would've made it through the day without his friendship.

"How goes the prom planning?" Tyler asks me now. "You have the whole night figured out yet?"

"Not exactly," I say. "We have a meeting during homeroom Tuesday to finalize some stuff."

Tyler's never seemed particularly interested in prom before, and that small, hopeful part of me rises to the surface. I slip into a daydream of the dance with Tyler. It's nearly as effective a distraction as cleaning is.

The candy is in order, and I'm restacking the soda cups when I hear the front door open. Not wanting to deal with anyone else, I double down on my stacking efforts and call over my shoulder, "Hey, Ty, can you get that?"

"Sure." He jumps down from where he was sitting on the counter, scrolling on his phone. We're not supposed to have them out while we're on shift, but we all ignore the rule.

A few seconds later, I nearly jump out of my skin when a figure leans over the counter to look down at where I'm now organizing the storage beneath the popcorn machine. "Hey," he says, and I smack the back of my head on a metal shelf.

"Hi, Kenyon," I say. "Um, what's up?" What is he doing here? He's standing there, staring at me with a goofy grin on his face. I try to covertly catch my reflection in the glass of the popcorn popper—do I have something on my face? Popcorn in my hair? It wouldn't be the first time. But the glass has too much oil splatter on it to make a good mirror. I smooth a hand over my hair, stopping at my ponytail. Just in case.

"Not much," Kenyon says. "I was in the area, and I remembered you said you were working tonight, so I thought I'd stop by and say hi. So . . . hi."

"Hi," I say back. Why is he still looking at me like that?

"I had a lot of fun last night. Maybe, uh, maybe we could do it again sometime?"

It takes a second for me to register what he's saying. When I do, a rush of elation fills my chest, and I'm not sure if it's because I'm getting another chance to find out if he kissed me at the party or simply because of the idea of spending another evening with him. My mind flits back to last night, and my cheeks warm with the memory of our date.

He's waiting for an answer. I glance over my shoulder; Tyler's standing by the box office, watching us with interest. Angling my back to him, I tell Kenyon, "Yeah, that'd be great. I mean, my friends are on this ridiculous crusade to set me up with, like, every guy in school, so my social calendar is suddenly very full, but I'd love to go out with you again, and . . . what?"

Kenyon stares at me, one eyebrow cocked. Crap, did I seriously tell him all that?

"Every guy in school, huh?" he says, way too loudly.

I shush him, glancing back at Tyler—his amused expression confirms he's heard everything. Great.

"Okay, not *every* guy in school," I say, giving up on being quiet—it's not like I have much to hide at this point. "A few guys. Like, four or five."

"Okay, and why?"

"It's a long story," I say. And one I'm absolutely *not* sharing in front of Tyler. What if it was him in the theater? I *hope* it was him, his hands in my hair, his lips on my own.

"We've got time," Tyler says from behind me. "Don't we, man?"

Kenyon looks at him then back at me. "Um, I guess?"

"Okay then," I say loudly. "Thanks for stopping by, Kenyon. Text me. Or call me?" What is the right way to do this dating thing? "Or I'll see you Monday? You're ready to start filming, right? Ezra seems nervous, but I think it'll be fine. Kira knows what she's doing, and they worked well together, so I think he'll be able to handle it . . ." I'm rambling. Ugh. Why is it so much harder to talk to him now than it was before our date?

Maybe because every time his lips quirk up into that half-smile of his, I can't help but wonder if they were on mine at Nana's party.

"Yeah," he says. "I'm ready. It'll be fine. I guess I'll see you at school then?"

Kenyon darts a quick glance at Tyler, leans across the counter, and plants a quick kiss on my cheek before walking out of the theater.

I brush the warm spot his lips left with my fingertips as I watch him leave. Then I see Tyler staring at me with that same amused expression he's worn for the whole exchange, and I force myself to drop my hand.

"Last night, huh?" Tyler smirks at me. "What happened last night?"

"Nothing," I say. I turn back to the cups and restack them.

"Didn't sound like nothing to me. He wouldn't want to be doing *nothing* again sometime soon."

"Shut up," I say, but not unkindly. "If you must know, my friends set me up on a blind date with Kenyon last night."

"And you want to go out with him again?" Tyler's sitting on the counter again now, but he's lost the chill vibe he had earlier. Instead of casually scrolling through his phone, his hands grip tightly to the countertop on either side of his thighs. Does he really care about my answer? Our regular flirting has never moved beyond lighthearted banter, but am I sensing potential jealousy here? Maybe I'm not the only one who's been hoping things would go further. The idea thrills me.

"Yeah, I guess," I say. "We had a good time. If he wants to go out again, I think it'd be fun."

"What's the deal with all these dates your friends want you to go on?"

"It's nothing. Just this stupid idea they have to find, um, the perfect guy for me, I guess."

He cocks his head to one side. "I thought you said it was a long story."

"It kinda is."

"That didn't seem so long."

"That was the *Reader's Digest* version."

"What the hell is *Reader's Digest*?"

Before I can explain, a man rushes out of the theater with his popcorn bucket, asking for a refill. I'm grateful for the distraction. Telling Tyler about my thrilling nightlife of lying on Nana's couch reading old copies of *Reader's Digest* doesn't exactly sound like the best way to win him over.

By the time I've taken care of the popcorn refill, a group of people has come in and clustered around the box office, taking Tyler's attention. Once they have their tickets, he pulls out his phone from his back pocket and hops onto the counter again.

I'm happy he's not pushing for details on Operation Mystery Kisser, but this feels like a dismissal. Like he's bored with me and would rather play on his phone than keep talking. Turning away from him, I duck back under the popcorn maker and resume organizing.

The longer I work, the more my irritation grows. I glare at Tyler, sitting there oblivious to the fact that I'm the only one working as he stares mindlessly at his phone, until I can't stand being in the lobby with him anymore.

In one quick movement, I jump to my feet and slam the little metal door to the compartment I was working in. Tyler looks up as I push past him, a question on his face, but I don't give him a chance to ask. Instead, I cross the lobby directly to the ladies' room, going through the door then leaning against it once it's fallen shut. *Deep breaths.* I can do this. I'm on edge because of the anniversary—that's all. I need a few minutes to myself to decompress.

The bathroom is surprisingly clean for how busy we've been tonight. I pick up a couple stray paper towels lying on the floor and move to check the stalls. The second one is . . . gross. Turning my head away so I don't have to watch, I lift my foot up to the flush lever and push down as my phone vibrates in my pocket.

I back away from the stall without risking another look before the door swings shut. If flushing didn't fix the problem, that stall can be out of commission for the rest of the night. I am not in the mood to deal with other people's literal crap. My phone buzzes again, so I pull it out and swipe away my lock screen. I have two new texts, both from Kenyon. A third pops up as I open the thread.

> **KENYON:** Hey, how about we see each other before Monday?
> **KENYON:** Like tomorrow?
> **KENYON:** Meet at Fort Fisher at 10 am?

A small thrill zings through me as I read his messages, which surprises me. I can feel a smile pulling at my lips as I type a response.

ME: What's at Fort Fisher?
KENYON: Will you come?
ME: I can't at 10.

As I hit send, disappointment swells in me, so I immediately start typing again.

ME: But maybe 11?

Three little dots bounce onto my screen, and I watch them with anticipation as Kenyon types. They disappear for a moment, then pop back up. The door to the bathroom swings open, and a group of slightly older girls rushes in, laughing and talking loudly. The movie must be letting out. Things will be busy again; I need to stop hiding in here and get back to work. I stare at the screen harder, willing the dots to be replaced by whatever he's been typing for so long.

KENYON: Sounds good, see ya there. Dress for exercise!

Wait. What? Why do I have to dress for exercise? I want to message him back and ask for more details, but when another group of women enters the bathroom, carrying the noise and chaos of the theater with them, I know I don't have time. Instead,

I slip my phone back into my pocket and weave my way through the crowd into the lobby, nervousness and excitement battling to become my primary emotion.

What did I just agree to?

When I get home from work, the TV is off and the recliner's empty. I'm so used to seeing Dad sitting there that I spin around to check the driveway before shutting the door. His car is parked in its normal spot.

I creep down the short hallway to his bedroom. The door hangs open a few inches, and I step forward to peek inside.

Dad's lying on his side on the bed, his back facing the door. I think he's asleep, but then I notice the glow of a phone in his hand. Shifting to the side so I can get a better angle, the screen comes into view.

It's a picture from their wedding, a candid the photographer caught at the reception. They're dancing, and Mom's head is thrown back in that laugh she had that could light up the entire world. Her hair is loose and wild, taken down from the updo she wore at the ceremony, and her bare feet are only just visible under the swishy hem of her gown.

In the picture, Dad's staring at her with such adoration that my heart aches.

A shadow slips across the screen, Dad's finger caressing the picture. It's then that I notice the shaking of his shoulders, and suddenly I feel like I'm intruding on the most private moment possible. He didn't forget. How could he? Of course this day is as hard for him as it is for me. Dad lost his *person*, his other half. He may not talk about it often, but that doesn't mean he isn't feeling it still.

Wiping a stray tear from my cheek, I back away from the door as quietly as I can and slip into my own bedroom.

chapter
SIXTEEN

"YOU AREN'T GOING ON A DATE DRESSED LIKE THAT, ARE you?" Nana's sitting in a wingback chair, an embroidery hoop in her hand, when I walk out of her bathroom dressed in a pair of shorts and an oversized T-shirt, my old gym shoes on my feet.

I look down at my outfit. The shirt has the words *Running Wild* in bright letters across the chest, as if I run. Ever. Exercise and I don't exactly get along, so it's not like I have a lot of options to choose from. I may not know what exactly Kenyon had in mind when he told me to dress for exercise, but I'm relatively sure one of Mom's old dresses isn't going to work.

"What?" I say, pulling the bottom of the shirt out so I can see it better. "He said I should dress for exercise."

Nana places the hoop on a small table next to her chair. She looks the epitome of a Southern grandmother sitting with her embroidery, but in the light of the library lamp she set it under, I can read the beginnings of the crude word she's stitching.

"Come here," she says, waving to me with an over-enthusiastic flick of her wrist. I trudge across the room until I'm standing right in front of her.

"Where is this boy taking you?" With deft hands, Nana grabs the waistband of my shorts, flipping it down once, then moves to the hem of my shirt.

"I don't know," I admit. "We're meeting at Fort Fisher." I check my phone as she twists my shirt into a knot above my left hip. "I actually better get going if I'm gonna get there on time."

"There's not much I can do about your shoes," she says with a weary sigh, "but go look at yourself." As I make my way to the bathroom, she adds, "And put a bit more blush on while you're in there. Look alive, girl!"

Inside the small powder room off Nana's entryway, I stand in front of the mirror and pull my hair into a quick ponytail. I left it down this morning, letting my natural wave air dry, so now it's bouncy and wild at the back of my head. I skip the blush Nana suggests, but I do slick on a fresh layer of Berry Burst lip gloss.

I take a minute to admire Nana's handiwork. Somehow, she's taken my ill-fitting, frumpy outfit and turned it into something cute. My shorts fit better with the waistband flipped down, and between that and the tied shirt, a narrow stretch of skin shows. This is about as date appropriate as workout clothes will ever be.

I snap a quick picture on my phone and send it to our group text. My friends would kill me if I didn't share my pre-date prep with them. The responses start coming in immediately, my phone dinging five times in rapid succession.

HADLEY: You look so cute!

NAOISE: You're wearing that on a date?

HADLEY: What? It's cute!

NAOISE: Y'all have no sense of fashion.

SHYLA: You look great Q! You gonna get your kiss this time?

My stomach jumps and twists at the thought of kissing Kenyon. By the end of our date Friday, I wanted to kiss him—maybe not just because of Operation Mystery Kisser, either. But now that I've had a full day to think about it, I'm not sure how I feel. I'd never gone on a date before Friday night; did I want to kiss Kenyon because of *Kenyon* or because I'd worked myself up to the idea of a first-date kiss? The date was fun, sure, but I don't know what to think about how it ended.

My cheeks warm with the memory, though, so maybe I *do* know what I think about it.

"You all right in there?" Nana's voice carries through the door, startling me back into motion. I wash my hands so it sounds like I'm doing something productive, then I type out a quick reply.

ME: He said to dress for exercise! This is the best I could do. And I dunno. I guess we'll see.

SHYLA: You HAVE to kiss him! How else will you know?

HADLEY: I guess she could go on a third date if they don't kiss today.

I can't even think about a third date right now. My nerves are ratcheting up the closer it gets to being time to leave. My hands shake as I swipe across my phone screen, responding.

ME: Well, I gotta go. I'll update y'all when I get back.

New messages flood in lightning quick. I'm pretty sure my friends are even more invested in the outcome of this date than I am.

SHYLA: Don't die. It's only a little exercise.
NAOISE: Have fun! We still on for later?

I'm going to her house after my date so we can work on fitting my prom dress. I can't wait to see what she's done so far.

ME: Very funny Shy. Yeah we're still on. See you then!
HADLEY: Okay Dad's calling me. Gotta go play. There's
   youth council after church so I won't see messages for
   a while but tell me EVERYTHING ok?

I don't answer but shut my screen off and slip my phone into the waistband of my shorts. That's another thing about exercise clothes: Where am I supposed to put my stuff? Would it be so hard for designers to throw some pockets into shorts?

"I better get going," I say as I walk toward Nana. She's still in her chair, embroidery hoop back in her hand, and she looks me up and down in one swift movement.

"You have fun, dear," she says with a smirk.

I don't like the look she's giving me. "What?" I say.

Her smirk shifts into a full smile. "Nothing, dear. Don't die out there, okay?"

"Ugh. Why do people keep saying that to me?" I mean, I know I'm not the most athletic person in the world, but I'm not going to *die* doing whatever it is Kenyon has planned.

At least, I hope not.

The Jeep is parked at the Fort Fisher Rec Office, backed in and facing the entrance to the parking lot. The top is off today, and it looks like it was made for the beach. Kenyon's sitting on the hood, his long legs stretched out in front of him, and he lifts a hand in a casual wave as I pull into the lot.

He's wearing a fitted V-neck shirt and slim board shorts, and . . . *wow.* He looks good. I'm suddenly even more self-conscious about my T-shirt and shorts. At least Nana's adjustments made the outfit a bit nicer. I lean to the side, trying to catch a surreptitious glance in the rearview mirror. As far as I can tell, my hair is still looking good, and my lip gloss has just the right amount of shine to draw attention to my mouth. Perfect. But maybe I should've taken Nana up on that blush tip after all.

The sun is warm on my skin when I step out of my car, and a gentle ocean breeze flutters my ponytail around the side of my face. For a moment, I let myself close my eyes and inhale deeply, savoring the salty tang in the air. Then I make my way toward Kenyon, who drops off the Jeep hood and meets me halfway.

"Hey," I say when we're standing in front of each other, closer than normal. A smile pulls up the corners of my mouth as I look up at him. Warmth kindles in my chest, and I realize I *missed* him—not that I'm ready yet to figure out what that means.

"Hey yourself," he says, his grin matching my own. "You ready to go? We gotta move if we want to beat the tide."

I lean, peering around him toward the park office and what I can see of the beach beyond.

Kenyon gestures to the Jeep, his arm wide and dramatic. "Your chariot," he says with a goofy half-bow.

Pulling my seat belt across my lap, I click it into place and ask, "Where are we going exactly?" The rec area is pretty much the last thing on the island, so I'm confused why he had me drive all the way here if we're going somewhere else.

"I thought we'd take a bike ride," he says.

"But I—"

"I borrowed my mom's bike for you." He jerks his head, and I follow the gesture toward the back of the Jeep, where—sure enough—two bikes are attached to a metal rack. Helmets, water bottles, and small backpacks fill the back seat.

"Okaaaay," I say, drawing the word out. "But where?"

In response, Kenyon takes a sharp turn out of the parking lot and onto a road that's not so much a street as it is an area of compacted sand in a road-like shape. Instinctively, I reach up and grab the Jeep's metal framing for support. Kenyon laughs.

"Relax, Quin. I've got this. We used to go off-roading back in Colorado all the time. The sand is nothing this old girl can't handle."

We follow the road until, before long, it fades away and we're left on the soft sand of a narrow beach. The Jeep's rear end swerves and fishtails, but rather than the fear I expected, my stomach flips in exhilaration. Kenyon seems to be in total control of the vehicle, and I feel safe with him. I release my grip on the roll bar and flex my fingers one by one. When we lurch into a dip in the sand then bounce back out the other side, I give a loud whoop of excitement.

Kenyon wears the same excited expression on his face that I can feel on my own. I'd never known you could drive out on the sand like this. Of course, my car would probably get stuck about three feet onto the beach, but maybe Mom's old truck could've handled this. She would have loved it too. She was the most adventurous of us all.

The sand is getting softer, the Jeep's tires slipping more as the engine revs and whines, trying to keep up. Eventually, we come to a stop, and Kenyon pops the stick into neutral before setting the parking brake and cutting the engine.

"Well, looks like that's as far as she'll go. It's all us now."

We meet at the back of the Jeep, where I watch as he lowers the two bikes to the sand. I've never seen bikes with such fat tires before; they are almost comical, like they were designed from a kid's drawing. Kenyon notices me staring and pushes one down with the palm of his hand.

"They're better for the sand," he explains. "You won't have to work as hard."

"Okay. You still haven't told me where we're going."

He's bent over one of the bikes, pulling a bungee cord tightly around a small bag he's attached to a rack at the back. Without looking up, he says, "Bald Head."

"We can do that?"

"Of course, why couldn't we?"

"Well," I say, wondering what I'm missing. "For starters, it's an *island*."

He stands, laughing, and runs a hand through his hair. The movement lifts his shirt, and for a second, a sliver of tanned skin shows between his shorts and shirt. I try not to stare. "Didn't you grow up here?"

"Yeah, so?"

"So, the islands are connected. A hurricane closed the inlet, and we can ride across now."

"Seriously?" I glance around the Jeep as if I'll be able to see the stretch of sand all the way to Bald Head Island. "When did that happen?"

"Before we were even born. Hey—catch!" He tosses a helmet my way, and by the grace of Lucille, I manage to catch it with only a bit of fumbling. I stand there, holding it numbly, and watch Kenyon as he wraps a thin piece of fabric around his forehead before lowering his own helmet onto his head, fastening it with a sharp *click*.

"Oh, hey," he says when he sees me staring, "let me help with that."

He's standing right in front of me faster than seems possible, reaching a hand toward my face. I freeze, standing like a statue as he stretches his arm out behind me and slips the ponytail elastic from my hair. My waves drop around my shoulders, free and wild. The ocean breeze whips them across my face, and a lock of hair sticks to my lip gloss. Great. That's sexy.

"Sorry," he says with a laugh, trying to free my hair. At some point, I convince my hands to move again and pull my hair into a low ponytail, where I hold it in my fist until Kenyon returns my elastic so I can secure it. By the time he places the helmet on the top of my head, I'm more than ready for this moment to be over.

Kenyon pulls a tube of sunscreen from his bag, and we both slather it on before strapping on hydration backpacks and climbing onto our bikes. It takes a few minutes for us to find our groove, but eventually we're riding alongside each other down the wet sand toward Bald Head Island. The sun is hot on my shoulders, but the salty mist hitting my face keeps me comfortable. I close my eyes for as long as I dare, soaking in the peace of being alone on this beach with Kenyon.

"What're you thinking about?" he asks, cutting through my reverie.

My eyes snap open. I'm riding so close to him that I'm surprised we didn't crash. "Um, nothing," I manage.

"Oh, come on. Nobody is ever thinking of absolutely nothing."

"I was," I insist. "My mind was one hundred percent empty."

He laughs. "If you say so."

"Well, what were *you* thinking about, Mr. Nobody-is-ever-thinking-of-nothing?"

He doesn't answer right away, and I watch him out of the corner of my eye as we ride along in silence. Apprehension slithers up my spine. I pull the mouthpiece of my hydro bag between my teeth to distract myself. The water is still cold, and I end up drinking more than I intended. I need to slow down; I can't imagine there's a toilet along this ride.

Finally, Kenyon sighs softly and says, "I was thinking . . . wondering really"—he hesitates, blowing breath between his lips in a long, steady exhale—"why we've never done this before?"

"This? Like bike to the island?"

"No, this." He gestures back and forth between us. "Why haven't we ever hung out outside of school? Gone out?"

"Well," I say, "we've not exactly been friends."

"I know. That's what I was thinking about. Why is that?"

It's clear what he's really asking, the question he can't quite bring himself to voice: Why have I been such a jerk to him since he moved here? Why did I write him off on day one as the enemy?

"I guess," I say, drawing the words out to buy myself time, "I was threatened by you. I've been working since freshman year to get into Mr. Welles's advanced film class, and here you come partway through first semester, waltzing in like you belong there."

"It's not like I—"

I cut him off, needing to finish this before I lose my nerve. "I know, I know. It wasn't your fault. And you're good, Kenyon. Really good. You should be in that class. But that didn't make it any easier to have you swoop in and steal the attention."

"Wow. I had no idea you had such a fragile ego, Quincy."

"Yeah, well, I'm a woman of mystery. Anyway, after a while, it became normal for us, you know?"

"What did?"

"Arguing. Fighting. It's what we do. Or did, I guess."

We fall silent, nothing but the sound of soft waves washing across the shoreline to keep us company. The tide is coming in, the bar of sand we're riding narrowing by the minute, and a mild panic that we won't make it to the island before the water totally covers our path starts to grip me.

"I have a confession," he says, breaking through my worry.

"That's a great way to start a conversation."

"Okay," he says, "here goes. I'm not in your group for *Maybe, Probably* by chance. I convinced Mr. Welles to let us work together."

"You did? But why?" This makes no sense, especially since all we ever did was argue in class.

"Because you're the best writer in the class. I knew your movie would be good, and I wanted to work on the best." He throws me a quick smile. "Plus, Donovan told me you were trying to get the Blackmagic, and there's very little I wouldn't do to be able to work with that camera."

His voice is teasing, so I match his tone. "Even work with your nemesis?"

"Especially that."

chapter
SEVENTEEN

LESS THAN FIFTEEN MINUTES LATER, WE REACH BALD Head Island, biking farther up the beach and away from the water. Kenyon slows, propping his bike up between his legs as it comes to a stop, and I drift next to him. Unfortunately, this bike is too big for me, and I can't stand astride the middle bar. As I start to tip, I suppress a squeal and fling one leg over the bar, jumping into the sand. By some miracle, I don't fall on my face, but I can't say the same for my bike.

I can hear the laugh Kenyon tries but fails to keep muffled. "That was the most graceful thing I've ever seen."

"Shut up," I grumble, but I can't help but smile. "You'd fall, too, if you didn't have daddy long legs."

He pulls the bag off the bike rack and digs through it, eventually revealing a small rainbow packet, which he shakes until it expands into what looks like one of the parachutes we used to play with in gym class as kids. It settles onto the sand, then Kenyon turns back to the bag.

"You gonna stand there all day, or do you want to join me?"

He's looking at me with an amused expression on his face, all raised eyebrows and half-smile, and *oh*. I've been staring at him this whole time. Standing here like a dork next to my fallen bike, watching this beautiful boy who's full of surprises.

I make my way to the parachute blanket and settle onto the edge of it, sitting cross-legged. Kenyon tosses two bottles of some sort of juice onto it then lowers himself next to me with the bag in his lap. It's not until he reaches in and pulls out a heavy paper take-out box that I see the bag is actually a cooler. He sets the box on the blanket in front of me then pulls a second one out for himself.

He pops open his box, so I do the same with mine. Inside is an assortment of food: a New England hot dog bun, toasted on both sides, a pile of lobster, a small plastic container with a yellow liquid in it, and a thick slice of cucumber.

"Oh my gosh, you brought lobster rolls?"

"No," Kenyon replies, picking up his bun, "I brought all the stuff to assemble them. They'd get soggy if I brought them this far already put together." He sets to work doing just that, stuffing the lobster into his bun and drizzling lemon butter over top.

"Where'd you even get this stuff?"

He shrugs. "Lobster Dogs had their truck out at Carolina Beach this morning, so I swung by and picked them up on my way to meet you. I also got"—he reaches back into the cooler and pulls out another container—"some of their pineapple cole—"

I snatch the new container from his hand before he can finish his sentence and pry the lid off. "This stuff is my favorite!"

He's already eating his roll, so I assemble mine, adding a scoop of the coleslaw to the bottom of the bun before topping it with lobster. We eat in silence, looking out over the water as waves crash gently across the shore.

This stretch of beach is totally deserted. I haven't seen another person since we left on our bikes. I know that only a mile or so south of here, the beaches are filled with people enjoying the heat of the early afternoon, but sitting with Kenyon, it feels like we're in a world of our own.

"Was it weird moving to a new school for your senior year?" I ask when we finish eating.

Kenyon leans back on his elbows, his legs crossed at the ankles, stretched out long in front of him. "I'm used to moving around. Dad was stationed in a new place every couple years when I was little. But, yeah, this was different."

"How so?"

"Well, for one, we've been in Colorado longer than anywhere else, so it was a lot harder to leave." He pauses, inhaling a long breath through his nose, and it makes me feel like this is hard for him to talk about. I consider changing the subject, but I remember how nice it felt telling him about my mom on our first date. Maybe he needs this. I wait.

"I've been with my dad ever since the divorce," he says finally, and his voice sounds strange, like he's working to push it through his throat. "They split up right after he got home from his last deployment. I'm pretty sure my mom was waiting for him to get back so she could leave."

"What's it like living with her?"

"Weird. She has a whole new family now. I was an only child my whole life, and now I have five younger brothers."

I try—and fail—to hide my shock. "Five? That's . . . a lot."

Kenyon laughs, rolling onto his side and propping his head up with his hand. Warm breath glides across my arm as he talks. "That's one way of putting it."

"I can't even imagine," I admit. "I only have one brother."

"Younger or older?"

"Older by three years. It's always just been us." The thought of Clark brings a rush of unexpected emotion—sadness mixed with anger—and I swing the conversation back to Kenyon. I'm not letting my brother ruin my day. "Having five little boys in the house sounds like a recipe for disaster."

"It is. Big time," he says.

"What about your mom? Is she remarried? I mean, duh, all those brothers came from somewhere, but . . ."

Kenyon takes my awkward rambling in stride, chuckling softly before saying, "Yeah, she got remarried years ago. I live in my stepdad's house now. It's . . ."

"It's . . . what?"

He sighs, running a hand over his face. "It's different. Like living with strangers. Even my mom. We say all the right things and make all the right moves, but it's like we're actors in a movie, simply reciting our parts. And when we go out, people try not to stare, but I know I stick out like a sore thumb. My stepdad is this blond giant of a man, the opposite of my dad in every way. So when we go out, it's him, my mom, and all these little blond-haired, blue-eyed boys. And then me." He gestures to himself.

I take in his tanned complexion, his unkempt black hair, those impossibly dark eyes. "Then your dad, he's . . ." I trail off, unsure how to continue.

"Adopted from Vietnam as a baby, right at the end of the war," he says. "He grew up here in the States, and it's all he's ever known, but still—" He cuts off abruptly, a muscle in his jaw tensing.

Kenyon huffs out a small, humorless laugh as he pulls himself back up to a sitting position. "But still, people don't care that he's American, that he fights for this country. They don't care that he's dedicated his entire life to serving. They see his skin and his eyes, and they—" He pulls the lobster roll box into his lap and starts picking at the edges of the paper. "When they see me with my family here, they assume I must be an exchange student or something."

"I'm sorry," I say. "That must be frustrating."

He shrugs. "Most of the time, it's no big deal. They ask where I'm from, and I say Colorado, and that's the end of it. But there's always that one person, the one who wants to know where I'm *really* from, you know?"

I don't know. How could I? But it seems to be a rhetorical question; he doesn't wait for a reply before continuing. "Anyway, I'm trying to get through this year so I can go back to Colorado for college."

Things may be strained between me and Clark, but my family is my world. The idea of feeling like a stranger in my own home, of having that kind of stiffness around Dad or Nana, of people thinking I don't belong with my own family—it sends my stomach tumbling. Part of me wants to reach out and grab his hand, to let him know I'm here for him. That I'll listen if he wants to talk. I may not understand where he's coming from, but I don't think he needs someone who understands as much as he simply needs someone who will listen.

But I don't because I let the pesky other part of me, the one that gets suddenly scared, take over. What if I reach for his hand and he pulls away? Am I reading way too much into the fact that he's opening up? I mean, that's kind of the point of a date, right? To get to know each other? And I did ask. Maybe he'll see me taking his hand as pushing this into the realm of too much too fast.

I focus on the last thing he said and ask, "Where in Colorado?"

His face morphs into an expression I can't quite read—disappointment? Relief? Something else entirely?—then relaxes back to normal. "Denver. The Colorado Film School."

"Oh, they are supposed to have amazing programs! What's your focus going to be?"

"Cinematography. I'm going to take some writing classes, too, though."

"Is that where you and your dad lived? Denver?"

"No," he says as he drops the take-out container onto the blanket. "We were in Colorado Springs, about an hour south. That's where the Air Force base is. But since Dad deployed from there, I still count as a Colorado resident, so I get in-state tuition, which is a huge help."

"That is nice. My dad teaches at the University, so I get a break on tuition. I don't know what I'd do without that."

Kenyon cocks his head to the side and looks at me with an unreadable expression. His mouth opens like he's going to say something, then closes again. One, two, three times. Then, finally, he says, "Can I ask something that's probably not appropriate?"

I mentally weigh my options. If I say no, will things get awkward between us? If what he asks really *is* inappropriate, that'd be awkward anyway, right? There's no way to know which way to go without knowing what his question is, and then it'll be too late to change my mind. After a seconds-long pause, I say, "I guess so?"

Kenyon looks as awkward as I feel. Seeing the unease on his face doubles my pulse. The muscles in my back tense as I wait for him to ask.

"Okay, so, your mom was an actor, right?" Before I answer, he talks over me. "I mean, I know she was. And she was pretty famous. In a lot of stuff. Like, some big movies. So, um"—he runs a hand over his head, like he's going to slide it through his hair, but he's still wearing his sweat band, so instead he sort of pats it and then drops his arm back across his knees—"didn't she leave you any money?"

My head jerks back like I've been slapped, and a sharp breath pulls through my teeth. I've not talked to anybody but my family and a lawyer about what Mom left me; not even Shyla, Naoise, or Hadley know. They've never asked, and now that the question is out there, hanging between me and Kenyon, I wonder if that's because they never considered it or because they didn't want to offend me.

"Yeah," I manage to say, the word feeling foreign in my mouth. But once it's out there, I find that I want to talk about it. "She did. A lot, actually." I try to shrug, like it's no big deal, but I'm afraid of his reaction. We're feeling out this new thing we have going on and I'd hate for things to get weird between us over something like money.

"Then why does it matter that your dad can get you a tuition break at the University? You can afford it anyway, right?"

Without warning, tears spring to my eyes as the memory of my mom floods over me. I turn my head, wiping at my face hastily.

"Oh, hey," he says, his voice soft. "I'm sorry. I shouldn't—"

Shaking my head, I wipe at my eyes, turn to him, and say, "No, it's not you. Um—you know how my mom died, right?"

He nods.

"Well, she was in the hospital for a few days first. I went to visit her the day before she—" Another wave of emotion threatens to topple me, and I squeeze my eyes against it until little bursts of white bloom behind my lids. "She'd been unconscious basically since she first went in, but she was awake then, so I got to talk to her."

She looked so normal when I walked into her room, sitting up in the bed with a soft smile on her face. Even covered in wires, monitors beeping around her, and under the harsh fluorescent lighting, she was the most beautiful woman I'd ever seen.

"Hey, Boop," she said, calling me by the nickname I hadn't heard since I was a little kid. She opened her arms to me, and I rushed into them, climbing up onto the bed with her. She held me so tight, as strong as ever, and my heart surged with the hope that she'd come home soon.

146

"How's it going at home?" she asked. "Are you taking good care of your daddy and brother?"

I laughed. "Dad lets us eat pizza pretty much nonstop. He's hopeless without you."

Her breath hitched, her chest stilling beneath me for a fraction of a second. "I'll have to harass him to make sure he cooks you a real meal."

"I like pizza," I said, and we both laughed.

We sat cuddled together for ages. She was so soft against my side, like her body was molded specially for me, and her familiar scent overpowered the antiseptic smell of the hospital. If I closed my eyes, it was like we were back in the bed of her truck, out on the back roads watching the fireflies.

Dad peeked his head in to ask if we needed anything, his face softening when he saw us together.

"Have you gotten ahold of Clark yet?" Mom asked him.

He shook his head, a sad smile pulling across his mouth. "I'll keep trying. We'll get him here."

We sent Dad off in search of hot chocolate and cookies, then Mom sat up a bit straighter. "Hey, Boop?"

I twisted to face her.

"Yeah?"

"I want you to do something for me." Before I could reply, she continued, "I want you to do something amazing with your life, baby. I want you to love bigger than you ever thought possible, and I want you to create beauty. Be fearless, my girl, and always, always be *you*. Don't play it safe. Take risks, make mistakes, and do incredible things."

Tears flowed down her face now, leaving tracks across her skin, and my heart clenched with a strange sort of longing—like I missed something I was still holding on to. "Mama?"

She smiled, tears still falling, and pulled me tight to her again, pressing her lips to my head through my hair. "I love you so much, baby."

"I love you too." Crying, I hugged her back, even tighter. I didn't understand what was going on. She would be coming home soon, right? So why was fear rising in my chest, wild and uncontrollable?

Dad came back in, a steaming cup of cocoa in each hand and a package of Grandma's cookies sticking out of his front shirt pocket. His face fell when he saw us, but he quickly forced a light-hearted smile. I tried not to notice how badly his chin wobbled.

"Any luck?" Mom asked.

He set the cups on the rolling table next to the bed and pulled the cookies from his pocket, tossing them to me. He shook his head. "He's not answering his phone. I tried some of his friends, but nothing yet." Seeing Mom's expression, he added, "He'll call back soon. Don't worry."

The three of us settled in for a movie—*You've Got Mail*, one of Mom's all-time favorites. She fell asleep less than an hour into the movie, and Dad took me home so she could get the rest she obviously needed. I've never been able to watch that movie again since that day.

"That was the last time I talked to her," I tell Kenyon now. I gave up on hiding my tears long ago. This couldn't be normal, right? I may not have a lot of experience with dating, but I'm relatively certain that crying on dates is not the way to go, and here I am with the waterworks for the second date in a row.

It doesn't seem to bother Kenyon, though. He listens to my story without interruption, and now he says, "That's why you aren't using her money for school? Because you want to do something amazing with it?"

I nod. "If I couldn't go to college any other way, then I'd use it. Like, that could be part of my amazing thing, you know? But I want to go to UNCW, and not only because my dad teaches there. Saving the tuition money is a huge bonus. That way, I can use my mom's money for something truly amazing. Something fearless."

"What's that going to be?" he asks.

"I don't know yet. Maybe I'll use it to make a movie—"

"Another movie."

I tilt my head in agreement. "Another movie. One I think is truly worthy of her legacy."

"Whatever that ends up being," he says, "I can't wait to watch it someday."

He's looking at me with such a soft expression that I want to lean forward, close the gap between us, and press my mouth to his. Not because of what happened at Nana's party or because of Operation Mystery Kisser. Not so I can find out if he's the one I'm looking for. I want to kiss him for *him*. For this amazing date he planned, and for wanting to know more about me and my mom. For a dozen small moments that I'd never have imagined happening with Kenyon.

Before I can, though, he twists away from me and pulls his phone out of his backpack. "Oh, man," he says. "We better get moving if we want to be able to check out Bald Head before we have to head back."

Reluctantly, I stand and help him clean up our picnic mess, shoving the blanket and empty containers into the cooler before he straps it onto the back of his bike. We slip our helmets on and click them into place. Then, before I turn to my bike, Kenyon reaches out and takes my hand in his. My heart stutters.

"Thanks for telling me more about your mom. I know it's not easy." He squeezes my hand softly, then drops it.

As we climb onto our bikes, I wonder again who this strange and wonderful person is. Has he been hiding there under the surface this whole time? I think back on the months we spent bickering in class, and I feel a small pang at the time we wasted. When he turns back to me and gives me a full-wattage smile, I promise myself not to waste any more.

chapter
EIGHTEEN

THE FIRST RAINDROP HITS MY CHEEK JUST AS WE GET BACK to the beach where we picnicked earlier. Kenyon and I spent the rest of the afternoon in Bald Head, exploring the island like tourists. We visited the Old Baldy lighthouse and the Conservancy and hiked around the marshland and maritime forest. We were at Sandpiper enjoying some ice cream when Kenyon's phone sounded an alarm letting us know we needed to leave if we were going to beat the tide. We could've ridden the ferry to Southport then Fort Fisher, but—tired as I was—I was enjoying our adventure, so we took our bikes back around the tip of the island and headed toward the Jeep instead.

Now, as more rain splatters across my shoulders and darkens the sand in front of me, I wonder if we made the wrong choice.

"You doing okay?" Kenyon calls over the sound of the waves, which is suddenly much louder than it had been all day. The wind's picking up, and the rain is rapidly shifting from a light sprinkle to a downpour.

"Yeah!" I yell back, unsure if I'm trying to convince him or myself. The darkening sky makes it hard to see where we're going, and all I can think about is the narrow strip of sand we crossed on our way to the island. Will it still be there in a storm?

We push forward, both of us leaning into our handlebars as if tucking ourselves closer to our bikes makes this any easier. I count my pedal strokes in my head—up to ten, then back down to one—over and over, telling myself each time that I only have to push for ten more strokes. I reassure myself with the thought that these storms usually pass through quickly. They come fast and hard, but they're over soon.

A sharp movement out of the corner of my eye catches my attention, and I turn in time to see Kenyon fall, his bike shifting underneath him. He hits the sand hard and rolls onto his back, foam clinging to him as the tide pulls toward the ocean. I stop my bike, careful to hop off before I fall too.

"Are you okay?" I call out as I rush to him.

He groans. "Just hurt my pride." Another wave rushes up the beach, soaking him and covering the tops of my feet. "The sand washed out from under my tires."

Kenyon rolls to his hands and knees and pushes himself onto his feet. The passage back to Fort Fisher is narrowing ahead of us, the compacted sand we rode out on completely covered by the waves. A dune to the left looks to be the only way across, and I don't know if I can handle the ride on such soft sand.

As if reading my mind, Kenyon says, "I don't think we can cross that."

"What do we do?"

He stares at the disappearing sand bar for a long moment, then turns back toward Bald Head. "I think we need to go back," he finally says.

"Seriously?" The last thing I want to do is get back on my bike, but at least we know we can make it to Bald Head. Who knows how long we'll be out here, getting soaked while we wait for the path to Fort Fisher to open up again.

The ride to town is exhausting, and by the time we get to the ferry launch, I'm about ready to cry with relief. The rain has subsided to a light drizzle, the worst of the storm already past. We lean our bikes against a wall, and I collapse onto a bench while Kenyon goes to find out about fares and launch times.

My legs tingle as they relax after the exertion of the day. I can't even remember the last time I felt this exhausted. Maybe I should've stuck with gym classes instead of dropping them after sophomore year as soon as they were no longer mandatory. I wonder if I should be stretching, but I'm too tired to care.

My phone dings, and I dig it out of my bag to find I've missed three calls and a pile of texts from Naoise. I scroll quickly to the last one.

NAOISE: Hello?? Where are you?!

I glance at the time—it's already after five. How did that happen? Last time I checked it was barely past two. Sliding my thumb across my phone screen, I scroll back through my missed messages.

Oh, crap.

> **ME:** I am SO sorry! I'm still with Kenyon. We're on Bald Head waiting for the ferry.
> **NAOISE:** So are you coming or not?

I try to calculate times in my head, but I honestly don't know how long the ferry takes. She lives only a couple minutes from where my car's parked, though, so I can swing by on my way home. As tired as I am, I don't want to ditch my friend. Plus, I want to see my dress.

> **ME:** Yeah but it'll be a while. Is that ok?
> **NAOISE:** Totally fine. See ya when you get here!

I slip my phone back into my bag and recline against the bench. I've got my head leaned back against the wall, my eyes closed, when I feel Kenyon sit next to me. He relaxes, and his leg presses against mine, warm on my cool skin. "Ferry leaves in ten," he says.

Finally, I open my eyes and turn to face him, and holy cow he is so close. He's mimicked my pose, leaning back against the wall with his legs splayed in front of him. My eyes are level with his shoulder, and I have a near-overwhelming urge to drop my head onto it and take a quick nap.

He nudges me lightly with his elbow. "Hey," he says softly, "sorry this turned into such a nightmare."

"It wasn't so bad," I say, leaning into him. I mean it to be nothing more than a nudge back, but now that I'm here, pressed against his arm, I can't bring myself to sit back upright. "I actually had a lot of fun."

And it was fun. As tired as I am, it's a good kind of exhaustion. My muscles simultaneously ache and feel like jelly, but I also have this incredible sense of achievement. I can't remember the last time I rode a bike, and now I've ridden all the way to Bald Head. Plus, spending the day with Kenyon didn't suck. At all.

"I'm glad," he says. Then he pulls my hand into his, so effortless, like we hold hands all the time. An electric tingle zips up my arm and warms my chest.

"Me too," I say before settling my head onto his shoulder to enjoy the wait for the ferry.

"We're here." Kenyon's voice pulls me out of the half-sleep I've been slipping into for the past thirty minutes. We managed to get to Southport in time to bike over to the Fort Fisher ferry launch and take the boat across the Cape Fear River to Fort Fisher. Now I'm leaning against Kenyon's chest, his arm around me holding me tight. He's let me nap on him for two ferry rides, and as I wake up somewhat, I reluctantly push myself away from him.

"Sorry," I say. "I didn't realize how tired I was."

"Don't be," he says and pulls me tight to his side in a quick hug before standing and heading toward where we left the bikes.

"How are we gonna get back to your Jeep?" I ask a few minutes into our ride along the Aquarium Trail. We're cutting across to the parking lot where we left my car, but now I'm remembering how far down the sand he drove us earlier and dreading having to cross that ground on these bikes. Today was fun, but my body is one hundred percent done with biking.

"I'm not sure," he says. He gives me a quick once-over, and I know he can see that I'm not up for a longer ride. "I guess I could drop you off at your car then I'll ride in for the Jeep?"

"Or I can give you a ride home, and you can come back for the Jeep, um, sometime?" We start filming tomorrow right after school, so I'm not sure when he'll be able to make it back out here. Still, I can't imagine adding more biking to this day. "There's a bike rack at the park office, right? Do you have a lock?"

"Not with me," he says, "but I can't leave my Jeep anyway. My school stuff's in it. It's okay, Quin. I really don't mind going by myself."

"Okay," I say, "but I'll wait at my car for you to get back."

In the end, it's a moot point. As we roll up to the parking lot, we see a group of people a bit older than us—University students, maybe—piling into an old Blazer.

"Hey, hey, hey!" Kenyon calls as we pedal toward them. "Hold up!"

A guy in slouchy jeans, a UNCW hoodie, and Birkenstocks turns to face us, his hand on the door handle. "What's up?" he asks.

Kenyon pulls to a stop next to the Blazer, and I somehow manage to stop and climb off the bike without making a complete fool of myself. My legs feel like they're made of rubber.

"You headed down the beach?" Kenyon asks, and the guy nods in response.

"Think I can catch a ride? We left my Jeep down there, and it'd be a huge help if you could get me back to it."

The guy glances past Kenyon to me, and I do my best to look pathetically exhausted. It's not hard. I *am* pathetically exhausted. "Yeah, sure," he says, "but we only have room for one."

"That's fine," I say immediately.

Kenyon turns to me. "You sure?"

"Positive. I'll hang out here and make sure the bikes are okay."

He gives my hand a quick squeeze. "Thanks. I'll be back as soon as I can."

Twenty minutes later, we have the bikes secured on the back of Kenyon's Jeep and our backpacks and helmets stowed inside. We're standing between our cars, neither of us sure exactly how to end a day as amazing and surprising as this one. I've not thought about what happened at Nana's party or Operation Mystery Kisser for hours, but now that our date is over, I'm acutely aware that I still don't know if it was Kenyon in that theater.

And I desperately want to know. At least, that's what I tell myself when the urge to kiss him overwhelms me.

"Well, thanks for today," I say. "I had a really fun time."

"Really?" His disbelief is clear.

"Really," I insist. "I liked it. It was hard, but I've never done anything like this before. I'm glad you asked me."

"In that case, you're welcome. I had fun too." He takes a step forward, taking my hand in his. My chest thrills with the contact, the same warm fluttering I get every time he does this. He tucks a stray curl behind my ear with his other hand. Then he's leaning in, and my heart leaps with excitement.

"Can I?" he asks. He rubs his thumb gently across my cheekbone. "I mean is it okay if—"

"Yes," I whisper.

His lips are on mine, warm and soft. Eager. His hand slides around the back of my head, and he pulls me closer.

Kenyon coaxes my mouth open with his, and a soft mewling sounds in my throat. His tongue explores my mouth. I melt into him. He is a *really* good kisser.

Then my brain catches up with what is happening, and all I can think is *I am kissing Kenyon!* Followed closely by *Kenyon is not the guy from the theater.*

I kind of want to keep kissing him anyway, so I push up onto my tiptoes to reach him easier.

As soon as I move for more, though, the kiss is over. Kenyon steps back and drops his hand from my hair. "Whoa," he says, "that was . . ." He shrugs and shoves his hands deep into his pockets, pushing his shoulders up by his ears.

"That was what?"

"Better than I expected?" he says it like a question.

"I'm not really sure if that's a compliment or an insult," I say.

"Oh, no, it's definitely a compliment. I didn't think you'd be so . . . good. For a first kiss, I mean."

I laugh. "Oh, that wasn't my first kiss."

"Oh, really?" His eyebrows rise until they push against his sweat band. "Here I thought I was something special, being your first date and all."

"Sorry to burst your bubble, Kenyon. Apparently, I'm just that kissable." This feels natural, joking with him. It's comfortable.

"You definitely are," he says and presses his lips to mine again.

I lean into the kiss, running my hands up his arms to grab his biceps. He rests his hands on my hips and pulls me toward him.

This is nice. I could keep kissing Kenyon forever, I think.

Except there's this nagging voice in the back of my mind reminding me that I've known he's not the guy I'm looking for since the moment his lips met mine. His kisses are great, but they aren't the ones I've been missing for the past week. My chest flutters at the memory of my mystery kisser, mixing with the swirling excitement of Kenyon's mouth on mine. I still need to know who was in that theater with me.

I break away from the kiss and take a step back. "I should"—I clear my throat, hoping my voice will come out clearer—"I should go. I promised Naoise I'd swing by on my way home."

"Yeah. Um, yeah, I should probably get back too."

"Today was great," I tell him again. "I really did have fun."

"Me too," he says. "I'll see you tomorrow, Quincy."

When he leans in to kiss me one last time, I know I should tell him no. He's not who I'm looking for, and I don't want to lead him on. But instead, I let him brush his lips across mine a final time before we both get into our cars and leave.

chapter
NINETEEN

"HOLD STILL," NAOISE MUMBLES AROUND THE LINE OF PINS held between her lips. She pulls a swath of fabric up to my shoulder and pins it to the thin strap there. She works faster than I can imagine, twisting and draping fabric this way and that, pinning as she goes.

The second I walked in their front door fifteen minutes ago, she and Shyla pounced, demanding details about my day with Kenyon. They hung on my every word, filling in the gaps with *awwww* and *that's so cute!* until I'd given a play-by-play of the entire day.

"And then," I said as my chest trilled with the memory, "he kissed me."

"That's my girl!" Shyla pumped her fist in triumph.

A giddy smile lit Naoise's face. "So . . . was it him?

I shrugged, a sudden rush of disappointment falling over me. "Nope. Not him."

"Are you sure?" Shyla asked.

"Positive." I nodded, emphasizing my point. "It was . . . great. But definitely not the same."

"Well, at least you know," Naoise said as she slid her thumb across her phone to unlock the screen. The calendar app popped up. "And now we can move on to the next one. Maybe we can squeeze two in next weekend?"

"I dunno," I protested. "Isn't that kinda fast?"

She flipped to our text thread and scrolled up to the schedule I sent her yesterday morning. "A bit, but if we don't do this fast, we won't find out who he was before everyone has prom dates."

She had a point. And it could be fun. After all, I had a much better time with Kenyon than I had expected.

"Fine," I said. "You're right."

Now I run my fingers over the fine tulle hanging from my hips and try to get a better look at the dress. She has me turned away from the mirror so I can't fully see what it looks like, but the way she's draping this fabric doesn't seem anything like the way Lucy's and Ethel's dresses looked in the show. "Are you sure, Neesh? Want to see the picture again?"

"Will you trust me? I know what I'm doing."

"I know. It's just that, well, the dresses in the show didn't have the color up here, you know?" I try to nod toward the magenta mesh she's draped over my left shoulder without moving enough to disrupt her work.

"I know," she says. She's out of pins now and steps back to get a better look at her work. "It's not going to be exact, okay?"

"What? I thought—"

Naoise holds a hand up to silence me. "Trust me. It'll have the essence of Lucy's dress but will be something new and special, just for you. Okay?"

"Can I at least see it?"

"Nope." She grabs the pincushion from the table behind her and pulls at the fabric by my hip. "You'll see it when I'm done."

Naoise is a magician with fabric, so I force myself to stop worrying. She works for a few more minutes, then helps me shimmy out of the half-finished dress, easing it carefully past my hips so I don't stab myself with any of the billion pins she's put in.

We're sitting on the living room floor watching *Project Runway* with a bowl of popcorn between us when Shyla comes in. "My turn!" she holds a box above her head like a trophy.

"What's that?" I ask.

"My lehenga!" She skips away to her room, and I turn to Naoise.

"Her prom dress," she explains. "She ordered it from India, from this little shop in the town *Dada* and *Dadi* grew up in."

"That's really cool." I raise my voice to call after Shyla, "You're putting it on, right? I wanna see!"

She comes out a few minutes later wearing the most incredible outfit I've ever seen. The skirt is high-waisted and full, gorgeous shimmering fabric flowing all the way to the floor. It's white with a delicate golden brocade stitched across the fabric. Her top is a deep royal blue, fitted and cropped a couple inches above the top of the skirt. It has elbow-length sleeves, and when she turns, I gasp with surprise. The back is completely open—a single band at the bottom and two triangles across her shoulder blades that meet at the base of her neck are the only bits of fabric holding it on. It's daring and unique and stunning.

I've never seen Shyla in traditional Indian clothing before. Her grandparents came to the States when Dr. Patel was only two years old. They are both gone now, and I don't know how much they told her about her heritage before they died. From the bits I've gathered, they didn't have a great life in India, and once they came here, they did everything they could to leave that life behind.

Shyla never knew her biological mother, but she did know that her mom and Dr. Patel met when he was in grad school, and their romance was a whirlwind. When her mom got pregnant after only dating for a couple months, she wanted to give Shyla up for adoption. Dr. Patel fought to keep the baby, and his parents agreed to help him raise her while he finished medical school. Shyla's biological mom went back to Delhi as soon as she could after Shyla was born, and as far as I know, she's never tried to contact her. Naoise's mom is the only mom Shyla's ever known.

When we were in middle school, Shyla did a research project on the region of India her family came from. She got all into it, learning everything she could about the history and the people there. By then, though, her grandfather was already gone, and her grandmother had dementia, so she couldn't ask them about their lives in India. I remember her being upset at the time, but I'd never given it much thought beyond that.

Now, seeing her in this beautiful lehenga choli, I wonder if she feels connected to the heritage she's never really known.

"It's gorgeous," Naoise coos. She stands and rushes across the room to her sister, circling her and looking at the dress from all angles. Shyla wraps her arms around the small bit of midriff showing between the two pieces.

"I dunno," she says, sounding more reserved than I've ever known her to be. "You don't think it's maybe too revealing?"

"Nope," I say. "You look hot." I steal the queso dip from where Naoise has been hoarding it and dip a piece of popcorn.

"If you're worried, we can wrap a dupatta to cover you up more, but I don't think you should. You look amazing."

"Really?" She drops her arms so we can see the full view again.

"Really," I say. I glance at my phone and see the time. "Oh, shoot. I promised Dad I'd be home by nine to watch the new Amelia Earhart documentary with him." I ignore my friends' smirks. They think it's hilarious that I spend so much time watching the History Channel with my dad, but I love it. "We still good for tomorrow? Have everything set?"

"Oh my gosh, Type A, we've got it. Relax," Naoise says with a tease in her voice. I know I've probably been a bit neurotic about the start of filming tomorrow. I'm sure I'm irritating everyone with my nonstop reminder texts, but until we have the first day behind us, I can't help it. I want everything to go perfectly.

chapter
TWENTY

SPOILER ALERT: THIS IS NOT GOING PERFECTLY. WE'VE BEEN shooting for almost two hours, and we're going to lose our light before we get this shot.

"Cut!" I yell for what feels like the thousandth time, and everyone deflates with a collective sigh. Kenyon turns to me from behind his camera and raises an eyebrow.

"What's wrong now?" His voice is casual enough, but I know he—and everyone else—wants to move on from this scene already.

"It doesn't feel natural," I say. "Ezra, you need to relax some."

Maybe I shouldn't have insisted on filming the big climax and resolution on the first day. With more time together, Ezra and Kira might have more natural chemistry, and this scene wouldn't feel so forced. But today is the only day I was guaranteed access to the gardens, and it is the perfect location for this scene. We need to take advantage of it while we have the chance.

"Um, okay?" he says.

Kira huffs in annoyance. "Look," she says, "we've been at this forever, and it's not getting better." She turns to Ezra and adds, "No offense," then swivels to face me. "I'm taking a break. You're the director. Direct him."

She breezes past me and Kenyon and wanders down by the water, pulling her phone out and tapping at the screen as she walks.

Everyone stares at me, waiting for direction, and I'm frozen to the spot. Kira is right. As the director, it's my job to get the best performance I can out of my actors. I need to fix this.

"Ezra, let's go for a walk. The rest of you, um, work on relighting the scene. We're going to get this done as soon as we're back."

Ezra's face flushes, and he rushes to my side. "I'm so sorry, Quin."

"Come on."

We walk in the opposite direction from Kira. We dip down a hill and out of view from the rest of the crew. I stop behind some trees and look around to make sure we're alone.

"What's going on?" I ask.

Ezra shuffles his feet in the dirt and shrugs. "I'm no actor. You know that."

"You were brilliant at auditions, though."

"That was different." He looks at me finally, his face open. Earnest in that way he's always been. "There was no pressure

168

then. I was doing you a favor. But now? People are going to watch this."

I take his hand in mine, the easy way we used to do as kids, and squeeze. "You're still doing me a favor. Forget about what's going to come when we're done. Pretend this is another movie only our parents will ever see."

He's nodding at my words. Because he believes me, or because he's trying to convince himself, I don't know.

"Think you can do that?"

"That's not all," he says, and I wait for him to continue. "I guess I didn't think through how hard the, uh, kissing part would be."

I almost laugh until I realize he's being completely serious. "Ezra," I say, "have you never kissed a girl?"

He stares at me, and for some reason, my cheeks flood with heat. "Yes, I've kissed a girl. But it's not the same. I don't know Kira at all. How do I make it look convincing?"

This is what happens when you're shooting a film with no budget and very little access to real actors. Without this kiss, the ending of *Maybe, Probably* will fall completely flat. I need to figure out how to help Ezra through this.

An idea forms in the back of my mind, and I almost laugh at the absurdity of it. It could kill two birds with one stone, though. If this works, I can get Ezra past his block and know for certain that it wasn't him who kissed me at Nana's party.

Unless, of course, it *was* him.

I drop his hand and take a step back. There's a tree stump to my left, and I step up onto it, raising myself a few inches so I'm closer to Kira's height.

"How'd you know I'd be here?" I ask.

Ezra stares at me in confusion, and I repeat the line. Recognition dawns on his face, and he says, "Quin, I don't think—"

"*Don't* think," I say. "Just practice the scene. No pressure. It's you and me. Nobody's watching. Let's do this."

I repeat the line, and, after only a moment's hesitation, he steps closer.

"You told me you would be," he says. I open my mouth to deliver my next line, but he cuts me off. "We were at that little café downtown. You were wearing the blue sweater I hate, and you said you were going to come out here and get pictures of the birds." He takes another step. He's impossibly close now. "I listen to everything you say, Addie. I know you think I don't, but I do."

"Sebas—"

His lips are on mine. This is nothing like the soft brush of a barely-kiss he gave me back in eighth grade. This kiss is confident and sure. A declaration. His arms wrap around my waist, and I manage to move my own to his neck.

He breaks away and steps back. I wobble a bit on the stump.

"How was that?" he says.

"That was . . ." I touch my lips. That was one hell of a kiss is what that was. Nothing like I would've ever imagined coming from Ezra.

"You think that'll work?"

Oh, right. The movie. Ezra wasn't really kissing me. *Sebastian* was kissing *Addie*. He was practicing. I force myself back to reality. "Yes," I say, a bit breathy. "Do it like that, and you'll be perfect."

"I messed up a bit there. Sorry, I got nervous, and I skipped your line."

"It's better that way," I say. "Seriously, do it *just* like that." We won't even tell Kira. It'll be more natural if he talks past her line the way he did to me now. "Are you ready for this now?"

We walk toward the group. Kira's back on set, chatting with Marcus and Naoise, who's pulling at her clothing, making sure all the costumes are perfect.

"Hey, Quin?" Ezra says as we join the others. "Why isn't there some big, grand gesture here? Isn't this scene a bit, I dunno, *chill* for a romantic comedy?"

"Thank you!" Kenyon turns from the camera and faces us. My Canon is in a different spot now, shifted to get better angles in the changing light. "I've been saying that from the start. Romantic comedies need the grand gesture at the end!"

I groan. This is an argument Kenyon and I have been having in class since the day he was put on my team. "It's cliché," I say.

"The airport chase, the big song, the thousands of flowers filling up her house—it's overdone."

"It's not a cliché," Kenyon argues. "It's a trope. Your audience expects it. Is it really a romantic comedy without it? The guy has to—"

"That's the other thing," I interrupt, my voice rising, "why is it always the guy? Like girls never screw up? They never have to make the grand gesture?"

"Okay," Kenyon says, "have Adalyn do it." Ezra stands between us, obviously amused by our exchange.

"That's not the point," I say. "Neither of them has to make a scene. Sebastian needs to show Adalyn that he loves her the way she expects. It's quieter, sure, but it's supposed to be."

"But you love the grand gesture," Ezra says. "I've seen you cry at too many of them to believe—"

"I love the grand gesture in *other* movies. But it's not right for *this* movie. I want to make something different. Something unique. It needs to stand out."

"If you say so, Miss Director," Kenyon says, but he's smiling in a way that tells me he's teasing. We've gone around this argument enough times that we both know how the other feels about it. In the end, he agrees that it's my call. And I say no grand gesture.

"Okay, let's do this," I say. "We're losing our light, so let's get this scene done, and we can all go home for the night. You good, Ezra?"

He nods. He looks confident now. Determined. He looks like Sebastian.

Kenyon makes one last adjustment to the Canon before he heads toward the Blackmagic. As he passes behind me, he runs his hand along my lower back, softer than a ghost, then gives my hand a quick squeeze. My stomach flips, and I feel the smile spreading across my face.

Across the park, I catch Naoise watching me, a knowing glint in her eyes. Her gaze follows Kenyon for a second then snaps back to me, the question clear. I give the tiniest shake of my head. I need to focus.

Kira is back in her spot, camera strapped around her neck, ready. I see Ezra, out of view of the cameras, hop from foot to foot as he waits for his cue.

Okay, this is it. Kenyon is behind the camera and Donovan's in place with his boom mic. I wait for Marcus to get out of the shot after adjusting his last light rig.

"And . . . action!"

chapter
TWENTY-ONE

"HOW OLD IS THIS GIRL GOING TO BE?" I ASK. I'M STANDING in front of a wall of Mylar balloons, trying to pick the perfect balloon bouquet for a kid I've never met.

"Five," Naoise says. She and Hadley pulled me away the second filming was done this evening to go shopping for decorations. Shyla's been babysitting for her dad's assistant for the past four years. The girl's birthday is coming up, and she wants to surprise her with a full day of birthday fun. She sent the three of us to the party store while she went to Sprinkles Bakery to sweet talk them into making a last-minute cake.

I pull a unicorn balloon from the wall. What five-year-old girl doesn't like unicorns? Then, after a moment's hesitation, I grab one with a cartoon ninja as well. Just in case. Hadley gets the rest of the balloons so we can fill in the bouquet with plain colors around the shiny picture balloons.

We stroll through the aisles, filling the cart with matching crepe paper, tablecloths, plates, cups, napkins, and forks. There's hardly anything pink, purple, or black in this store that we don't take. This is going to be one incredibly over-decorated party.

"What about this?" I ask. It's a giant, inflatable Pin the Horn on the Unicorn game. The unicorn looks like it's probably bigger than I am when blown up, and the horns all have this weird goo on the bottom so they'll stick to the unicorn wherever they're put. "It's probably too much, right?"

Without a word, Hadley grabs the massive box off the shelf, struggling under its bulk until Naoise helps perch it precariously across the top of our cart. We make our way to the checkout stand to pay and get a helium tank.

As we leave the store, it's clear we made an error in judgment. We left Hadley's Bronco parked at the end of the street, and now we have to lug all this stuff more than a block to get to it. I'm sure we look quite the sight walking down the sidewalk laden with bags, a helium tank, and a giant box containing an inflatable unicorn.

"You have Saturday off for your birthday, right?" Naoise asks. She shifts the unicorn box to the side so she can see me better.

"Oh, yeah," I say. Truthfully, I've been so focused on *Maybe, Probably* and Operation Mystery Kisser that I haven't given much thought at all to my birthday this weekend. But I have the day off, anyway. "My manager gave me the day for filming. I took the night, too, in case it goes long. Why?"

She shifts again, and I move to stabilize the box. "Thanks," she says, and we waddle together, the box held awkwardly between us. "We need to make sure filming doesn't go too long. You have a date Saturday night."

I stop dead in my tracks, and the box slips from my fingers as Naoise takes another step. It tilts dangerously between us, and she fights to get a better grip, but it's too late. The box falls to the sidewalk. Half a dozen sparkly unicorn horns scatter across the cement.

Hadley steps on one and lunges forward, slipping, the helium tank stretched out in front of her as she tries to regain her balance. The canister hits me in the chest, and I let out a loud "oof" with the impact.

"I'm so sorry," Hadley says once she's firmly back on her feet. She sets the helium tank down carefully and chases after a stray horn.

Across the street, a family sits at Sprinkles, staring openly at the Three Stooges act we put on. The door opens with a soft tinkle of bells behind them, and Shyla steps out. She barely glances across the street before running toward us.

"Got the cake ordered," she says. She looks around at the horns scattered across the sidewalk and asks, "What happened?"

Naoise gathers three horns in her arms and shoves them back into the box. "I told Q about her date this Saturday and she flipped."

"Did not," I say. "I was just surprised. And, hey, if it's with Ezra, you can go ahead and cancel. It's not him."

"You don't know—" Naoise starts, but I cut her off.

"I *do* know," I say before quickly filling them in on what happened with Ezra earlier.

"Whoa," Shyla says. "Look at you getting it."

"Ew . . . don't say it like that. You make me feel dirty." I bend down and pick up a horn, rolling it between my palms. "But anyway, I've checked him off the list, so maybe we should just take the weekend off."

Naoise pulls the horn from my hands and tosses it back into the box. "If you want to find your mystery kisser before prom, you need to put yourself out there, Q. We're running out of time."

"Yeah, but . . . it's my birthday. I thought maybe . . ."

Naoise cocks her head to the side and gives me a knowing grin, and my sentence fades away, unfinished. "No, that's not it. Why don't you want to go, really?"

"No reason," I say way too fast. Hadley and Shyla look at each other, confused, but Naoise never takes her eyes from my face. She doesn't miss anything; I know she saw what happened with Kenyon on set today, and she probably has big ideas about what's going on.

Here's the thing about Kenyon: not even I know what's going on with us. The subtle touches and hand squeezes are something he's never done before, obviously. I know I had a great time with him this weekend, and I know he's a freaking great kisser.

But I also know it wasn't him in the theater at Nana's party. He's not who I've been looking for.

"Can I at least know who I'm being set up with this time?" I ask. "It was super awkward going in blind last time."

"That's the point of a blind date," Hadley says. "You have to go in not knowing."

"But there're only so many options, so I may as well know, right? Is it Tyler?" I can hear the hope in my voice.

Naoise rolls her eyes. "It's not Tyler. Let's go."

The four of us gather up the party supplies and walk toward the Bronco. It's a lot easier now that Shyla's here to help Naoise with the unicorn box.

"When is my date with Tyler?" I ask.

"I don't know yet," Naoise says. "We'll see."

"Maybe you'll find your guy before that, and you won't even have to go on a date with him," Hadley says.

"But I *want* to go out with Tyler. It's these other guys I'm not so sure about. Just because you don't like him for some reason—"

"I like him fine," Naoise says, sounding not at all like she likes him. "But I don't think he's your guy."

"Okay, so who am I going with on Saturday? It's my birthday after all. The least you can do is tell me."

"You may as well," Shyla says. "He already knows." At a look from her sister, she says, "Sorry. He wasn't really into the whole blind date thing. I really had to push him to agree to it, and I eventually had to tell him the truth." She turns to me. "It's Donovan, okay?"

"You told him—"

"Not all of it," she says. "He doesn't know about the kiss or anything like that. Just that it's a date with you. You'll have fun. Hey, what's that noise?"

We all stop, listening. After a moment, we hear it too. A weird, hoarse *maaaaa* sound.

"I think it's coming from behind your car," Naoise says. Hadley hesitantly walks around the side of the Bronco, the rest of us following.

"Oh my gosh," she says when she reaches the back of the car. She sets the helium tank on the sidewalk and rushes behind the Bronco, out of view.

Naoise, Shyla, and I share a look and, in unison, drop our own stuff on the sidewalk next to the car, following Hadley. We find her kneeling in front of a—

"Is that a goat?" Shyla says.

It's the tiniest, cutest goat I've ever seen. It's mostly white, with black ears and nose and calico spots on its back. Three of its four legs have black socks, as well, and the fourth is white.

Inexplicably, it's tied to the hitch at the back of Hadley's Bronco.

"It's a goat," I confirm. I look around for anything that might explain the presence of this random farm animal.

"Look at this," Hadley says. She lifts a string from around the goat's neck. There's a small card attached to it. She reads it to herself and smiles, then reads it again, aloud. "Will you goat to prom with this kid?"

At that moment, the door to the law office we parked in front of opens, and Tanner lopes across the sidewalk toward us. "Well, will you?" he says.

"Yes!" Hadley jumps to her feet and runs to her boyfriend. He grabs her in his arms and spins her around before setting her back on the sidewalk and pressing a kiss to her lips. "I'd love to go to prom with you."

chapter
TWENTY-TWO

ON SATURDAY MORNING, DAD PLACES A TOWERING STACK of pancakes in front of me. There's a single candle poked into the top one. We learned when I turned twelve that pancakes can only handle so many candles. Ever since then, I've always gotten one candle to blow out on my birthday morning.

Mom used to make them for me—my favorite rainbow sprinkle pancakes, the only thing she ever really mastered in the kitchen. When she died, Dad insisted on continuing the tradition. He burned the pancakes the first year, and they still aren't quite as good as Mom's, but I love them all the same.

"Make a wish," Nana says. She's sitting across from me in Mom's old seat. She has her hands clasped below her chin, and her collection of rings reflects the flicker of the candle back to me. I glance to my right, where Clark's chair sits, empty.

I wish Clark were here, I think to myself. *I wish I had my family back.*

I know Dad and Nana are thinking the same. More than once, I catch them eying his empty chair. I want to text him— maybe even call him—and ask where he is and what's important enough to miss this, but I refuse to let myself be even more disappointed by my absentee brother. It's clear he doesn't want to be here.

The three of us talk about our plans for the day as we eat. I tell them about the scene we're shooting later and mention that I'll probably be spending the evening with my friends. It's not exactly true, but I don't want to deal with all the questions that'll come from telling Dad and Nana I have a date.

"Unless you want me to come home?" I ask Dad. "We can hang out."

"Actually," he says, rubbing a hand across the back of his neck, "I figured you wouldn't want to spend your eighteenth birthday at home with your boring old dad—"

"You're not boring," I say automatically.

"Whatever you say, kiddo. But I have plans tonight, so you don't need to worry about hurting my feelings." I stare at him over my glasses and gesture for him to continue. "There's a showing of *1776* at Thalian Hall. I told my freshman lecture they can get extra credit if they go, but it'll probably only be me."

"That's nonsense," Nana says. "What could all those youngsters have to do on a Saturday night besides watch a bunch of people sing about American history?" Her eyes twinkle as she teases him.

"Very funny." Dad turns to me. "You have fun with your friends."

"I will."

We finish our breakfast, then I kiss Nana goodbye and give Dad a quick hug before heading to my bedroom to get ready for the day. Donovan and I are supposed to be going on our date directly after the shoot, so my outfit, hair, and makeup need to work for both filming and whatever we might be doing after . . . and I have no idea what that is.

I dig through my closet, trying to find the perfect birthday outfit. I've pulled about six of Mom's dresses out before deciding on a high-waisted plaid skirt and a slouchy crop top that hangs off one shoulder and shows a thin sliver of skin above my skirt. Just enough to be flirty and fun without overdoing it. I feel like I could be in *Empire Records*, another of my mom's movies that Ezra and I used to watch all the time.

A few hours later, Hadley and I pull up to Dr. Patel's office, and the cast and crew sing a rousing—if terribly off-key—version of "Happy Birthday to You." A huge bundle of balloons sways by the door, and I notice the unicorn and ninja balloons among them. I give Naoise a questioning look, gesturing at them, and she shrugs and beams her braces-filled smile at me.

We're filming at Dr. Patel's office tonight, thanks to her and Shyla. His office is closed on Saturdays, and he was nice enough to let us rearrange his reception area furniture so we could fake a restaurant scene. We've moved a small table in front of the window, and I watch as Marcus places a single flower in a vase and a candle in the middle of it. Naoise helps him fold some cloth napkins, and the two of them finish setting the scene together.

It's been fun seeing Marcus and Naoise become friends as we make this movie. They have a natural banter about them, and she seems comfortable with him, which is huge. Naoise doesn't always let her guard down around guys. She's been hurt too many times—people tend to think because she's beautiful, she should be in a relationship. They don't understand her disinterest. It's easier for her to shut herself off than to deal with the insensitive comments she used to get all the time.

I don't think I've ever seen her be so open and *herself* around someone who isn't me, Hadley, or her family. I'm happy for her. She could use another good friend.

"Sound is good," Donovan says. He's standing behind Naoise, his boom held out over the table. "I can pick y'all up perfectly."

"How's the lighting, Marcus?" I ask.

He gives me a cheesy thumbs-up and smiles, the light reflecting off his teeth, making them ultra-white against his dark brown skin. "I've got it covered. Don't you worry." He pulls a cord, and the window dims. The candle is lit, and he brings his softbox tripod in closer to the camera.

It's meant to be a romantic candlelit dinner, and if we keep the framing tight, I think we can pull this off. I've already decided to shoot the exterior shots at Black Sea Grill, and once we cut to this scene, I don't think anyone will be able to tell we aren't in a real restaurant.

"Okay then," I say. "Let's do this."

"Ready?" Donovan asks once we finish pushing the furniture back where it belongs. The scene went amazingly well. Even when the girl who was supposed to play the server didn't show up, we managed to move along with no problem. Hadley stepped in and played the part like it was written for her. She only said like five words, but still. It saved us today. Maybe I was simply emotional after my birthday breakfast, but I nearly choked up when I called cut for the last time. I have the greatest friends in the world.

We've been so busy this afternoon that I've not even had a moment to be nervous about my date. Donovan gave me a quick smile and a wave when he arrived on set, but then he went straight to work, not once mentioning the date during the shoot. But it's time now.

"Just about," I tell Donovan. "I have something I need to take care of really quick, then I'll meet you outside, okay?"

I slip into Dr. Patel's office and search his desk for a notepad. I know he has one—he used to bring extras home for Naoise and Shyla to color on all the time—and sure enough, I find a small stack of them nestled under his computer monitor.

I'm scribbling a quick note of thanks when I hear the door click shut. I look up. Kenyon's standing there, his back leaning against the heavy wooden door. "Hey," he says.

"Hi?" Why does that sound like a question? "What's up?"

"I wanted to say happy birthday before you head out on your big date."

Ugh, of course Kenyon would know about my date with Donovan. They are best friends. How did I never consider how weird this might be for him—and for me? At least I gave him fair warning that I'd be going on a lot of dates.

"Thanks," I say. "Any idea where he's taking me tonight? Nobody will tell me anything."

He grins, and there's a playfulness in his eyes. "Oh, I know where you're going. But I'm not telling."

"Spoilsport."

He's standing close now, with only the corner of Dr. Patel's desk separating us.

"You'll have fun, I promise."

"I hope so." Part of me is ready for this whole Operation Mystery Kisser thing to be done, to tell my friends to stop the plan. But the thought of never finding out who was in the theater that night leaves me with a hollow sensation deep in my chest, and a bigger part of me wants to find him. I want him to kiss me again with that same passion—I want him to take me to prom.

"Well, I guess I better get going." I put the note in the center of the desk where Dr. Patel will be sure to see it Monday morning.

Kenyon grabs my hand as I walk past him. An excited thrum starts at the base of my throat. I do my best to ignore it. He pulls gently, stopping me and turning me around. I look up at him.

He's staring at me with an emotion on his face that I can't place. He drops my hand, and the disappointment that floods me is surprising. He looks past me to the door.

"Happy birthday," he says finally.

"Thank you." Why am I hoping for more? I gesture toward the door. "I really should g—"

Kenyon threads his fingers into my hair and tilts my face up toward him, his mouth on mine, cutting off my words. He kisses me so gently it almost hurts, and I lean into him for more.

I grab his T-shirt and twist it into my fist, pulling him closer as I open my mouth to his kiss. A soft warmth builds in my chest, and I wrap my other hand around his where he holds my face so gingerly.

Kenyon breaks away and steps back. My hand slips from his and falls to my side. "Sorry," he mumbles.

"Don't be." I force myself to drop my grip on his shirt, even though all I really want is to pull him closer again. "That was . . . nice." Truthfully, nice doesn't cover it, but I don't have the words to express myself right now. Not when all I can do is wish for him to kiss me again.

"You're going on a date with my best friend," he says. "He sent me in to see if you were ready or if you needed any help."

"He did?"

Kenyon nods and runs a hand through his hair as he lowers himself to half-sit on the edge of the desk. "Yeah. Pretty sure this isn't what he meant."

"Hey," I say, stepping closer. "You know I'm only going out with Donovan tonight because my friends have this thing about setting me up on all these dates, right?"

"Isn't that the only reason you went out with me too?" he says.

"Well, yeah," I admit. "But . . ."

"But what?" He's leaning closer. I could lift myself onto my toes and press my mouth to his again. But I don't.

"I didn't expect . . ." I trail off. I don't know how to finish my thought. Not really. I didn't expect any of this. But mostly, I didn't expect the warmth that's glowing inside me right now.

I didn't expect fireflies.

"What didn't you expect?" Kenyon asks. Our lips are only a breath apart, and his words caress my skin as he whispers them. My heart trills in my chest, a fluttering so intense it's almost painful.

"This." I wrap my arms around the back of his neck, sliding my fingers into his hair, and pull his mouth to my own again.

chapter
TWENTY-THREE

WHEN WE LEAVE, I CAN STILL FEEL THE SENSATION OF KEN-
yon's lips on mine. His taste lingers in my mouth, a combination
of coffee and the cinnamon bears he's constantly snacking on.

We walk together, but with enough distance between us
that I can't feel his body's heat anymore. When we step outside
and I see Donovan waiting for me, my gut twists with guilt.

Kenyon gives Donovan a fist bump when he walks past, telling him he'll see him later. Kenyon calls out, "Happy birthday,
Quincy," one more time as he climbs into his Jeep.

"Ready?" Donovan asks.

I nod. "Sorry that took so long."

He shrugs. "It's fine." He opens the door of his car for me,
and I climb in.

We've been driving for a while when Donovan asks, "You
okay?"

"Yeah," I say, but the word sounds hollow. When did I
become the kind of person who kisses one boy minutes before
going on a date with another? And not just any other, but that

first boy's *best friend*. Three weeks ago, I'd never even been kissed properly. Now I'm juggling two guys in one night?

"You and Kenyon seem to be getting pretty close," he says, and the guilt twists even deeper. I might be sick.

"I guess," I say. I can't change the subject fast enough. "Where are we going?"

"I thought we'd grab some food then hit up the beach."

We drive to town in excruciating silence. Any small talk we try to make fizzles out almost immediately. Clearly, I didn't think this through. I should've driven myself to Dr. Patel's office instead of riding with Hadley—then I could've met Donovan when we both got back from filming. Anything to save me from this painfully awkward car ride.

Finally, he pulls to the side of the road and cuts the engine. In front of us stands a red food truck with a crowd of people surrounding it. When we make our way close enough for me to see it, I notice that the menu is in Spanish; the only word I recognize is taco.

Thankfully, Donovan knows what he's doing and orders for both of us before we head to the only empty table in the grassy area behind the truck. After a minute of waiting, he looks at me.

"Is it me or is this super awkward?"

"I'm sorry," I say. "I'm a terrible date tonight."

He flips his hand like he's waving away my apology. "You're fine."

I try to make more of an effort, but the truth is, my heart isn't really in this. I like Donovan, but I don't feel much of a connection with him. Not romantically, at least. I get the feeling I'm not alone.

Eventually, we fall into comfortable conversation about school and music, and I learn Donovan's going to Appalachian State next year on a partial scholarship to study music production.

"What do you want to do with that?" I ask.

"I'm not really sure." He takes a huge bite of his enchilada and chews thoughtfully before continuing. "I used to want to be a big-name producer, but I've been thinking a lot lately about doing scores for movies or something."

"Oh my gosh," I say, "do you want to write something for *Maybe, Probably*?" Having an original score would elevate the movie way above what we would be able to do by piecing together a soundtrack with music licensed for free.

"Sure," he says with a shrug. "I'll start tinkering tomorrow and see what I can come up with."

"That'd be amazing," I say.

We finish eating, and by the time we walk back to his car, the awkwardness between us is nearly gone.

"Okay," I say as Donovan shifts his car into park. "This is unexpected."

We're stopped in front of Naoise and Shyla's house. There's only one light on, in the upstairs hallway. I know I've not been on a lot of dates, but isn't taking your date to her best friends' house kind of weird?

"I wanted to go to the beach," he explains, "and Shyla said we could use their place for access. Is that okay?"

"Yeah. You surprised me a bit, but this is fine." I still think it's weird.

"Okay, then, let's go."

Donovan grabs a bag from the trunk, and we walk together to the Patels' front door. He pulls a keychain from his pocket and flips through it until he finds the right key.

"She gave you her house keys?" I had no idea they knew each other well enough for something like this.

He shrugs and twists the key in the lock, pushing the door open as soon as it gives. Grabbing my hand, he pulls me through the front door.

"Okay," he says into the dark foyer, "now we have to figure out how to get to the back door and outside again."

I laugh. "Come on," I say, taking the lead. I know this place nearly as well as my own home. I don't even need to turn the lights on as we wind our way through the huge house.

We step into the great room, the ocean coming into view through the floor-to-ceiling accordion doors. The café lights Mrs. Patel strung along the second-floor deck are lit, their glow illuminating the room enough for me to make out the furniture.

A movement catches my eye, and I turn toward it. Something isn't right, but before I can figure out what it is, the overhead lights flick on and a chorus of voices shouts, "Surprise!"

I jump and spin back to see Donovan standing behind me, laughing. "Happy birthday, Quincy," he says.

"Did you . . . ?"

He shakes his head. "I was only the distraction."

The room is packed with bodies. Everyone from the movie is here, along with some other people from school. I scan the faces in front of me, trying to take in everyone who came. My eyes lock with Kenyon's where he stands across the room, and a jolt of electricity shoots through my body. Suddenly, I'm hyper-aware of Donovan standing only a step behind me.

Before I can process the feeling, Naoise runs from the kitchen and tackles me into a hug. "Are you surprised?" she asks.

Now that the shock is wearing off, I'm able to fully take in the scene. Purple, pink, and black crepe paper streamers cover the room, and a giant inflatable unicorn takes up the entire corner opposite the fireplace.

"Oh my gosh," I say, smacking her on the arm playfully. "I thought you said this stuff was for a five-year-old!"

"Close enough," Shyla says as she joins us. I hug her tightly.

"Y'all are the best," I say into her hair.

"Never forget it," she says back. "Now, let's party!"

We play several rousing games of Pin the Horn on the Unicorn then dig into the cake Shyla ordered from Sprinkles. It's the only thing at this party that doesn't look like unicorn puke. The cake is in the shape of a stack of film reels with an old-fashioned 35mm projector on top. Next to it stands a minia-ture Oscar statuette. On the base, it reads *Best Director, Quincy Walker.*

It's the most magnificent thing I've ever seen.

"There's no way Sprinkles made this in two days," I say as I pass a piece to Ezra. "How long have y'all really been planning this?"

Hadley drops a scoop of ice cream onto a plate and passes it over for cake. "About a month," she says.

"I can't believe nobody spoiled the surprise," I say.

"Are you kidding? And face the wrath of Neesh?"

"Hey," Naoise calls from across the room, "I heard that!"

Donovan takes a couple plates of cake and ice cream off the kitchen island. "Want to go outside?" he asks.

I pass the cake knife to Ezra and follow Donovan outside. Shyla pushed the accordion doors wide open shortly after we got there, so now the deck is an extension of the interior.

Donovan leads me down the steps and onto the long pier leading across the marshy area to the beach. About halfway down, he hops onto the railing then helps me up next to him.

"I needed to get away from the bustle for a bit," he says as he hands my plate back to me. "I hope that's okay?"

"No problem. You okay?"

He nods and we eat our cake in companionable silence. I swing my legs like a little kid. "So . . ." I say.

"So," Donovan repeats.

"How long have you known about this party?"

"Since Monday." He takes my plate from me and stacks it on top of his. "Shyla thought our date would be a good way to keep you away until it was time to arrive."

"Well, it worked."

My stomach flips. I know the reason I'm on this date: Donovan was helping at Nana's party. If I kiss him now, I'll know if it was him. We're not exactly in the kissing place, though. I need to turn this date around.

I lean toward him until my arm is resting against his. "I've had a good time," I say. I try to make my voice alluring, but I'm pretty sure I fail.

"Yeah, me too. This has been fun."

I shift to face him, angling myself on the railing as much as I can without falling off. When he looks at me, I lean toward him.

Can I do this, really? Donovan's a great guy, but there's not been a single spark between us all night. Dinner was nice, and I love my party, but it's been like hanging out with a friend. Nothing more.

I can't. He's *Donovan*. Maybe it was him in the theater at the party, but does it really matter? What if all this chasing I'm doing is for nothing? Sure, it was an amazing kiss. Mind-blowing, really. But that's all it was. A single kiss. Is it worth chasing down a phantom, especially when I find myself having all these strange feelings about someone else? When that *someone else* is back in the house?

"We should go back in." I hop off the railing, and Donovan follows. We head toward the house. The sounds of my surprise party float across the air to my ears, my friends having fun and playing silly games.

A weird sense of longing washes over me as I cross the pier back toward the house. Just like that, this thing that's consumed me for the past two weeks is gone, and I feel like I've lost a part of myself with it. I'm surprised to find I'll miss it.

I'm on the last step to the upper deck when I come to an abrupt stop. I hear Donovan's step falter behind me. He's a couple stairs down when I turn around, so for once I look him directly in the face.

"What's—"

Before I have a chance to second-guess myself, I lower myself to the next step so I'm close enough to reach him. Then I lift up on my toes, wrap one hand around his neck to pull him down to my level, and press my lips to his.

Donovan freezes, his body turning to stone. I feel the muscles in his neck tense beneath my hand, and his mouth opens in shock for a second before he pulls back.

We break off the kiss and I take a step back, rising to the deck, moving away from him as I do. Donovan stares at me, stunned, but he doesn't seem to be upset or offended. If anything, he looks embarrassed.

"Um," he says, not looking directly at me. He scratches the back of his head. "Look, Quincy, I think you're great and all—"

"Sorry," I interrupt. "That's something I needed to do." I grimace at how ridiculous I sound.

"Why?" he asks. "I mean, not that I'm not flattered, because I am, but . . . why?"

There's no way out of this—I'm not nearly a good enough liar to come up with a story on the spot. And I still can't tell if it was him at nana's party. Not based on that non-kiss. He froze so completely that it was like kissing a mannequin.

"Donovan?" I take a slow, shaky breath to steel my nerves. "At my Nana's party did you—"

"Quincy?"

I spin at the sound of Kenyon's voice. He's standing behind me on the deck, and I catch the look of pain on his face before he shutters his emotions.

"Ken—" I start at the same time Donovan says, "Hey, man."

Kenyon looks from me to Donovan and back to me before turning and disappearing into the house.

"Crap," I groan.

"I'll talk to him," Donovan says.

When he steps past me, I grab his forearm, stopping him. "Let me. I'll talk to you later, okay?"

He nods, and I see the understanding wash over his features. "We good?" he asks.

I nod. "Yeah. We're fine."

Back in the great room, Naoise and Marcus are spinning a blindfolded Kira in circles. She holds a unicorn horn above her head like a javelin as she turns. I skirt around them and search the rest of the room, but I can't find Kenyon anywhere.

"You okay?" Ezra pulls me over by the fireplace, away from the unicorn commotion so it's easier to hear. "You look lost."

"Yeah, I'm fine," I say. He pierces me with a stare I've not seen in years but immediately recognize. He doesn't believe my lie for a second. I sigh. "Actually, no. Did you see where Kenyon went? I need to talk to him."

"I think he left," he says. My stomach drops. What he saw on the deck—me kissing his best friend—I need to explain that.

"You can probably still catch him," Ezra says, "if you hurry."

"Thanks," I say over my shoulder as I rush toward the foyer and out the front door.

I scan the driveway and street, but Kenyon is nowhere in sight. Finally, I turn toward the neighbors' house and see him standing next to his Jeep.

"Kenyon, wait!" I yell as he pulls the door open. I rush down the porch steps and jog across the expansive side lawn to join him.

"Hey," I say when I get to him. I take a few measured breaths, trying to regain control. My heart pounds against my rib cage, only partly from the exertion. "You're leaving?"

Kenyon tilts his head back, pulling in a deep breath through his teeth. He huffs it back out and finally looks at me. "I'm all partied out," he says, his voice flat.

"Look, about what happened," I say, but Kenyon holds up a hand to stop me.

"Don't," he says. "I get it. You told me you were going on a bunch of dates. I knew you were going out with Donovan tonight. But I never thought that meant . . ." He turns back to the Jeep.

I grab his arm. "Kenyon, please, listen for a second. It's not what you think."

"Quin, stop." He shakes my hand off. Then he climbs into the Jeep and shuts the door. I stand numbly beside the vehicle as the engine roars to life. Kenyon doesn't glance my way once, but simply eases the Jeep onto the road and leaves me standing alone in the dark.

chapter
TWENTY-FOUR

"DID YOU FIND HIM?"

Ezra is waiting for me in the foyer as I come back inside.

"Yeah."

"Everything okay?"

Even after these years apart, Ezra still knows me too well, so it's no use lying to him. I shake my head and say, "I just want to go home."

"But it's your party," he says.

"I know, but it's about over anyway, right?" Half the crowd has already left, and the rest have mellowed out. "I need to find Donovan so we can go." I didn't think it could get more awkward than the drive from Southport earlier, but I'm pretty sure the ride home is going to beat that, hands down.

"I think I saw him and Shyla heading upstairs a few minutes ago."

I thank him and head for the staircase. Upstairs, I hear laughter coming from Shyla's room. The door is open a few inches, and I push my way in.

"Hey, Shy, have you seen—" My words freeze in my throat. Shyla's on her bed, lying back on a mountain of pillows. But that's not what catches me off guard.

Donovan is leaned over her, propped up on one forearm. He sweeps her hair back from her forehead then leans down and kisses her, so tenderly I almost swoon. I back out of the room and walk to the staircase. This night can't possibly get any weirder.

I'm halfway down the stairs when I hear Shyla calling my name. Her voice quavers. She's scared—of what I'll say and how I'll react. I turn and see fear etched on her face. She pulls the corner of her lip into her mouth and bites it, the same nervous tic she's had since middle school, and she stares at the floor right past me, not ready to meet my eye. Seeing her standing there, so vulnerable, my shock fades. Behind it isn't the anger I'd expect, but a small thrill of joy for my friend. Beneath her fear, I can see the excited flush still in her cheeks and neck, and I'm suddenly incredibly happy for her. The emotion rushes through me, knocking me a bit off-kilter.

"Hey," I say softly.

Finally, she looks up, her eyes catching mine. "I'm so sorry, Quin. Please, please don't hate me. It's just—"

"Shy, it's—"

"You know how hard it is to be Naoise's sister? She's so beautiful, and tall, and thin, and everyone who sees her loves her, and then there's me"—she gestures to her whole self—"nobody sees me when I'm with her."

"Shyla—"

"Wait, let me finish." She steps down to join me. "But Donovan sees *me*. He doesn't look at me and see Naoise's less-pretty, fat sister. He sees me, and he likes me, and he thinks I'm beautiful. I know that doesn't excuse me kissing him when you're on a date, but I—"

"Shyla!" I finally have her attention, and she snaps her mouth shut, tears shining in her eyes. I pull her into a tight hug.

"You are *not* Naoise's fat sister. You are one of the most incredible people I know." I pull back and hold her at arm's length so I can look her in the eye. "Donovan is lucky to have you, Shyla."

"You're not mad?"

I shake my head. "I was," I say. "Or I thought I was. But mostly I'm surprised. Not mad. But . . ."

"But what?"

"We kissed tonight. Just a few minutes ago. If I had known how you felt, Shy—"

"I know," she interrupts. "He told me."

"He did?"

She nods, a smile spreading across her face. "He said that kissing you made him realize he doesn't want to waste his time anymore. The reason he didn't want to go on a blind date was because, well, he wanted to ask me out." Her blush deepens, and she tries to hide her smile. "Sorry. I know you wanted to find out—"

"It's fine," I say. "Really." And it is. I'm happy for her. But as the shock continues to wear off, I'm left with the memory of what happened with Kenyon. I hurt him, and for what? To kiss a guy who only wants to be kissing my best friend? I can't get the image of his pained expression out of my head.

"What about Operation Mystery Kisser?" Shyla drops her voice to a whisper.

"It wasn't him," I say, though I'm not totally sure. What happened on the deck wasn't a real kiss and didn't at all help me know if he kissed me at Nana's party or not. Maybe he did, but I'll never know. Because when I look at Shyla's face, filled with the giddiness she has when talking about Donovan, I know I won't take a second chance at kissing him. "That was the most awkward kiss of all time."

She laughs. "Yeah, that's what he said too. You're really not mad?"

"Really. I'm happy for you, Shy. Donovan is great, and you two will be great together."

She hugs me again. "Thank you." Her voice quavers.

"Hey, I'm actually gonna get out of here. Can you tell Donovan?"

"Oh, yeah, I'll go get him."

"No, don't. Go have fun. I'll get another ride."

Pulling my phone from my bag, I head downstairs. I've somehow missed six calls, the noise of the party apparently drowning out my ringtone. Four are from a number I don't recognize, and two are from Nana. I check the time on them—9:42 p.m. and 9:45 p.m. My heart drops when I see her name. I can't believe I missed these, so caught up with my party that I didn't keep track of the time. Every year on my birthday, Nana calls to celebrate me being an *official* year older, right when I was born—at 9:42 p.m. I stop in the stairwell to call her back, looking out over the end of my birthday party as the phone rings in my ear.

Marcus, Naoise, and Kira are all piled in a heap on a couch, and Ezra sits on the arm, laughing. The rest of the house appears to be empty. Ezra catches my eye as I drop my phone back to my side. Voicemail. I'll have to try again later. I step into the room and give him a small wave and a smile before heading to the front door. I pull up a rideshare app and start typing in the Patel address.

"Need a ride?" Ezra pushes the door shut behind him and joins me on the front porch.

"I'm fine," I say, waving my phone. "I'll call a rideshare."

Ezra takes my phone from me. "Come on," he says. "I'll give you a ride."

"It's okay. You stay."

"I need to get home anyway. I have an early class tomorrow."

He hands my phone back and leads me to his car. Once we're settled in and headed toward my house, I ask, "How many more classes do you have?"

"This is the last weekend."

"Then you'll be a full-blown paramedic?"

He shrugs. "Only an EMT, and I can't actually work with the EMS until I'm eighteen, but I'll be qualified at least."

"Only a few weeks to go, then," I say. "That's pretty awesome. But why EMT?"

He shrugs. "Why not?"

"That's not an answer," I say. "It's a pretty big thing to do at our age."

"I guess I thought it would be a good job for summer and during school. And it'll look good on med school applications later."

"You want to go to med school? Since when?"

He looks at me with a wry grin. "A lot's changed since we were kids, Quincy."

"Oh, yeah? What else has changed?"

Ezra stares straight ahead, and I can see the muscle in his jaw working. He stretches his fingers out straight then regrips the steering wheel.

Finally, he sighs, and the tension leaves his shoulders. "I found him," he says.

"Found who?"

"My dad."

"What?" I'm shocked. I had no idea he even wanted to find his father. In all our time as friends, he never once hinted about looking for him. "Where? How?"

"He lives in Charleston." Ezra stares straight ahead as he talks. "He has a whole new family. A wife and four kids. He's a doctor now."

"Is that why you want to go to med school? Because your father's a doctor?"

Ezra pulls into the other lane to pass a truck. He doesn't answer until we are back in the right-hand lane, the truck fading in the distance behind us.

"At first, yeah. It's silly, I know, but I thought that, maybe, if I could get into med school . . . maybe I'd be good enough for him."

"You *are* good enough, Ezra. It's not your fault your dad is a douchenozzle."

He smirks, but I can still see sadness on his face. "I know. I do, really, but when I found out about his new life, it's like something in me snapped. I found the EMT course that same week. Oh, shoot, I missed the turn. Sorry."

"It's fine." Truthfully, I didn't even notice when we drove past my street. Ezra's revelation about his dad had me too distracted to pay attention to where we were.

We drive across to Wrightsville beach, where Ezra pulls off on a side street and flips a quick U-turn. When we're on the right road headed toward my house again, he says, "It's not about him anymore, though."

"What isn't?"

"The med school thing. I signed up for the EMT classes on an impulse, but I ended up really loving it. I'm good at this, and I think I'd really like to be a doctor."

"That's great, Ezra." I can't imagine what it must have been like, searching for the dad who chose not to stick around. Finding him. Seeing the new life the man was living without him. I can't help but wonder if Ezra's absolute silence on the matter over the years wasn't because he didn't care, but because he cared too much.

"Does your mom know?" I ask as we turn onto my street.

He shakes his head. "I thought about telling her, but I can't. She's in a really good place, and I don't want to ruin that."

"You're going to keep this to yourself, then?"

"I think I have to. Hey, who's that?"

There's a vehicle in my driveway, some kind of vintage car I don't recognize. Ezra pulls in behind it, and the headlights illuminate midnight blue paint and an Iowa license plate.

"Who on earth?" I whisper.

"I'll walk you up," Ezra says, and we climb out of the car at the same time.

"Oh, thank goodness," a voice calls from the front porch.

A girl bounces down the steps and rushes to us, meeting us halfway across the yard. She's gorgeous, with blonde hair piled in a messy bun on the top of her head. She's wearing a casual sundress. "Are you Dr. Walker's daughter?"

"Yeah?" I say.

"What's going on?" Ezra asks.

"Your dad's in the hospital," she says. "We were at this play for extra credit, and I was driving behind him on my way home, and there was this truck, and . . ."

She keeps talking, but I don't hear anything. A loud whooshing sound fills my head, an ocean blocking out the rest of her words. Dad's in the hospital. I need to go. Right now.

"I'll take you," Ezra says, a reply to my unspoken thought. He presses a hand to my lower back and guides me to his car, helping me into the passenger seat.

I hear Ezra and the girl talking for a moment before he gets in and backs out of the driveway.

"It's gonna be okay, Quin."

I wish I could believe him.

chapter
TWENTY-FIVE

NANA'S AT THE HOSPITAL WHEN WE ARRIVE, AND I RUN into her arms as soon as I see her. She holds me tight. I fit her body like I belong there.

"Shhhh," she whispers into my hair. "I've got you, baby girl. I've got you."

When I calm down, we head to the waiting area, and Ezra goes off in search of coffee for the three of us. Nana fills me in on what she knows so far: the girl at the house—Anna—is in Dad's freshman lecture and was at the play with him and some other students to earn extra credit.

"She waited with him until the ambulance came," Nana explains, "and then she found his cell phone and called me."

"Where is he? How bad is it?"

Ezra returns and hands us each a paper cup filled with coffee before sitting in a chair across from us.

"He's pretty banged up," Nana says, and I gasp, less from the words than from the quiver in her voice. Nana's always so strong and seeing her this affected scares me. Tears fill my eyes. "I don't know much yet, but the doctor says he's stable. We should be able to see him soon."

I stare at the coffee in my cup. The surface of the liquid shivers with the shaking of my hands. "Where's Clark?" I ask.

"I don't know," Nana says. "I left him a message. Seems you both have a problem answering your phones tonight."

"Sorry," I mutter. I think back to the calls I missed earlier.

Nana pats my knee, leaving her hand there to calm me. "Don't you apologize. You didn't know. I hope you were having a good birthday party."

"You knew about that?"

She nods. "I figured that was why you weren't answering. That sweet girl offered to go wait for you. She seemed really shaken up by the whole thing. She didn't want to go home until you and your brother knew."

"I should call Clark," I say, but before I can pull out my phone, a man in dark blue scrubs walks into the room and I freeze.

"You can see him now," he says, and Nana and I rise together.

"Give me your phone," Ezra says. "I'll try to get ahold of Clark."

"Thanks," I say, passing my phone to him. Nana grabs my hand, her grip like a vise, and we follow the man to go see Dad.

I'm curled up in the chair next to Dad's bed when the door creaks open and Ezra peeks his head in. "Up for more company?"

"Ezra," Dad says, his voice bright. "Come in. Maybe you can convince this girl of mine that I'm fine."

"Sure you are," I say. It's been an ongoing argument between us for the past hour. Dad acts like nothing even happened, despite the hospital bed and all the monitors he's hooked up to. Despite the massive splint wrapped around his left leg, bracing a broken femur, and the gauze covering the side of his face and head.

The doctor gave us a quick rundown of what to expect as he led us to Dad's room. His leg is stabilized as well as possible while we wait for the orthopedic surgeon to arrive and evaluate it. Until then, the focus is on pain management, decreasing the swelling, and monitoring Dad's head. He's showing signs of a mild concussion, and he's got a line of stitches under the gauze running from the peak of his cheekbone in a high arc over his ear.

I try not to think about the implications of that. Possible concussion, head trauma—the memories of Mom came at me as the doctor spoke, fast and brutal, and I forced my eyes shut against those stored-up images.

"How long are you stuck here for?" Ezra asks as he steps into the room. Behind him I see Anna enter as well.

"Miss Holloway," Dad says, surprised. "What are you doing here?"

"I wanted to make sure you're doing okay," she says. Her cheeks darken with a blush.

"Anna stayed with you until the ambulance came," Ezra says, "then went to the house and waited for us to get home."

Dad props himself up on his elbows so he can get a better look. "You did? I don't know what to say."

Anna smiles softly. "It was nothing." But something in her face, the far-off focus of her eyes, tells me what happened tonight affected her more deeply than she's letting on. She twists her hands in her dress. "I'm glad you're doing better," she tells Dad. "I should get going. I don't think I'm actually supposed to be here this late." She glances out the door to the hallway, like she's worried security is going to come after her, and I notice she's not wearing the *visitor* sticker the rest of us were given when we got here.

Dad waves away her concern. "That boyfriend of yours coming down again this weekend?"

"Nope. Not until after finals." She shrugs. "It's probably better. I never seem to study enough when he's here." Dad laughs hard, then presses a hand to his chest. I'm instantly on high alert. I shoot upright on the bed and reach for the call button.

Dad swats my hand with his own. "I'm fine," he gasps. "Nothing's wrong. I'm fine," he says again.

Anna leaves, and I snuggle back into the chair. Dad has the History Channel playing on the TV, the volume silent and the subtitles turned on. We've seen this show before, but there's nowhere I'd rather be than here watching with him.

"I should probably get going too," Ezra says after a minute. He turns his head and stifles a deep yawn. "I'm glad you're still with us, Rob." He gives Dad a quick hug and heads toward the door.

"Ezra," Dad says, "take Quincy with you."

"I wanna stay," I argue, but Dad's already shaking his head.

"Go, sweetheart. I need to sleep. Sorry I ruined your birthday."

I've sent half a dozen texts to Clark and called him twice. I stare at my phone, my thumb hovering over the dial button, but I can't bring myself to push it again. Anger burns my skin. Where the hell is my brother? It's bad enough that he totally ignored my birthday, but this is too much.

"Take a left here," I tell Ezra as we pass a familiar street. I've only been to Clark's apartment a handful of times, but I'm sure I can find it, even in the dark.

We weave through the streets of Wilmington until I locate the right cul-de-sac. Clark lives with his roommate, Eric, in a small two-bedroom over an elderly couple's garage. As we pull up, I noticed a light on in his apartment. I jump out of the car and slam the door.

Ezra joins me at the top of the stairs as I start pounding on the door. He stands beside me, and I can tell he's not sure whether he should stay or drag me away before I make a scene.

"Coming," a deep voice calls from inside. As the lock clicks, I barely hear through the sound of my palm hitting the door the same voice mutter, "Calm down already." I drop my hand and it tingles with the aftermath of my attack on the door.

The door swings open enough to show me the guy standing there in low-slung sweatpants and no shirt. He's not surprised to see me.

Clark and Eric have been friends since high school. They got this apartment together two years ago when Clark decided he didn't want to live at home anymore. Eric's always been nice to me, and I feel a twinge of guilt for interrupting his night.

"Where is he?" I ask, my voice icy.

The conflict on Eric's face is clear, but in the end, he swings the door open without a word and steps back for me to enter. Ezra stays put on the porch.

The apartment is tidy, with nothing out of place. This must be Eric's doing. Clark's room at home always looked like a hurricane had just blown through. The living room is empty, so I head to the hallway, following the soft glow cast by a light.

Clark's sitting up on the bed, back propped against a pillow. His hair is a mess, and he wears the thick glasses he only ever puts on before bed. He's holding his phone, scrolling through something on the screen.

"It's not broken, then," I snap from the doorway.

My brother startles and drops the phone into his lap. "What are you doing here?" he asks.

"Why are you ignoring my calls and texts?" I hate the whine that creeps into my voice when I talk to him.

"Quincy, not now." He groans and presses his fingers into his eyes, his glasses moving up to his forehead as he rubs. "I had a really long day, and I don't want—"

"*You* had a long day?" I scream at him. "Dad's in the hospital, Clark! A truck ran a red light and barreled into him. He could've died, and you can't even be bothered to answer your phone!"

Clark stares at me, his jaw dropping open. I watch the color drain from his face. "What?" It's only one word, but his voice cracks, and my heart instantly breaks with it.

I cross the room and sit on the edge of the bed. "Yeah. Broken leg, possible concussion. Lots of stitches."

"How long will he be in the hospital?" he asks.

"I dunno. A couple days probably. He needs surgery."

He nods, staring straight ahead. His emotions show clearly: fear and regret are transforming his features. Softening them. It makes him look more like the brother I grew up with.

"I'll visit him in the morning," he says finally.

"Good." I stand to leave. The anger I came with has melted away, and suddenly all I want is to go home and curl up in my bed. I could sleep for a week. When I reach the bedroom door, I turn to him. "And answer your phone from now on, okay?"

He gives me a half nod. He at least has the decency to look sheepish. As I step into the hallway, I hear him say, "Quin, wait."

I turn, one hand on the doorframe, and look at him. It isn't until now that I truly take in this room. It's as neat as the rest of the apartment, the walls decorated with black-and-white pictures I immediately recognize as his work. Clark has always looked at the world differently, and the photos he takes give a little glimpse into how he sees things.

A red chair sits in the corner of the room with a gray blanket draped over it. A paperback lies open on the chair, face-down to hold the spot. Clark's bed has a crisp blue comforter and striped sheets, and everything is so neat that I start to think I don't know him at all anymore. This isn't the same Clark who lived in the room next to mine.

"What?" I ask when he doesn't say anything else.

He stares at me, his face twisted with an emotion I can't quite place. His eyes shine with what might be tears, but he presses his fingers into them before I can be sure. I watch as his glasses rise to his forehead again, the frames pressing into the skin. His hands fall to his lap, and for a second, I'm sure he's going to tell me something important. But then he sighs and drops his gaze to the bed. "I'm sorry I missed your birthday," he says finally.

chapter TWENTY-SIX

"ENJOY YOUR SHOW," I SAY AS I HAND A BAG OF POPCORN across the counter to the middle-aged couple.

"Thanks," the woman says, "you too." Her husband laughs, and she reddens.

"Happens all the time," I assure her, and I watch as they walk into the theater. As soon as the door swings shut, I pull my phone from my back pocket and check the screen.

I canceled filming yesterday so I could spend the day at the hospital with Dad. Nana brought breakfast up for us. It wasn't the same as going out, but I liked that she tried to keep our tradition going. Clark even came, eating silently in the chair next to Dad's bed. When Nana left, she made me walk her all the way to her car so Dad and Clark could have some time alone together. I don't know what they said, but when I made my way back up to the room fifteen minutes later, Clark was in my spot on the bed, hugging Dad tightly, his eyes rimmed red. Before either of them could see me, I backed away from the room and went to hang out in the waiting area until I saw Clark leave. I didn't like seeing him so vulnerable after our fight the night before. It's easier to be mad at him.

It's going to be a nightmare to reschedule everyone for filming, especially with what little time we have left to finish the film, but the cast and crew were thankfully very understanding. We'll need to shoot every night for the rest of the week. So far, I've heard back from almost everyone that they can make this schedule work—everyone except Kenyon, that is.

The theater is making me twitchy tonight. I love this job, but it's the last place I want to be right now. I tried to call my manager to bail on my shift so I could go straight to the hospital from school, but Dad insisted I go to work instead.

Right as I'm about to slide my phone into my pocket, it vibrates, and a text message pops up.

EZRA: How's your dad?
ME: Stubborn. He hates being in the hospital.
EZRA: When's he out?
ME: Probably Wednesday
EZRA: Keep me updated. Mom's already cooking up a storm. She's making freezer meals. Y'all won't have to cook for about a month.
ME: I will. Thanks.

A month of Lylah's cooking sounds like heaven, but it's not quite enough to distract me from what's going on with Dad. The doctors told us he'll be fine and that the chances of complications beyond this point are slim, but a few minutes on Google reading about possibilities after a femur fracture was enough to make me wish I'd never looked it up.

"What's with you tonight?" Tyler asks. I jump at the sound of his voice.

"Nothing."

"Sure," he says. "You're always like this."

"Like what?" I snap.

"Distracted. Quiet." He pins me with a pointed stare. "Grumpy."

I've been storm-cloudy since the second I walked in the door, and it's not gone unnoticed. Both Tyler and our other coworker, Pennie, have been skirting around me for the whole shift, but now that Pennie is upstairs to start the show, apparently Tyler's going to face me head-on.

"Just a bad weekend," I mutter.

He hops onto the counter and lets his legs dangle. "Can't have been all bad," he says, throwing me his trademark smirk. "I heard you got some lip action from Donovan at your party."

"What?!"

"And here I thought you were all about that Kenyon guy," he says.

"It's not like that," I say, even though I'm starting to wonder if it really *is* like that.

He pops a piece of popcorn into his mouth. "If you say so."

My cheeks blaze, and soon the heat spreads through my whole body. "Anyway . . . how'd you know about Donovan?" I ask, cringing inwardly at the memory of the most awkward kiss ever—and Kenyon's face after.

He laughs. "Who didn't tell me? I'm sorry I wasn't there."

"Yeah, why weren't you?" I ask, but then I counter, "You know what? It doesn't matter."

"You're a little ball of sunshine today, aren't you?"

I glare at him. I don't want to talk about this. I shake my head, trying to banish the memory of Kenyon's pained expression.

"So are you and Donovan gonna do the prom thing?" He asks it casually, like he doesn't have a care in the world, but I notice he's not quite meeting my eye. Is he trying to feel out if I have a prom date? A surprise rush of hope trills in my stomach. I was beginning to think these feelings had been buried under whatever's happening with Kenyon, but they bubble back to the surface, alive and well.

"Definitely not," I tell him. "He'll probably be going with Shyla."

Tyler winces. "Whoa. Isn't she your best friend? Tough blow, Walker."

"Not really." I shrug. "The whole date with Donovan was only this thing I had to do for a night. He's much better off with Shyla. I'm not interested in him." I emphasize the word *him* and look Tyler straight in the eye, trying to convey my message.

Ask me to prom.

"Oh, cool, I guess." He picks up a cup from the counter beside him and starts flipping it between his hands.

Why won't he just ask me already? Almost every time we're together, he brings up prom. What guy does that unless he's interested?

My phone vibrates, and I slip it out of my back pocket as fast as lightning. Every text or call that comes through, I get a jolt of terror that something's happened to Dad. I remind myself that he's going to be fine, but I can't help but worry. I can't lose him too.

There's a text message, and my stomach twists when I see the name.

KENYON: We still on to shoot tomorrow or do we need to reschedule?

I want to lay it all out for him, explain what he actually saw between me and Donovan, tell him how sorry I am. But I already did that. I sent message after message after message, telling him there was nothing between me and Donovan. He ignored everything I sent, and my calls went straight to voicemail.

The only message he answered was the one canceling Sunday filming, and to that he only responded, "OK."

So instead of explanations and apologies, I give him what he asked for.

ME: Yeah. Hadley's after school.

My phone is still clutched in my hand, and I wait too long for a reply that isn't coming.

"What's going on?" Tyler asks from his perch on the counter.

"Nothing," I say.

"You look like you want to murder that phone," he says with a chuckle. "That's not *nothing*."

Irritation ripples under my skin. Yeah, maybe I shouldn't have kissed Donovan on Saturday night, but it's not like Kenyon and I are officially together. He knew I was going on other dates—he *knew* I was going out with Donovan. It's not like I did anything all that wrong. He's acting like a baby and refusing to talk to me. I suddenly realize that the longer I stand staring at my blank phone screen, the more the guilt I've been feeling is morphing into anger.

"Yoo-hoo, earth to Quincy." Tyler waves a hand in front of my face, and something inside me snaps.

"Can I ask you something?" I say, my words quick and harsh. "Are you ever going to ask me to the stupid prom?"

His eyebrows shoot up in surprise. He opens his mouth to respond, but I continue my tirade.

"You ask about it every time we're together. You flirt with me and drop little hints. What is this? Do you get some sick pleasure out of leading me on?"

Tyler's eyes are huge as he stares at me. "Uh, I, um . . ." His gaze slips from my face to beyond my right shoulder, and he grimaces.

"Can I, um, get a refill, please?" I freeze in place, squeezing my eyes shut. *Of course* someone would come out of the theater at this moment. Two hours of run time, and this person picks this exact thirty-second window to get more popcorn. My face burns, and my chest feels all jittery.

Tyler's a statue, so I take a deep breath and plaster my best customer service smile on my face. "Sure," I say, turning around. I grab the bag from the girl's hands. "You want any butter on that?"

Once I finish, I notice Tyler's squatting down in front of the low cabinets counting inventory. He never does inventory. Tyler would rather do pretty much anything than count cups and popcorn bags. Most nights, he volunteers for bathroom duty to get out of this chore.

He's avoiding me—that much is obvious. I don't blame him. Now that my anger has ebbed away, I'm left with the hollow realization of my outburst, and embarrassment floods over me. I used to think I didn't get embarrassed easily, but I may be changing my view on that after today. I'd be totally okay if the floor opened wide and swallowed me whole.

chapter TWENTY-SEVEN

"THERE YA GO, LITTLE GUY." KENYON HOLDS A SMALL square of watermelon out to the parrot in front of him, and the bird grips it tightly in one of its taloned feet. I watch as it sticks a leathery tongue out the side of its beak and gives the fruit a small taste. Its pupils constrict and dilate, and it licks again before finally sinking the pointed end of its beak into the fruit.

"Thanks again for letting us do this," I say to Hadley's neighbor, Samantha.

"Oh, it's no trouble at all," she says. "It's the least I can do after y'all helped me rescue this knucklehead. I can't believe you're going to put that in your movie."

I laugh. "I couldn't help it. It's the perfect meet-cute moment."

Kenyon's petting the bird now, with slow strokes starting at its head and running the full length of its shiny green back. Every time he raises his hand, the bird tilts its head, waiting to push it back into his palm for the next stroke.

"He's such an attention hog," Samantha says, nodding at the bird. "He'll keep you here forever if you let him."

The rest of the cast and crew are next door at Hadley's, setting up her barn for the scene we're shooting today. In the movie, the bird is in the rafters of the old barn, and Sebastian's trying to coax it down when Adalyn hears him and comes by to see what's going on. I plan to intercut the scenes we shoot in the barn with the close-ups of Oscar, the parrot, that Kenyon and I just filmed.

"We should get going," I say. Without a word, Kenyon gathers up his gear and follows me out of the house. We set across the wide lawn to Hadley's, and no matter how many times I try to fall into step with him, he stays either slightly ahead of or behind me.

"Are you ever going to talk to me again?" I ask. I try not to show my irritation, but it's hard.

"What do you want to talk about?" he says, not unkindly, but without any warmth either.

I grab his forearm and force him to stop. "Look, about Saturday night—"

"Nope. New subject." He pulls his arm from my grip. "I was thinking about our ending, and I'm pretty sure I figured it out."

"Our . . . ending?"

"For the movie," he says. "I know you don't want a grand gesture, but I really believe we need one. It's not a romantic comedy without it. I was thinking we could bring it back to the bird. Sebastian could train the bird to say—"

"We don't need a grand gesture," I say for what feels like the thousandth time. "I like my ending. It's quiet. Understated."

"It's not what rom-com viewers want, though."

"So what? People don't ever know they want something until they see it. Look at *The Shining*. That movie transcended the genre, and people love it."

"You know Stephen King hated that movie, right?" Kenyon throws back.

"Not the point."

"Okay," he says. "So what is the point?"

We're almost to the barn now. I can hear the cheerful voices of our friends as they wait for us. I'm so sick of arguing over the end of this movie. I know I wrote a good script. Sure, it might not turn out to be the conventional romantic comedy, but I'm confident about it. It's good. I *know* it's good.

"The point," I say, fighting to keep my voice calm, "is that we agreed to film the movie I wrote. This is my movie, and we're going to do it the way I want."

Anger flashes in his eyes, quick and hot, before he turns away and speed-walks to the barn without me. Good. I'll take anger. Any emotion from him is better than the stoniness he's been giving me since Saturday night.

I shake my hands by my sides and hop on my toes. Rolling my chin to my chest, I let my head sway from side to side.

Tension releases from my shoulders, and I take a deep breath, forcing myself to stop thinking about Kenyon.

I have a movie to make.

Nana's car is in the driveway when I get home from school the next day. Heart in my throat, I race up the front steps and through the door. Dad's sitting in his normal spot with the recliner fully extended to support his leg. A fluffy blanket is pulled up to his chin. There's a small table next to his chair, and on it rests a huge cup of ice water with a straw next to a bowl of popcorn.

"Oh, hey, John," he says when he sees me. "You okay?"

I manage a nod and what I think is a smile but feels more like a grimace. "I saw Nana's car and thought—"

"You don't think I'd let my own son take a cab home from the hospital, do you?" Nana breezes down the hallway. As always, she's dressed like she's going to a fancy event. She's the only person I know who puts on a full face of makeup and heels to sit around the house with her son and granddaughter.

Dad pulls the blanket up and pats the empty spot on the chair next to him. Hesitantly, I cross the room and climb in.

"How are you feeling?" I ask.

"Bored out of my mind," he says.

There's a documentary playing on the TV, something about Cambodia as far as I can tell. "Oh, like you don't love getting to watch your documentaries all day long?" I tease.

"Okay, that part is pretty nice," he admits, "but I'd like the option to be able to do something else."

"Quit your fussing," Nana says as she walks by to sit on the sofa. She swats Dad's good leg as she passes. "You'll be back to work tomorrow."

"Seriously?" I look to Dad for confirmation, and he nods.

"Doc says I'm fit as a fiddle—"

"Except for that whole bum leg thing," Nana interjects.

"Yes, except for that. I'll have to sit for my lectures, but I'm cleared to work."

I look from Dad to Nana and back again, disbelief washing over me. "How can you two be so flippant about this? You could've died."

"But I didn't. And now I'm bionic." He gently pats his left thigh, where I know a metal rod sits beneath his skin. "You don't have to worry about me, Quincy."

I lay my head on his shoulder. "Too late," I say. "I don't want to lose you too."

"You won't, kiddo. I promise."

chapter
TWENTY-EIGHT

"NO. NOT A CHANCE."

We're in the cafeteria on Thursday finishing our food—I have spinach and mushroom tortellini, thanks to Lylah's freezer meals—when Naoise announces that she's set me up on another date for Saturday night.

"I'm done with these blind dates," I say.

"Nuh-uh," she says, pointing a fork at me. "You promised. I've been busting my butt on your dress. You have to hold up your end of the deal."

"Come on, Neesh. With all the stuff with my dad and the movie schedule, I really can't."

"I thought your dad was fine," Hadley says. "My dad went to visit him yesterday, and he said he's healing up really well."

"Sure, he's fine," I say, "except for the part where he can't walk and do basic stuff around the house." I shove my Tupperware into my backpack and stand, waiting for my friends to take care of their messes. We make our way to the recycling and garbage cans, then we head into the hallway to hang out until the bell rings for our afternoon classes.

We've only been there for a few minutes when the guys walk toward us. They have the second lunch period but get here early if they change fast enough after weight training. Tanner folds his arms around Hadley, pulling her against his chest, and plants a sweet kiss on her temple. Marcus and Kenyon hang back, waiting for him.

"Ladies," Tanner says dramatically, and Hadley's face breaks into a love-silly grin at his over-the-top tone. "What are we discussing? It looks very serious." Hadley rolls her eyes.

"Nothing," I say quickly at the same time as Shyla says, "Just Quincy's big date this weekend."

I see the hurt flash across Kenyon's face before he's able to shutter it. Without a word, he turns and walks into the caf. Marcus watches him go then turns back to the group.

"Date, huh? Who's the lucky guy?"

Naoise says, "It's a surprise."

"It's always a surprise," Hadley says. Tanner nuzzles his face into her neck, and she giggles.

"I'm not going," I say.

"It's not too late to find a dress at Dillard's," Naoise says pointedly.

Marcus watches our back-and-forth with amusement. "Okay, then," he finally says, turning to Naoise. "We still on for Saturday?"

She nods as the bell rings. Tanner and Hadley separate reluctantly, and we watch the guys head to the caf.

"What's happening Saturday?" I ask. We have a full day of filming planned—our final day of shooting if everything goes right. Neesh and Marcus better not have made plans during our filming time. Marcus's grade depends on him being at the shoot.

As if she can read my mind, Naoise says, "Calm down, Sophia Coppola. We have plans in the morning, before we need to be on set."

"Doing what?" Hadley asks. We drift toward the stairs. At the rate we're going, we'll be late for our next classes.

"He's coming over so I can measure him. We, um, we're going to prom together, and I'm going to make him a vest."

"You're going to *prom* with *Marcus*? Since when?" I say a bit louder than I mean to.

"Monday," she says. "We thought it'd be fun. And easier, you know?"

"Easier than what?" Hadley asks.

Naoise sighs and spins the combination on her locker. "Easier than going with someone who doesn't get what it's like."

"Whoa," Shyla says, her face full of glee. "He *is* ace, isn't he? You all really do have a club now!"

"Very funny," Naoise deadpans. She pulls her books from her locker, hugging them to her chest. "It's nice having someone who gets it."

233

"I think that's great," Hadley says. "You two are going to have an absolute blast. You should do dinner with me and Tanner before!"

Shyla nudges her sister with her foot. "I'm happy for you," she says.

chapter
TWENTY-NINE

DAD AND NANA TAKE ME TO THE SET EXTRA EARLY ON SAT-
urday morning. It's our last day of shooting, and I want to do
something special for the cast and crew, so we stopped at Sprinkles for donuts and coffee for everyone.

Maybe I should be embarrassed to have my dad and grandmother on set with me, but I'm happy to have their support.
Plus, our set today is the courtyard gardens at Nana's condo
complex, and she was the one who arranged for us to use it.

Together, Nana and I set out the treats on a folding table as
Dad watches from where we parked his camp chair, grumbling
about his inability to help. We turn in unison at the sound of the
wrought iron gate clanging. Kenyon stands behind it, one bag
strapped to his back and another hanging at his side.

He goes to work without a word, setting up the Blackmagic
for the first shot. I unfold my tripod, pull the Canon from my
bag, and attach the quick-connect plate to the tripod head.

"Where do you want this one?" I call to Kenyon.

He gives me the barest of glances then turns back to work on
his camera. "Leave it," he says. "I'll get it when I'm done here."

We finish setting up and Dad, Nana, and I start chatting. Kenyon stands with us, not willing to be rude to my family, but he doesn't say a word until the cast and crew show up. Then he walks Kira and Ezra through their scene a couple times, adjusting the cameras to get the best angles, and before I know it, everyone is ready and looking to me for direction. I can't believe it's already our last day. I'm not sure I'm ready for this to be over.

I look around at all the people who have rallied behind *Maybe, Probably*: the family that supports all my big dreams and ideas; the friends who show up, day after day, to help me when I know they have other things they'd rather be doing; the cast and crew, without whose incredible talents *Maybe, Probably* would never have gotten off the ground. All these people, here because I have a dream.

Today, if only for a little while, I get to fully live that dream. "Action."

"Hey, can we talk?" I ask, a trash bag stuffed with the remnants of our wrap party hanging loosely from my hand.

Kenyon stiffens at my voice. He's packing the Blackmagic into its case for the last time. We wrapped on filming half an hour ago, and after a small celebration—Nana got us sparkling cider and plastic champagne flutes—we set to work tearing our equipment down.

"What do you want to talk about?" He replies like we're reciting lines from a script.

"Come on, Kenyon. I miss—"

"You still have a date this weekend?"

I snap my mouth shut. *I miss us*, I was about to say, but I wonder now, was there ever an *us*? Part of me is wondering if I imagined the connection I felt we had.

But I didn't imagine the way he made me feel, the warmth inside me when we kissed. There's no imagining fireflies.

"Well?"

"Yes," I say. My voice is barely a whisper.

"Then I don't think there's anything for us to talk about."

"Don't be like that. I told you I would be going on dates with other guys. You knew that from the start."

"You didn't tell me you'd be kissing them all," he says.

I tilt my head back and close my eyes against the brightness of the afternoon sun. I want to argue but I can't. The whole goal of going out with these guys was to *kiss* them, to find who gave me my first real kiss in that theater. Now it all seems so silly and juvenile. Nana's party feels like it happened in another lifetime. And if I really think hard, I can barely remember what that kiss even felt like. All I remember is kissing Kenyon.

"You're right," I say, "but I can explain. There was this guy at my grandma's party, and—"

"Stop," Kenyon snaps, his voice harsher than I've heard before. "I don't need explanations or excuses. Let's just call this what it is, okay? We had fun, and then you moved on."

"But I didn't move on. Can't you see that?"

"Could've fooled me."

I open my mouth with a retort, but before I say anything, my jaw clamps shut, the click of my teeth impossibly loud in my head. He's *right*, I realize. No matter my reasons, no matter how badly I wanted to find out who my mystery kisser was—or how desperately I still want Naoise to finish my perfect prom dress—I was careless with his heart.

"I'm so sorry," I whisper.

"Don't be." Kenyon latches the camera case shut and stands. "You don't owe me anything, Quincy. We're not together. You can kiss whoever you want."

With that, he walks out of the courtyard, leaving me and our borrowed camera behind.

chapter
THIRTY

"PUT THE BLUE ONE BACK ON," HADLEY SAYS, HER VOICE tinny through the phone speaker.

I texted Naoise during the ride home from filming, trying to back out of tonight's date. After my talk with Kenyon, going out with another guy was the last thing I wanted to do.

My phone rang seconds after I hit send. "No," Naoise said as soon as I answered, not giving me a chance to talk. "You are not backing out of this."

"Come on, Neesh."

"No," she repeated. "I stayed up half the night finishing your dress—it's amazing, by the way, and you have to come try it on Monday to make sure it fits, okay?"

"Okay. Thanks. But I'm really not up for a date tonight."

"We had a deal, Q. I make the dress, and you let me set you up on dates. I did my end of the deal. You are not backing out of yours."

Dad watched me from the corner of his eye, an amused look on his face. Did we really have to be having this conversation while I was in the car with him and Nana? I turn toward the window and lower my voice.

"There's a lot going on right now, and I'm not feeling up to it tonight. I think I'm just gonna spend some time with my dad."

"Oh, no," Dad said, his voice way louder than necessary in the tiny car. "You are not using me to get out of anything. In fact, I forbid you to stay home tonight."

"You forbid it?" I rolled my eyes at him, and he laughed in response.

Nana joined in his laughter. Traitor.

"Thank you, Mr. Walker!" I pulled the phone back from my ear until the yelling stopped. Quieter, Naoise said, "Tyler will be at your house at six thirty."

"Tyler?" My stomach dipped, a not-unpleasant flutter rising in its depths.

"It was supposed to be a surprise," Naoise said, "but your neurotic butt won't stop trying to back out. So there you go. The date you've been waiting for."

Now, with Hadley on video chat helping me pick out the perfect outfit, I can't place a finger on what I'm feeling. I've daydreamed about going out with Tyler for so long that I can't quite believe it's really happening.

I slip into the blue dress, another of my mother's. It slides over the cap-sleeve crop top I'm wearing and falls right below my knees, with tiny buttons all the way up the front. I spin in front of the phone, letting the soft fabric swish around my shins.

"Perfect," Hadley says. I put my glasses on, and she squints, leaning closer to the camera. "No, not those ones. Wear the clear frames."

I do what she says, switching my glasses for clear acrylic frames before grabbing the phone from where I'd propped it on my bookshelf and falling onto my bed.

"Hey, Had, how long ago did Naoise plan this date?"

"I'm not sure," she says. The image shakes as she changes positions, and even though I can't see anything beyond her face, I know she's sitting cross-legged in the middle of her bed. "Maybe Tuesday? Tanner's been trying to get him to do it for weeks now, but that boy of yours refuses to do the blind date thing."

"Does that mean he knows it's with me?" Suddenly, my nerves are at an almost unbearable level. It was bad enough knowing I was finally going out with Tyler, but it's somehow worse knowing he agreed to this after my prom outburst with him at work.

Hadley's laughing on the other end, her face scrunched up and head thrown back.

"What?" I say.

She struggles to control herself enough to say, "Of course he knows the date is with you. He's picking you up at your house, dingleberry."

Oh. *Duh*. I was so wrapped up in the fact that I was finally going out with Tyler that I never stopped to consider the fact that he was coming *here*. That he'll be here in—I check the time on my phone—less than ten minutes.

"Did you call me a dingleberry?" I ask, desperate for a distraction. "What even is that?"

She doesn't take the bait. "You don't need to be nervous," she says. "It's just Tyler. You'll be fine. Unless . . ." She gives me a knowing smile.

"Unless what?"

"Unless there's another reason you're so nervous about tonight?"

With a groan, I instantly blurt out the story of my outburst to Hadley. "That was the last time we talked, and now this whole date there's going to be this prom pressure hanging over us."

"Good alliteration," she says, "but that's not what I meant when I said maybe there's another reason."

"I don't follow."

Hadley gives me a pointed look through the phone. "Kenyon? I'm not naive, Q. I see the way you two look at each other, the subtle touches when you think nobody's watching. You like him. And he likes you."

"Liked," I correct. "He doesn't want anything to do with me now." Tyler will be here in less than five minutes, so I give her the basics of what happened between us, ending with me kissing Donovan and the hurt look on Kenyon's face. As I finish, the doorbell rings.

"I gotta go."

"You don't have to go, Quin," Hadley says.

I listen as Dad opens the front door and invites Tyler into our house. "I really do," I say. "Tyler's waiting. I'll talk to you later, okay?"

"Wait," she says as I reach for the End Call button. "What are you going to do about Kenyon?"

I shake my head. I can't think about Kenyon right now. I can't think about anything other than the fact that Tyler, the guy I've wanted for so long, is standing in my living room, waiting to take me on a date.

"Nothing," I say finally. "He made his choice."

"We're going to a movie?"

Tyler pulls his car into a spot toward the back of the full parking lot. It's a Saturday night, so the AMC megaplex is busy.

When I got off the phone with Hadley and came out to the living room, I found Tyler and Dad bantering about basketball. Tyler is a Duke fan, and Dad couldn't let him go without trying to convert him to the Heels.

"I remember you were bummed when we couldn't get *Walking to Rwanda* at the Orpheum, so I thought you'd like to see it."

"Oh. That's great. Thanks!" Truthfully, Shyla and I went opening weekend, but I'm so touched by Tyler's thoughtfulness that I don't tell him.

About halfway to the theater, Tyler's hand bumps against the back of my knuckles. Before I have even a moment to question it, his fingers wrap gently around mine. I turn my hand so we can lace our fingers together, and suddenly there's a bullhorn screaming in my head: *Tyler is holding my hand!*

In the theater, we settle into seats toward the back. Tyler places our drinks in the outer cup holders, leaving the middle armrest up so that when we sit, our arms touch. I let my legs drift to the side until my thigh rests against his. When the lights dim and the screen lights up with the trailer reel, Tyler reaches his arm around me and pulls me to his side. With my head resting on his chest, we watch the movie.

I could get used to this.

"What do you want to do now?" Tyler asks as soon as the movie is over. I shush him automatically, then cringe at myself.

"Sorry," I say. "I like to watch the credits."

He's already starting to stand, and he hovers in this half-standing, half-seated crouch. "Like, in case there's an extra scene at the end? There's not in this movie. I checked."

"Not for that. I like to stay until the very end is all."

He sits down and takes my hand in his. The way he does it without a thought throws me off. We've spent months dancing around this, and now that we're here, he acts like we've been going out for ages.

My family and friends are so used to my insistence to stay to the end that I don't really know how to explain it to someone new. "It's silly, really, but I feel like I need to stay to support everyone who worked on the movie. Just because they aren't top billed, it doesn't mean they didn't work hard."

"You know they don't know if you stay to see their name in the credits or not, right?"

"Yeah, I know." I'm watching anyway.

"Okay, well, I need to use the restroom." Tyler stands. "Meet you in the lobby?"

chapter
THIRTY-ONE

I'M THE ONLY ONE LEFT IN THE THEATER WHEN THE SCREEN
finally blackens and the house lights go up. An employee has
been cleaning the aisle behind me, so I rush out before he gets
to my row.

The lobby is packed with people waiting to go into the 9:00
p.m. shows. I stand on my tiptoes, craning my neck to spot
Tyler, but it's no use. You can't really see over anyone when
you're five-foot-two.

When I'm reasonably sure he's not in the waiting area near
the restrooms, I make my way to the main lobby. There's a huge
cardboard standee for the latest Tarantino film blocking my
view, so I skirt around it—and directly into a hard body.

"I'm so sorry." Large hands wrap around my upper arms,
steadying me before I completely lose my balance, and I look up
into a face that immediately makes my heart skip.

"Oh," I say, realizing at the exact same time Kenyon does.
He drops my arms and steps back like I've burned him.

"Um, hi," I say. "What are you going to see?" I try to look
around to see if he's with someone without being too obvious.

"*Mass Grave,*" he says. "Donovan really wants to see it, so . . ." He shrugs.

"Oh, well, that's cool. You'll have to let me know how it is."

He laughs, but it's reserved, not the carefree laugh he used to have around me. "I can tell you now. It's bloody and over the top, and it has very little character development."

"Sounds fun," I deadpan.

"Nah, it's fine. I'm sure it'll be entertaining at least. How about you? What are you seeing?" Warmth floods me when I notice him do the same check-for-companion that I did.

"I saw *Walking to Rwanda.*"

"Oh, I want to see that one. How was it?" His body relaxes some. This is comfortable ground for us. As long as we stick to movies, things don't have to be painful and awkward.

"It's *so* good," I gush. "Shyla and I actually saw it already, but it was as good the second time. Maybe even better because—"

"There you are," Tyler's voice interrupts me, and then three things happen simultaneously: he drapes an arm around my shoulders, Kenyon's face turns hard as he looks away, and my heart cracks in my chest, pain flooding my body.

"You ready?" Tyler asks, completely oblivious to what just happened.

"See you later, Quin." Kenyon steps around us and walks toward the theater without another look. I turn and watch him go.

Tyler drops his arm to my waist and guides me outside. For so long, all I wanted was for him to hold me like this, but now it feels all wrong. I squirrel my way out of his grip by feigning an untied shoe, and when I stand up, I make sure to keep some distance between us.

Back in the car, Tyler starts the engine but doesn't back out of our space. "You okay?" he asks. "I thought maybe we could go grab some food or something."

He sounds so sincere that the fissure in my heart gets a bit wider. This isn't fair to anyone, and the longer I go on with this ridiculous game, the more people I'm going to hurt.

"Actually," I say, "I'm not feeling so great. Could you take me home?"

"Thanks for the movie. Sorry to bail on you."

We're standing on my front porch with the sounds of whatever documentary Dad's watching drifting out through the open living room window.

He grabs my hands in his and leans in so he can look me in the eye. "No need to apologize. I had fun."

"Yeah. Me too." I try to inject some pep into my voice. It's not Tyler's fault this date turned into a disaster. As far as he knows, it didn't. "Well, I better go in. See you Monday?"

"Have a good night, Quincy." And then he leans forward, and adrenaline floods my system. He's going to kiss me.

This is it: the moment I've been wanting for months. Tyler is going to kiss me. Will his kiss be the same as the one from Nana's party? I've been hoping so hard it was him in that room that I've nearly convinced myself it was. This is my chance to find out. My eyes drift shut.

Kenyon's face flashes in my mind, the hurt expression he wore when I kissed his best friend. The stony coolness when he saw who I was with tonight.

At the last second, I turn my head to the side, and his lips brush my cheek.

"Good night," I say. I squeeze his hand quickly then let go and head inside.

Dad looks up when the door opens. "You're home. I didn't expect to see you so early."

I push the door until I hear the soft click of the latch and turn the deadbolt. "Didn't feel great. I think I'm gonna head to bed."

I hear Dad calling to me as I exit the bathroom, face washed and teeth brushed. I make my way to the living room and stand by his chair.

"Did he hurt you?" For a second, I think he's joking, until I see how serious his expression is.

"What? No. Tyler's fine. I really just don't feel well." I climb onto the chair, cuddling against him.

"If you're sure," he says, and I can tell he doesn't fully believe me.

"I am. I'll be fine in the morning."

"Okay, then. Goodnight, John." Dad smooths back my hair from my face the way he used to when I was a kid. He presses a kiss to my forehead. "You know where to find me if you want to talk."

"I know. I love you, Dad." I slip off the chair and pad back toward my room.

"Love you too, kiddo. Have a good night."

As I slip beneath my comforter and sheet, I pull up our group thread and type out a quick text to my friends.

ME: It wasn't Tyler.

Whether it's true or not doesn't matter anymore. Not after I've messed things up so badly. I just want to be done with it all, and now I am. Before the deluge of responses has a chance to blow up my phone, I switch it to Do Not Disturb and drop it to the floor next to my bed. I'm ready for this night to be over.

chapter
THIRTY-TWO

ON MONDAY AFTER SCHOOL, I FOLLOW SHYLA TO HER CAR.
She's been jumpy and distant all day, and I can't figure out what's
going on. If I ask, she laughs it off and says everything's fine, but
I know her almost better than I know myself. I've never seen
her act so nervous.

We swing by a drive-thru coffee kiosk, and while we're
waiting to get back onto the main road, she takes a shuddering
breath and says, without looking at me, "I think I'm going to
India."

I sputter, inhaling a sip of latte. My throat spasms and I
hack and cough until my eyes are watering, tears streaming
down my face.

"When?" I manage between coughs.

"You gonna survive?" She passes me her open water bottle,
and I take a gulp. The cool water soothes the burn in my throat,
but the impulse to cough still catches me.

"There's this program at the University of Delhi for
English-speaking undergrads studying psych. They teach in
English only, but there's a track to learn Hindi as well. Only a

handful of people get in every year, but I checked into it, and it looks perfect for me."

"That's really great, Shy." I remember the way her face beamed when she put on her prom dress, how she seemed both shy and confident in the traditional Indian lehenga. She's embracing her heritage, and I can tell this program in India means a lot to her.

"When will you find out?"

Without a word, she reaches behind her seat and rustles through her backpack. A thick envelope drops into my lap. I pull the papers out and skim over them quickly. The letterhead tells me they're from Indraprastha College for Women, part of the University of Delhi.

"You're already in?"

Shyla blushes, her tan skin deepening, and a wide smile breaks out on her face. I squeal in excitement. "This is incredible, Shyla!"

"Yeah," she says, but I can hear the doubt creeping into her voice. "I guess so."

"Hey, what's going on? This is a good thing, isn't it?"

She doesn't answer for a moment, and I watch the scenery pass by as we get closer to her house. Shyla's never been an open book; she tends to hide her real thoughts and feelings behind her humor and wit. If I press her, she'll make a quick joke, and it'll be over, so I wait.

"It's that"—she pulls her bottom lip into her mouth and bites down, sucking a deep breath in through her teeth—"I haven't told my parents. Or Naoise. We were supposed to be roommates in Nashville next year. How am I supposed to tell her I'm bailing to go to India?"

"Neesh loves you," I say. "She might be upset at first, but she'll come around."

"Maybe," she mutters.

"She will. I promise. Plus, isn't Marcus going to Fisk next year? They're becoming pretty good friends."

"That's true," Shyla agrees. She squints at something through the windshield. "Hey, what's that?"

I follow her gaze to the side of the road. Up ahead, there's a white sign attached to the mile marker. The sun glints off it, and I squint against the brightness until we get close enough to see. In huge letters, taking up the entire poster, is one word: SHYLA.

"What the heck? Is that duct tape?" She looks at me, and I shrug.

"Keep going. Maybe there's more."

Sure enough, there's another sign on a reflector post. WILL.

We drive, the suspense heavy in the air around us. The only sound in the car is us whispering as we read the signs in unison, post after post.

SHYLA WILL YOU GO TO PROM WITH ME?

"That is so romantic!" I squeal. Promposals are a big deal around here, and this is one of the best ones I've seen. It must've taken hours to pull off. Jealousy churns in my gut, and I hurry to tamp it down. Just because I've imagined my own promposal for so long—and it looks like it'll never be coming—there's no reason for me to not be thrilled for Shyla.

A horn blares behind us, and Shyla jerks in her seat. A glance at the speedometer shows that we've slowed to nearly half the speed limit. She grips the wheel hard and pushes her foot on the accelerator.

"Who do you think did it?" she says when we get back to speed.

"I know who did it, and so do you."

"I don't know . . ."

"Donovan! He obviously adores you." Since my party, I've been watching the two of them, noticing the coy looks and subtle flirting. Now that I know they like each other, I can't believe I didn't see it before. They are perfect together, and I'm truly happy I caught them kissing while I was supposed to be on a date with him.

Sometimes life is super weird.

"We've not even talked about prom yet," she says. "He's never even hinted about it."

"Because he wanted to surprise you!"

We turn into her driveway, and Shyla cuts the engine. She looks stunned, like she can't quite believe what we saw.

"Come on," I say, and we head into the house.

Naoise is in the foyer, bouncing on the balls of her feet, a huge smile lighting up her face. "Finally! I've been waiting forever!"

Dropping her keys onto the table by the door, Shyla says, "It hasn't been forever."

"Feels like it," Naoise mutters.

"What's going on?" I ask

"Come on, come on, come on!" Naoise grabs her sister's hand and drags her to the staircase. I follow them upstairs and down the hall to Shyla's room.

There's something attached to the closed door, and I need to stand on tiptoes to peek over Shyla's shoulder and see what it is. Stuck there with duct tape is the biggest pushpin I've ever seen. A purple scrap of paper hangs from it. *Use me,* it says.

"Okay . . ." Shyla pulls the pin off the door and twists the knob.

Inside, her room is a rainbow of balloons. They spill out into the hallway when she pushes open the door. "What the—?"

She walks into the middle of the room, spinning a slow circle, balloons bouncing around her legs as she moves. She has this expression of wondrous delight on her face that makes her look like a little kid.

"Pop them!" Naoise is still bouncing on her toes, excitement radiating from her.

Shyla looks at the pushpin in her hand like she forgot it was there, and then a sly smile spreads across her face as she jabs it into the nearest balloon.

Pretty soon, all three of us are wildly popping balloons, our laughter mixing with the bangs. We're down to the last dozen or so when I stomp on a bright green one and a small scrap of paper flutters to the ground.

"Look!" I pick up the paper and wave it in front of Shyla, who pops her last balloon and grabs it from me. Naoise and I watch her as she reads it. Her face flushes with a deep blush.

"It's from Donovan," she says.

"I told you!" I yell triumphantly.

Naoise pulls her into a tight hug. "I'm so happy for you."

Shyla catches my eye over her sister's shoulder, and I can see the guilt and fear mixed into her happy expression. She and Naoise have been inseparable since even before their parents got married. They aren't only sisters; they're best friends.

Being apart next year is going to be hard on them, but I'm proud of Shyla. She's always been there for the rest of us, the first one to help when anyone needs something, the peacemaker and the supporter. She is constantly pushing us to follow our dreams: me with my films, Hadley and her music, and Naoise's fashion design.

It's her turn to follow her own dream, and, hard as it may be, going to India is something she needs to do. She'll do amazing things over there. It's finally Shyla's turn to shine.

In Naoise's room, I stand in front of her full-length mirror, staring at my reflection. This dress is the most amazing thing I've ever worn. It's not exactly what Lucy and Ethel wore when they sang "Friendship" at the variety show—it is so much better. Naoise was right. Of course.

It has the basics of Lucy's dress: white with a fitted bodice, a tulle princess skirt, and simple half-inch straps. Magenta and deep-purple mesh cascades from my right hip down the skirt to the floor. It may not be the exact colors from the show—every colorized photo I found showed them a bit differently—but they look amazing together.

If she'd stopped there, she could have made a great replica of the dress. Instead, she pulled the color up, draping the fine magenta mesh diagonally across the bodice and over my left shoulder. A flutter sleeve falls, light as a feather across my upper arm and just past my hip. She's added the tiniest sparkly crystals to the right strap, and I dip my shoulder now, loving the way the light plays over them when I move.

"Neesh, this is seriously amazing!"

"As good as Lucy's dress?" She's perched at the edge of her bed, her back straight and hands in her lap. Her words have a teasing tone to them, but I can tell how much my answer really means to her.

"It's better." I turn a slow circle, twisting my neck as I do so I don't lose sight of the dress. Running my fingers through my hair, I try to envision how I'll style it. I'd planned to twist it up in a retro look to really embrace the Old Hollywood theme, but with this dress, maybe soft curls and a semi-casual ponytail would be the way to go. Mom had these beautiful pearl and crystal bobby pins, and they'd be the perfect addition.

Prom is less than two weeks away. Over the past week, I've seen more and more promposals going up as everyone's excitement for the big day grows. As happy as I am for my friends and classmates, each one is a crushing reminder that I don't have a date. And if the past few weeks are any indication, I won't have one.

"What's wrong?" Naoise asks, and I stop my spin.

"Nothing. It's . . ." Crossing the room, I smooth the back of the dress so I won't mess up the basting stitch Naoise did to fit it perfectly to my body. When we're done here, she'll reinforce it, and my dress will be complete. I sit next to her.

Naoise loops her arm around mine and leans into me. Head close to mine, she says, "What?"

I sigh. "It's just that this is such a gorgeous dress, and it's going to be a shame that I won't have a date to impress with it." Shaking my head, I force myself to laugh it off. "Never mind. I'm sure I'll have a great time stag anyway."

"You would, if you were going stag," she says. "But you won't be alone."

I pull back from her, turning so I can look her in the eye. "What do you know that I don't? Because last I checked, I'd pretty much burned my best chances at having a prom date."

"I know nothing," she says with mock seriousness. "It's only a hunch I have."

I can tell I'm not going to get anything more out of her, so I drop it. The dress really is amazing, and I know how lucky I am to have a friend like her. And, truthfully, I'm happy she seems to have forgotten about Operation Mystery Kisser for the time being. It helps that the last guy on the list from Nana's party is *her* prom date now.

Maybe I'll never know who kissed me at the party. It's only been three weeks, but somehow it feels like a lifetime ago. Already, the memory of the kiss is fading, and my stomach no longer dips when it crosses my mind. I think a part of me will always wonder who it was, but I've realized I don't want that kiss. Not anymore.

Now, as I sit with Naoise in the most amazing dress I've ever worn, the only kisses I want are Kenyon's.

chapter
THIRTY-THREE

"I THINK WE SHOULD INTERCUT THE SCENES HERE." I REACH for the computer mouse, trying not to show how hurt I am when Kenyon flinches away from me. Reminding myself it doesn't have to be perfect at this point, I make quick work of piecing the scenes together, alternating between Adalyn and Sebastian to illustrate what I mean.

"I don't know," he says when I'm finished. "It works, but is it too busy? We lose some of the emotion this way, and this is the time where we really need to see what Adalyn's feeling."

I consider his point, looking at the image I've captured on the school's iMac screen. Kira did an amazing job with this scene, and the guilt and heartbreak are clear on her face. But we get that still if we intercut Sebastian's part of the conversation, right?

"We need Sebastian's part of the call, though," I say. I flick to the next cut, a close-up of Ezra's face. He's gripping the phone to his ear so hard his knuckles shine white next to his cheekbone. He's hurt, bewildered, and angry. This is the phone call that changes everything for the characters, and both actors did an incredible job at evoking their emotions. "The sequence doesn't make sense if we only hear Kira's side, and I was watching Jamison Beck's YouTube channel, and he says phone voice-overs are—"

"Well, if Jamison Beck says it, then it must be true." Kenyon's voice holds a hard edge to it.

I lean into my chair and stare at him. "What is your problem today?"

"I don't have a problem. Let's do this. The bell's gonna ring soon."

Mr. Welles gave us a free period to work on whatever we needed today. Donovan headed straight for the music wing with a laptop and a bundle of recording equipment. He won't show us what he's been working on, but he's tinkering every chance he gets. He promises he's almost ready to share, and I can't wait to hear what he's put together.

Marcus isn't at school today, so that leaves me and Kenyon to work on edits alone. To say this has been the most uncomfortable class period of my life would be an understatement.

"Okay," I say slowly, "if you don't have a problem, what's with the sarcastic barbs?"

"This is *our* movie, Quincy. Not Jamison's. I know you have some kind of massive crush on the guy, but he's not always right, you know."

"I do not!" I'm nearly yelling, and I take a quick look around the room to see if anyone is watching us. I lower my voice. "I do not have a crush on Jamison Beck. I don't even know him. But his work is amazing, and he obviously knows what he's talking about. He's one of the judges for the festival, so we should do what he—"

"We don't need to do everything he says on his YouTube channel just because he's a judge. We've got this."

I watch as Kenyon deletes the cuts I added in, pulling the scene back to only Kira's side. I hate to admit that he has a point—we do need to see her emotions here. But I still think we lose impact by cutting Ezra completely out as well.

"He may not always be right," I say, my words spiky and hard, "but the idea isn't only bad because it came from him either."

Kenyon's face flashes with something I can't quite place. Is he embarrassed? With a sigh, he pushes his hair back. "Fine. You're right. What if we did something like this?"

He turns to the computer and sets to work, lightning fast, and I watch as he cuts scenes in and layers audio. Kenyon doesn't speak, but works furiously, checking the time every so often. I try to watch what he's doing, but he angles his body, blocking the screen from my view. I relax into my chair, trying to be patient.

Eventually, I pull out my physics homework and start working on the problems our teacher gave us. If I'm going to be stuck here, unable to work on the movie, at least I can get through some of my other classwork. Kenyon's talking to himself, too softly for me to make out what he's saying.

The bell is going to ring any minute now, and I don't know if he'll finish in time. "Almost done," he says. Then, with a flourish, he scrolls to the beginning of the sequence and pushes play, falling back into his chair like he just ran a marathon.

The bell rings, and the room explodes to life around us, our classmates packing up and hurrying out the door. Kenyon and I stay where we are, watching our movie on the computer screen.

The scene starts with Adalyn dialing. The camera is tight on her, so we can't see her location. She pulls the phone to her ear, and there's a slight tremble in her hand. Fear transforms her face.

Cut to a wide shot of Sebastian at a park, throwing a Frisbee for his dog. The brightness of the colors brings a cheeriness to the shot that's in direct contrast to what we saw with Adalyn. A phone rings, and he throws the Frisbee once more before answering.

The scene cuts to a close-up as he checks the caller ID. His face lights up, and he answers, "Addie."

We watch, close up on his face, as elation turns to confusion before we cut back to Adalyn. She has tears in her eyes as she talks. The shot stays tight on her, catching every tiny shift of her features. Kenyon put Sebastian's lines as voice-over, slightly muffled so it sounds like they are coming from the other end of the phone.

We stay with Adalyn for the duration of the scene, watching as she breaks Sebastian's heart, and her own, in the process. When she hangs up, she dissolves into tears and the camera slowly pulls back from her face. We see that she's standing on the curb with a suitcase at her feet. A taxi pulls around the corner, giving us a glimpse of its yellow sides. It's enough to cue the viewers that she's leaving.

I think that's it, but then the scene cuts again, and we're back in the park with Sebastian, the same wide angle we started with. He pulls the phone from his ear and stares at it for a moment in disbelief. At his feet, the dog nudges the frisbee toward him, begging for attention, but he's too lost in his own heartbreak to notice.

The screen freezes there and then flickers back to the editing software. Kenyon spins in his chair to face me.

"What do you—are you crying?"

I touch a hand to my cheek and am surprised to find that it's wet. With an embarrassed laugh, I wipe the tears away.

"That was incredible. How . . . ?"

The dog belonged to a guy who was at the park when we got there to film. Ezra played with him before we shot his scenes, and I had no idea Kenyon had caught any of it on camera until I checked over the dailies that evening. It was supposed to be nothing more than a lighting test, something to scrap for the real material. When the dog came back to beg Ezra to play more, right in the middle of filming his scene, I thought it was a ruined shot and we did it again. I never imagined something I thought was a blooper would heighten the emotion of this scene.

"You were right," Kenyon says. "I wasn't giving your idea a chance." He gives me a sheepish grin. "But you were right. We needed to see Sebastian's reactions. We can cut more into the conversation if you want."

"No," I rush to say. "This is perfect. So much better than what I thought it could be."

Kenyon's smile broadens, and my heart soars with hope that the wall he's built between us is starting to crumble. "I guess we make a pretty good team?" he says.

I nod, not trusting my voice to speak. Could we go back to the way we were? I don't even know what we were, exactly, but I want to find out. I want to erase everything that's happened since my birthday party. I want to explore whatever it was Kenyon and I could have had.

And the way he's looking at me tells me that he might want the same things.

"Hey," I start, but a deep voice talks over me, and I jump.

"You two need to move out," Mr. Welles says. He looks between me and Kenyon with a knowing smirk. "I've got another class to teach now."

And like that, the spell is broken. Kenyon turns from me and saves our work before shutting down the program and disconnecting our external hard drive. I watch in silence as he shoves it into his backpack and tosses the bag over one shoulder. I'm still sitting there when he walks out of the classroom without even a backward glance.

After school, I'm in the AP English classroom with the Prom Committee. It's our final meeting, the last chance to hash out details for the big night—a night to remember, and all that.

"Ticket sales are holding strong," Naoise says, checking her notebook. "Let's give it one more good push this week and see if we can get a few more people to come, okay? We don't want anyone to be left out. Hadley, how's the fundraising looking?"

Hadley pulls a stack of papers from her backpack. "Great! I got Santos Photography on board for pictures at a discount by trading an ad spot for senior portraits on next year's football programs. And Pier 23 wants to give free prom tickets and dinner to four couples, so if any of you have talked to someone who wants to come but can't afford the ticket price, please let me know."

"That's excellent," says Mrs. Anderson, our committee advisor. "We don't want the budget to be the reason anyone misses out. Our current ticket sales should cover the venue and DJ, right?"

Naoise turns to me, questioning.

"Yes," I say. "We're able to keep our decoration budget down by using the Rialto. It's basically all we need for our theme as is."

"That's all set and ready?" Naoise asks.

"Yep."

"Can you confirm that for us really quick?"

Suppressing a sigh, I pull out my phone and stand up. Naoise has been getting more and more sassy about the Rialto this past week. I know it wasn't her first choice of venue, but it's going to be great. As we get closer to prom, the pressure is molding her into a prom dictator. I know she wants the night to be perfect, though, so instead of the sarcastic retort I feel like making, I force myself to smile as I slip out of the room to call the Rialto and confirm our reservation.

"You've reached the Rialto Events Center. Our menu options have recently changed, so please listen . . ."

I type in the number for the reservations extension and wait while the line rings in my ear.

"Hello! Rialto Theater reservations," a perky voice on the other end says. "What can I do for you today?"

"Hi, this is Quincy Walker at Port City Christian Academy. I'm calling to confirm that our prom reservation is all set and ready to go."

Faint clicking carries across the phone and into my ear. "Port City," she mumbles to herself, and then she says, "Okay, here we go. Everything's confirmed. You'll have access to the building starting at 10 a.m. the morning of Saturday, June fifth."

"Did you say June fifth?" I say over whatever she's saying next.

"Yes, ma'am. You have the theater all day."

"But prom is May twenty-ninth."

"It says here that you're booked for the fifth," she says firmly.

I lean my back against the cool lockers and slide down until I'm sitting on the hard hallway floor.

"That's graduation," I tell the woman on the phone. "We have to do it on the twenty-ninth. It's the only day that works." All our vendors are booked for the twenty-ninth—our photographer and our DJ, the catering company that's providing snacks and drinks. The chaperones—everything. It's all set for the twenty-ninth. "Can we bump it up a week? Please?"

"Sorry, ma'am, but we've got a wedding here on the twenty-ninth."

My heart clenches tight, freezing in my chest before picking up at double speed. What am I going to do? What am I going to tell Naoise? I was the one who convinced her to pass on the Ballast to try something new and go with the Rialto. And now I'm the reason we don't have a prom venue.

"Ma'am," the woman says, and the tone of her voice tells me it's not the first time she's tried to get my attention. "Is there anything else I can do for you?"

"No," I say. Numbly, I pull the phone from my ear and hang up.

In the classroom, the rest of the committee is talking and laughing. Naoise has her head thrown back, a look of glee on her face. A hard lump lodges in my throat, and my stomach rolls over, threatening to be sick. How did this all get so messed up so quickly? My hands shake as I numbly push the door shut with a click. I lean against it, breathing slow and steady in an effort to calm my nerves until they notice I'm back.

"Well?" Mrs. Anderson says when she sees me. "Are we good to go?"

"Um," I say, "not exactly."

Naoise freezes midway through straightening a pile of papers and cuts her eyes to me. "What does that even mean?"

I sigh and wave my phone as if that explains anything. "The Rialto . . . they have the wrong date."

The room explodes into a flurry of questions. Voices fly around, each trying to be heard first. My face burns, and my vision blurs as tears rush to my eyes. Through the chaos, my focus never leaves Naoise, her incredulous stare burning through me.

Finally, Mrs. Anderson stands, raising an arm into the air until the rest of us notice her movement and quiet our frenzy. "Let's all calm down," she says, lowering her arm and pressing both palms onto the table. She turns to me. "How did this happen?"

"I . . . I don't know," I admit.

"What are we going to do now?" Hadley asks. Red splotches rise in her cheeks, and I can tell she's moments away from panic. "Maybe I can ask my dad about using the church's cultural hall?"

"We can save some money by holding it in the gym," someone suggests, and the rest of the room boos.

Mrs. Anderson lowers herself into her chair. "Okay," she says, "good. Let's brainstorm and figure this out. Everyone, give me your ideas. If we need to hold it in the gym, we will, but I'm sure you all can come up with something better."

Slowly, I make my way to the empty chair next to Naoise and sit, listening to the conversation flow around me. As the new venue ideas get more and more outlandish, I sneak a glance toward her, but she stares resolutely ahead, watching Mrs. Anderson scribble all the suggestions into her notebook.

After the meeting, Naoise drives me home in excruciating silence, her anger crashing into me like waves for the entire ride. When she pulls into my driveway, she doesn't even put the car into park. Without a word, she hits the unlock button and waits for me to leave.

I don't move. I can't make myself leave without trying to smooth this over. "I'm so, so sorry, Neesh. Really," I say.

"You're sorry? Well, that's just great, Quincy. Maybe sorry will magically get us a new venue."

"I didn't think—"

"You're right," she spits out. "You didn't. You didn't think about anything other than what you wanted. You got to pick the theme. You got the venue you wanted. And now what? We have 300 students who paid for the perfect prom night that won't happen. Did you think about any of them?"

Ouch. "That's not fair, Neesh. I didn't ask them to mess up the dates."

"Of course you didn't," she snaps. "Because nothing's ever your fault, is it? Quincy never screws up."

Rage rolls off her, filling the car. Is this really what she thinks of me, or is it her anger speaking? There's no way I'm going to fix this by talking right now. Grabbing the door handle, I finally turn to her.

"I'm really sorry, Neesh. I'm going to fix this. I promise."

chapter
THIRTY-FOUR

DAD HAS AN APPOINTMENT WITH HIS ORTHOPEDIST THIS afternoon, so I'm surprised when I find the front door unlocked. I push it open, glancing at his empty chair before stepping into the house. It's not like Dad and Nana to forget to lock the door.

With a sigh, I drop into the chair-and-a-half and close my eyes. How did prom get so messed up? I rack my brain, trying to find any solution to our lack of venue, but I come up completely blank. What happens when this gets past the Prom Committee, when I have to admit my screw-up to the entire school? There must be some way to fix this. I need time to think clearly.

"Hey," a voice says, and I scream, nearly falling out of the chair as I spin toward the kitchen.

"Clark," I breathe out. "What are you doing here?"

"I came to visit Dad. Where is he?"

"Doctor," I say. "You can go. He won't be back for a while." I stand and start toward my bedroom.

"Quin, wait. How are you doing?" The chair screeches across the floor as he pushes away from the table and follows me. He stops at my bedroom doorway and watches as I pull my homework from my bag, spreading it out in front of me. "Quin, talk to me."

"You want me to talk to you? Now?" I laugh a cold, humorless laugh. "Okay, Clark. What do you want to talk about?"

He stares at me, wide-eyed, and a part of me loves that I've shocked him. This has been building up inside me for so long, and now that I'm starting to let it loose, I crave more. Part of me recognizes—through my building rage—that I'm not being fair. I'm still riding high on the anger and pain of my fight with Naoise. That's not Clark's fault, but he's the only one here for me to let loose on.

"Oh, I know," I say with mock-elation. "Let's talk about how you totally abandoned your family. Let's talk about how you're never here anymore. How you'd rather hang out in your little apartment and never come home. How you ignore all my calls and texts and never talk to me anymore."

"Quin—"

"I'm not done." Anger burns hot in my veins, and I want to lash out at him, to hurt him the way he's hurt me for so long. "You said you wanna talk, so I'm talking. Where the hell have you been the past two years? It's like you don't even care about us anymore. It's like you don't even care that Mom's gone!"

A sob escapes me, and I drop to the bed. The rage seeps from me, and suddenly I feel more tired than I can ever remember being. Clark still stands at my doorway. He stares at me with hard eyes.

My brother steps into my room. "You really think I don't care that Mom's gone?"

I cross my arms over my chest. "That's what it seems like."

In one swift movement, Clark grabs the bottom of his dark T-shirt and pulls it over his head and down to the top of his shoulders. When he turns, showing me his side, I gasp.

His entire rib cage is inked with the crisp black lines of a tattoo. It's an elongated diamond stretching from right below his armpit to the subtle curve of his waist. The top is simple lines and dashes, and the bottom is two hands cupped toward each other.

Between the hands is the most beautiful firefly I've ever seen, forever imprinted on my brother's skin. It's gorgeous.

"Clark," I breathe. "When did you do this?"

I reach to touch the lines, my hand drawn to his skin without thought, but he flinches away and pulls the shirt over his head.

"The day of Nana's party," he says. "It's why I was late. The appointment ran over."

"I had no idea," I say.

"Of course, you didn't. You don't think about how Mom's death affects anyone else but yourself."

"That's not fair," I say.

"It might not be fair," he says, "but it's true. You complain about me staying away and not coming back home, but did you ever for a second think I don't come back to this place because it's too hard? Look around, Quin"—he waves his arm toward my bedroom door and the rest of the house—"she's everywhere in this house. I can't look anywhere without being reminded of her."

"And that's so bad? Is it really such a bad thing to be reminded of your mother?"

Clark rubs a hand over his face. "No," he says. It's more a groan than an actual word. "It reminds me that I wasn't there. She was dying, and I wasn't there. I never got a last conversation, a last hug. I never got to"—his voice cracks, and he wipes a tear from his cheek—"I never got to say goodbye."

"Then where were you that night?" I ask. I've wondered for years what kept him from being with us—with *Mom*—after the accident.

The bed creaks when he drops to sit next to me. Our arms touch, and I realize this is the closest I've been to my brother in years. My chest aches.

"I can't . . ." Clark drops his head into his hands, hunching forward. His shoulders shake. He looks broken.

I hesitate, unsure if he'll want me to touch him, but then I simply wrap my arms around him in a hug. Clark leans into me, his whole body convulsing as he cries. My own tears fall onto the back of his shirt. All this time, I thought he left because he didn't care about me and Dad. I've been so angry with him, mad because he left me alone, but I never considered that he was even more alone than I was.

"You can talk to me," I tell him. "Whatever it is, you can tell me."

Clark shifts, and I let go so we can sit side by side. "I was staying at Eric's that weekend," he says. "I saw the calls from Dad and Nana, but I ignored them because"—he pulls in a deep, tremoring breath—"Eric kissed me for the first time, and I didn't know what to do."

"What?" I turn to look at my brother, but he stares at the floor. I study his profile, the straight nose and gentle curve of his lips and chin. How could I not know something so big about my own brother?

"So, Eric's, like, your boyfriend?"

"Yeah."

"I thought he was just your roommate."

Clark looks at me. "He is," he says firmly. "As far as Dad knows, Eric is my friend and roommate."

"Clark, Dad won't care." I put a hand on his and squeeze. "He wants you to be happy."

Clark pulls his hand away and stands up. "Look," he says. "I'm sorry I've not been around. I can't be in this house. It's too much, Quin. I need some space to figure all this out, okay?"

"Okay."

"Can you let Dad know I came over? I'll try again tomorrow maybe."

"Okay," I repeat.

chapter
THIRTY-FIVE

SUNDAY MORNING, NANA MARCHES INTO MY BEDROOM, clothed in a fine dress and sweater combo, her hair styled like she just walked out of the salon. She's wearing pearl drop earrings and a matching necklace, and her wrist shines with a tennis bracelet.

"Up!" She claps her hands then pulls the quilt off the bed. The cool air-conditioning raises goose bumps on my bare arms.

"I'm tired," I groan. I'm curled on my side, knees to chest, facing the wall—the same position I've been in nearly every minute since Clark left Thursday night.

I told Dad I had cramps Friday, and while I'm not sure he completely believed me, he let me skip school. I couldn't face Naoise. Not without a solution to our prom dilemma. I called Pennie to cover my weekend shifts and spent all day Friday locked in my room calling every venue I could think of and begging them to take on our prom, to no avail. Yesterday, I finally went to Nana for help. She has connections all over town. If anyone could make this work, she'd be the one.

After calling her, I went to work online, scrolling on my phone until well past midnight, trying to come up with any possibilities I might have missed. I saw a show once where a prom was held on a boat, so I scoured yacht rental listings. There were a few possibilities, but I quickly pushed them out of my mind when the first "Request a Quote" form revealed a price more than double our entire budget. The sun was already casting a soft light on the eastern horizon before I drifted off to sleep.

Now, without turning to Nana, I ask, "Any chance you have good news for me?" My voice comes out all cracked and croaky, like it's not been used in months.

Nana grabs my ankles and pulls my legs straight, flipping me onto my back in the process. "Maybe, maybe not," she says. "It's time to get up, scrub your face, and get dressed. We have breakfast in twenty minutes. We can talk then."

Flinging an arm over my eyes, I say, "Just tell me now. I want to sleep. We can miss breakfast this week."

"We most certainly cannot. I am not going to let you waste away in this room. Get up and get dressed, or you'll be eating in your pajamas."

With that, she breezes from the room, leaving nothing but her familiar perfume lingering in the air.

Five minutes later, I roll out of bed and drag myself into the bathroom. One glance in the mirror confirms that I look exactly like someone who's been hiding in her bedroom for days, but I don't have time for a shower. Nana doesn't mess around with Sunday breakfasts. She'll be dragging me out the front door in fifteen minutes regardless of whether I'm dripping wet with shampoo in my hair.

I splash cold water on my face and twist my hair up in a way that almost hides how greasy it is, then I set to work on my makeup. Normally, I wear more on Sundays to fit in with Nana's socialite country club set, but this morning a bit of crème blush, mascara, and a swipe of lip gloss will have to be enough.

"I was beginning to think you'd chosen the pajama route," Nana says when I rush into the living room. "I almost can't tell you haven't bathed in days."

"Okay, okay," I grumble. "Point taken."

"She lives!" Dad says from his chair. He's been sleeping there since his accident, more comfortable reclined with his leg propped up.

"Very funny," I say and press a kiss to the top of his head. "I'll see you later. Maybe we can watch that Rasputin documentary together."

"Well?" I prompt the second we're seated with our menus.

Nana takes her time reading hers, slowly scanning this week's offerings. "Well what, dear?"

"Very funny," I say. "Please tell me if you have a lead." A small spark of hope ignites in my chest—surely she wouldn't tease and drag things out if the news weren't good—but I try to tamp it down. The disappointment will be that much harder if I let myself expect too much.

She closes the menu, lowering it to the table before finally looking at me. "I spoke with someone at the studio. Lovely man. He was a PA on that film I did when you were a kid. Well, his crew is starting production on *Before Us* next week, and they're already getting sets together. There's a big gala at the end of the movie, and that happens to be what they're filming first."

Shut up. Is she saying what I think she is?

"Can we . . . do we get to have prom on an *actual* film set?"

Nana nods, a sly smile on her face.

"Oh, my gosh!" I squeal. "This is amazing! How big is it? What kind of decorations do we need?"

"That's the best part. They're filming at Airlie Gardens. Everything is set up outside. You'll have tents and an outdoor dance floor and the whole nine yards."

Airlie Gardens is iconic. It's been in the pivotal scenes of so many shows and movies that I can't keep track of them all. The Greek-style fountain will make the perfect backdrop for pictures. It may not be what one would imagine with a theme of Old Hollywood, but this will be better than anything I could've pulled together at the last minute.

There's just one problem.

"That sounds really expensive. We don't have a huge budget to work with."

"Oh, that's all taken care of," she says with a flick of her wrist.

Nana's good, but I'm not sure she's *that* good. No matter the history she has around here, movie studios aren't in the habit of lending their sets out for free.

"What did this cost you?" I hate the idea of her paying for my mistake.

Nana takes a slow drink of her water. "Nothing. Simply the promise of a cameo from an old icon."

"You're gonna be in *Before Us*?" Nana hasn't acted in a movie since I was twelve.

"They need someone to play the cooky old grandmother." She waves a hand above her head in a flourish. "I, for one, couldn't think of anyone better suited for the role."

I laugh. "Me either. You'll be perfect. Thank you so much for this."

"It's nothing, dear."

We order our food, and I pull my phone into my lap, hiding it from Nana's view while I type out a quick message to Naoise.

ME: We have a new venue. It's going to be incredible!

Nana holds up a bejeweled hand in greeting to a passing couple. They stop, and she falls into conversation about art classes and embroidery circles and whatever else her active social life entails. I tune them out and focus instead on my phone, hoping for a response from Naoise. Nothing.

"How's the movie going?" Nana asks after the server drops off our food and the couple makes their way to another table.

I wave the question away with my fork then pop the strawberry crepe into my mouth. "I don't wanna talk about it."

"Too bad. Talk." Nana is sassy today.

I sigh. "We're almost done. It's going to be really good, but . . ."

She stares at me over her glasses, her expression the only prompting I need to continue. Before I know it, I've spilled everything that's happened since the night of her party, leaving nothing out aside from Clark's admission from Thursday night. It's not my place to out him, even to Nana, who would probably be ecstatic about the news. She listens quietly, eating her quiche and fruit while I talk. When I pause, she doesn't push for me to continue, but simply waits until I'm ready to keep going.

"I don't know what to do," I say finally.

"I can't tell you how to fix this," she says. "That's all on you."

I give her my best puppy dog eyes. We're both wearing thick, red-framed glasses today, and as I stare into her face, I can only hope I still look as great as she does when I'm eighty. "What would you do, Nana? I mean, if you were me?"

"Well," she says before taking a long drink of club soda. It has lime wedges and a sprig of mint in it, the closest thing she's had to a mimosa since she sobered up when Dad was a kid. "I'd go talk to that boy, Kenyon, the one you're obviously crazy for. Tell him how you feel, sweetie."

"But what about Clark?"

"What about him?"

"He's my brother! How do I fix things with him?"

She shrugs and takes another drink. "You don't."

"But—"

"Give him time. Clark will come around. He needs to grieve in his own way. Don't try to force him. He'll open up when he's ready."

"But what if he's never ready?"

"He will be," she says, voice firm and sure, and I know the conversation is over.

We finish our breakfast in silence, her words tumbling around in my mind. I know I need to talk to Kenyon. I've known for a while now—maybe even since our first date—that I want to be with him, and I let my stupid theater kiss fantasy get in the way of that. Life would be so much easier if I'd let go of Operation Mystery Kisser and let myself fall for Kenyon all the way.

I know what I need to do. I just don't know if I'm brave enough to actually do it.

chapter
THIRTY-SIX

I'VE DRIVEN PAST KENYON'S HOUSE FOUR TIMES ALREADY, and now I'm parked outside, but I can't quite bring myself to walk up to the front door.

My stomach is twisting so hard that I feel like I might be sick. Maybe I should've done this right away after breakfast instead of giving myself the whole day to think and worry about it.

I watch a shadow move across the windows of Kenyon's house. I need to do this. Now.

The door swings open before I've even finished knocking. Kenyon looks good in dark jeans and a fitted T-shirt. His hair is as unruly as ever, falling over his eyebrows as he looks down at me. He doesn't say anything.

"Hi." The word hangs empty between us. I have so much I need to say, but I have no idea where to start. In a whole day of stressing about this moment, how did I not come up with a plan of action?

Kenyon leans against the door frame, arms crossed over his chest. I can hear the chaos of his younger brothers yelling and laughing in the background. There's a loud crash from somewhere deep inside the house, but Kenyon doesn't even flinch. He stares at me, his face blank, waiting. He's not going to make this easy for me.

"I've been thinking about *Maybe, Probably*," I start. "And I think we should revisit the dating sequence. The way we show Sebastian and Adalyn getting—"

"Quincy," he says, cutting me off. "Why are you really here?"

"No, really," I say. Movie talk is safe. If I can talk about the movie for a while, maybe we can find a comfortable place, and then telling him how I feel won't be quite so terrifying. "I couldn't stop thinking about it, and I thought we could—"

"It's too late," he says. "I gave the hard drive to Donovan already. He's putting the score in."

"But—"

"Quincy, stop." He doesn't sound mad. Just tired.

"Okay," I say. I stare at his feet, unable to look him in the eye. A deep breath does nothing to calm my nerves; there's never going to be a right time. It's not going to suddenly become comfortable and easy. I need to say the words.

"I'm sorry, Kenyon. Really, really sorry. I had this stupid idea in my head about finding this guy from my nana's party, so when I started to fall for you, I ignored it." Finally, I look at his face. It's guarded, his normal softness morphed into hard lines, and I hate that I'm the one who did that to him. "I shouldn't have kissed Donovan."

"You seriously think I'm mad because you kissed Donovan?"

Wait. That's not why he's mad? "I mean, I don't . . . he's your best friend. I shouldn't have—"

"You told me you'd be going out with other guys. You can kiss them all if you want. But you can't expect me to sit around waiting for you to date every other guy in school until you're ready to give me a chance."

"No, I know—"

"Do you? Because I honestly can't tell if you're here because you're sorry I got hurt, or if you're sorry that not everyone adores you."

"That's not fair," I say, anger sparking in me. This is so not going how I wanted it to.

Kenyon shrugs. "Are we done?" He moves to shut the door.

"Wait!" I put a hand on the door, stopping its progress, and step a bit closer to him. "I'm sorry," I say again. "If I could take it all back, I would."

It hits me then what I need to do. I don't have time to think it out, to plan the perfect promposal, but this will have to do. Kenyon's hand is still on the doorknob, and I make myself reach for it before I have time to second-guess myself.

My heart pounds against my rib cage. My throat is growing tight, and I'm suddenly scared I won't be able to say the words. Kenyon lets me take his hand in mine, a mixture of longing and fear crossing over his face. I look him in the eyes and take a deep breath.

"Go to prom with me," I say.

Finally, a soft smile breaks on his face, and my heart soars a bit.

"Is that a question or a command?"

I laugh. "Which one means you'll say yes?"

He tilts his head to the side, and the look in his eyes melts me. How could I ever have imagined that some random dude from Nana's party would be better than the amazing guy standing in front of me?

But then he stiffens, and his face hardens back into a mask. My breath catches in my throat when he drops my hand.

"I can't," he says, and his voice holds none of the warmth I'm used to.

"What? Why?"

He laughs without humor. Tears spring to my eyes. "You really *did* think I'd wait around for you, didn't you? Are you really that selfish, Quincy? I already have a date for prom."

"You do?" My voice is tiny.

He doesn't answer but moves to close the door again. This time I don't stop him. "Have a good night," he says in a formal tone, and the door shuts in my face.

I stand on his porch for a long time, frozen to the spot, staring at the dark wood of his front door. He's not coming back, that much is obvious, and when I notice a neighbor giving me strange looks from the driveway next door, I force myself to turn and walk down the sidewalk to my waiting car.

I drive around for nearly an hour, numb to my surroundings. I have no idea where I'm going, but I can't bring myself to go home yet.

When I get to Tara's Diner, I pull into a spot at the back of the lot. I can't remember ever coming here without my friends, but the familiarity of the building is like a warm hug.

Inside, it's busier than normal, and our usual booth is taken. An unfamiliar server tells me to sit wherever, so I make my way toward a small two-person table by the back wall.

"Hey, Quin."

I turn at the sound of my name, surprised to find Ezra sitting in a booth with a milkshake in front of him. He smiles and waves, so I change course and walk to his table.

I don't see who he's with until I'm standing at the edge of the booth, and I startle when I notice her.

"Oh, hey Kira." I look from her to Ezra. I didn't know they'd kept in touch after we finished filming.

"Hi," she says. "How's it going?"

"Fine," I lie. She doesn't need to know about my awful evening.

We make small talk for a few minutes—I fill them in on the screening we're going to have at Hadley's right after graduation. They both agree to come, and they seem genuinely excited to see the finished film. I feel the tension and sadness lifting from me as we talk. I've been so caught up in Operation Mystery Kisser and trying to make things right with Kenyon that I let myself forget about the good parts of my life. We made a great movie with *Maybe, Probably*.

"Well," I say finally, "I should go. Have a good night." I plod over the rest of the way to my table, slumping onto one of the chairs and sighing deeply.

My server has barely dropped off water and a menu—not that I need one—when Ezra slips into the chair across from me.

"Hey," I say hesitantly. My eyes flick to his table. Kira's still sitting there, tapping away on her phone screen with a smile on her face.

"How are you *really*?" he asks.

"Fine," I repeat.

"Look," he says. He leans forward, forearms resting on the table. "I know we've not been best friends for a long time, but I still know you, Q. You're not fine. Not by a long shot. Is it your dad?"

He clearly does still know me, and my chest aches with all the time we've lost as friends. Years we'll never get back because

I pushed him away. He tried to be there for me, and I wouldn't let him. But I can change that this time around.

"Dad's okay. He's getting restless, but he'll be fine."

"So if you're not upset about your dad, what is it?"

It only takes a few minutes for me to tell Ezra the story. Condensed down like this, it doesn't seem nearly as big as it feels. He listens silently, nodding as I talk.

"So, yeah," I say when I finish. "I basically ruined things with Kenyon."

"I thought you said he turned you down for prom because he already has a date." Ezra looks genuinely confused.

"Well, yeah, but that's just a line, right? He wanted me to go away. I could tell."

Ezra narrows his eyes. "He really does have a date. He asked Alicia Short in calc last week."

"He did?"

"Yep. He did it with this big equation on the whiteboard. Got the teacher into it and everything so he could be sure that Alicia was the one to solve it and get—"

I hold a hand up to stop him. "I don't need all the details."

"Sorry."

He asked her last week, and his promposal obviously took some time to work out. How long had he been planning to ask her? Maybe I'd totally misread everything between us.

He seemed so hurt when I kissed Donovan, but maybe that was the excuse he needed to stop whatever it was we had going on.

"Hey, Q?"

I snap out of my thoughts and focus back on Ezra.

"I gotta get going," he says, tilting his head back toward where Kira's waiting for him, "but can I say something?"

I nod, and he continues, "I need you to promise me something."

"That sounds ominous."

"It's not. Trust me."

"Can I at least hear what it is before I make promises?"

He shakes his head, a soft smile spreading across his face. I've missed this. The teasing banter Ezra and I have always had, the way we knew when to push each other and when to pull back and give space. That part of me that's aching with regret grows bigger.

"Okay," I agree. "I promise."

"Ezra!" Kira calls from their seat, and he turns for a second to assure her he's coming. She smiles at him, and I can't help but smile too. They are cute together. I hope this goes further than one date at the diner for the two of them.

He turns back to me. "Don't push Kenyon away."

"But he—"

It's Ezra's turn to stop me with a hand. "You need to fight for what you want. It might be hard to see him, but don't give up because it hurts. Okay?"

"I dunno."

"You promised," he says, and I can see the challenge in his eye.

"Fine." I have no idea how I'll do it, and I have no idea if it'll work, but I won't run from this. I'll take Ezra's advice and fight for what I want.

And what I want is Kenyon.

chapter THIRTY-SEVEN

TUESDAY MORNING, I'M ALMOST LATE FOR SCHOOL. I FOR-
got my phone in the living room, so I slept right through my
regular alarm, not waking up until Nana got to the house to drive
Dad to work. I rushed to get ready—barely taking a second to
glance in the mirror and clean up yesterday's makeup from under
my eyes—then hurried into the living room. My phone was buried
deep in the chair-and-a-half, muffled under Dad's fuzzy blanket.
I grabbed it, gave Dad and Nana both a quick kiss goodbye, and
ran out the door.

Now, I rush across the parking lot, trying to smooth the
frizziness of my hair as I walk-run. My ballet flats slap the pavement, and the hem of my dress flutters across my thighs with the
breeze. A couple of girls I vaguely recognize from the soccer team
pass me, giggling and shoving each other. One of them gives me an
excited smile as I pass.

"So romantic," she breathes.

Uh, what?

I keep walking, but now I notice how many people are looking at me. One of the guys from my fourth period US Government class whoops when I step onto the sidewalk.

Shyla and Hadley rush toward me. Behind them, I see Naoise walking briskly the other way. She's been ignoring my calls and texts since Thursday afternoon, not even answering when I sent her the details about Airlie Gardens. They announced the change of venue over the PA system during first period yesterday, so I know she got the news and passed it on, but she's still pissed. As much as I'd hoped finding a new place to hold prom would fix things, I can't blame her. I pushed her into my theme and my venue, and I nearly ruined everything. Still, I could really use my friend right now.

"Who do you think it is?" Hadley asks when they reach me. She loops one arm through mine and does a little skip step next to me.

"Who what is?" I look at her face, the goofy grin she's giving me, and turn to Shyla, who's beaming in the same silly way. "What's going on?"

Shyla turns and waves her arm, drawing my attention to the scrolling marquee. It was a gift from the senior class a few years back, and it runs through the calendar of upcoming events at the school. Hardly anybody even looks at it anymore now that the school is set up with text message announcements.

I glance at Shyla, confused, and she nods at the sign. I read the words as they scroll by, excitement building in me as I do.

ROSES ARE RED,

VIOLETS ARE BLUE,

QUINCY FAITH WALKER,

I WANT TO GO TO PROM WITH YOU.

"Oh my gosh," I breathe. "But, who . . . ?" I've ruined my chances with the one guy I want to go with, and I can't imagine who else would've done this. Or maybe I just don't *want* to imagine someone else doing it.

Hadley squeals and throws her arms around me, jumping up and down. Shyla joins our hug. When the shock starts to wear off, their excitement washes through me, and I jump with them. The students still hanging around outside clap and laugh at our display. It's like we're in a movie, and it's everything I could have dreamed of.

A movement over Hadley's shoulder catches my eye, and I look up in time to see Naoise turn away from us, a sad smile on her face as she slips into the school.

"Who do y'all think it is?" I whisper to my friends in the back of AP English class during second period. Shyla, Hadley, and I are all in Mrs. Anderson's class; it's the only one I have with them both. Naoise tried to get the same schedule as us, but second period was the only time the Textiles and Design class met, so she had to take English during fifth instead.

"It's gotta be Kenyon, right?" Hadley's face is hopeful.

I shake my head.

"Nah, he asked Alicia," Shyla says.

"Yeah, thanks for the warning there," I tell her. She has calc with Ezra and Kenyon and was there for his promposal. I can't believe she didn't tell me.

"I didn't know there was anything to tell," she says. "You've been all about Tyler for so long that I didn't think you'd care who Kenyon asked to prom."

Mrs. Anderson shushes us from the front of the room, and we pull our books closer to us. We're on our last big paper of the semester, and she's giving us an extra period of free work time. My paper is about the feminist themes in *Little Women*, but now I'm wondering why I picked such a long book to work with.

A couple minutes later, a piece of folded paper lands on my desk, and I snap my head up. Hadley's still focused on her copy of *East of Eden*, but I see a sly smile cross her lips. She nods toward the paper, and I open it.

Maybe it's Tyler.

I'm surprised by the jolt of excitement that hits me. What if it is Tyler? After he never responded to my outburst about prom—not to mention what ended up being the biggest dud of a date I've ever been on—I figured he'd never ask me. And I've been okay with that. My crush on Tyler has been going on for so long that I am starting to think I only liked him because that was what I was used to.

But now the idea of him asking me to prom brings back all those fluttery feelings I used to get. Could it be him?

There's a note taped to my locker before lunch. I dump my books onto the shelf and grab what I'll need for my afternoon classes, shoving them into my backpack as fast as I can. Pulling the paper off the door, I spin and lean against the cool metal so I can read it.

> *The time's almost here*
> *To reveal my face.*
> *Meet me after school*
> *In your favorite place.*

My favorite place? My mind flashes to the wide field Mom and I used to park at whenever we needed girl time. It was my favorite place in the world, once upon a time, but I've not been there since she died.

There's another verse, so I read on.

Don't leave campus,

Or I might turn shy.

Go to your favorite classroom

To meet your dream guy.

This is maybe the cheesiest thing ever, and I love everything about it. I hug the paper to my chest, ignoring the curious looks I get from the other students, then I head toward the cafeteria. I feel like I'm floating, and I can't help but think that Naoise was wrong. Prom can be just like in the movies.

chapter
THIRTY-EIGHT

"EVERYONE READY?" MR. WELLES STANDS IN FRONT OF US holding a huge bowl of popcorn. When we got to class today, all the tables were pushed to the side of the room, and the center was filled with soft chairs, beanbags, and a long couch. I have no idea where this all came from, but he's obviously very excited about his temporary theater setup.

We're showcasing our projects today. Our group is the only one that made a feature rather than the required short film, so Mr. Welles had us pick a twenty-minute segment to watch. As a group, we decided Marcus could pick our sample for us, and I have no idea what he chose.

As we all finish settling into our seats, my nerves run haywire. This will be the first time we show *Maybe, Probably* to anyone, and the first time I see it with Donovan's scoring. He was working on it until late last night and didn't have time to send it back to us before class today.

I'm sharing a giant beanbag with Marcus, the two of us pressed side to side as the bag forms a little cocoon around us. Kenyon sits as far from me as possible on the opposite side of the room. He hasn't looked at me once since I came to his house Sunday night. Alicia Short is perched on the armrest of his chair, and my chest gives a pained twist when I see them laughing with each other. I dig deep into my memory, trying to recall any time he's shown interest in her, but I come up empty. How did this happen?

"You ready?" Marcus whispers.

"Not really."

He laughs and nudges my side with his elbow. "Relax. It's gonna be great."

Mr. Welles shushes us and turns off the lights. The room's silent for a moment, the only sounds the crunching of popcorn all around me, and then the projector flickers to life as the first film starts to play.

It's another group's film, and I can't decide if it makes me more or less nervous that our movie isn't playing first. I do my best to push my nerves down as I settle myself against Marcus's side and try to enjoy watching the screen.

When their clip ends, we all clap, and I watch as my classmates adjust their positions and grab more snacks. We have a five-minute break, then Mr. Welles pushes play.

My heart leaps into my throat when a close-up of Ezra comes to life on the screen. It's a profile view, and he's looking up at something beyond the frame. His Adam's apple bobs as he swallows deeply.

Marcus picked the meet-cute between Sebastian and Adalyn, the scenes we filmed in Hadley's barn. I don't know if it's the segment I would've picked to showcase, but it's a good one. It gives a feel for the characters and sets the tone of the film. He did a great job.

When Adalyn gives Sebastian a slice of watermelon, and he thinks it's for him instead of an offering to coax the parrot down from its high perch, the class breaks into laughter. I can feel the smile on my face, huge and giddy, and my chest about bursts with excitement. I can't believe we really pulled it off.

My gaze flits to Kenyon, and I will him to look at me. To acknowledge me and all the work we put into *Maybe, Probably*. I want to know that no matter what happened between us, he can see how good we were together. At least for this. We made something amazing.

But he doesn't. His eyes remain glued to the screen as the rest of the scene plays out—never once glancing my way—and the fissure in my heart widens with every passing breath. I've ruined this, and I'm beginning to think there's no way to fix it.

After school, I stash my stuff into my locker and head back toward Mr. Welles's room. I spent last period working on my English paper in the library. I could've stayed in Mr. Welles's room to work, but I knew I wouldn't be able to focus knowing my prom date would be arriving at any moment. I thought I'd be nervous to find out who the promposal is from, but now that I'm almost to the room, the only thing I feel is excitement.

I can't wait.

The room seems empty when I get there, but then I notice one of the iMacs at the back of the room is on, a familiar shape behind it clicking away on the mouse.

"Oh, hi." My steps falter when I see him.

"What are you doing here?" Kenyon asks, not unkindly.

"Um . . . I'm supposed to be meeting someone here. What are you doing?"

"Tweaking some of the transitions, trying to smooth some things out," he says. "A couple cuts seemed a little choppy during class."

Kenyon's probably the only other person in our class who loves filmmaking as much as I do, but I'm somehow surprised by the extra time he's putting into this project. We're already getting a good grade on it, and the festival this summer won't give him anything. Even if we submit it in both of our names, all the prizes are for people who are here in North Carolina, and he told me he's headed off to Colorado in the fall.

"Who are you meeting?" he asks.

"I'm, um, not really sure—"

"Quincy," a voice says from behind me, and I turn.

Tyler's standing in the doorway, his standard smirk on his face. My heart thrills, excitement jump-starting it into furious pounding. Behind me, the clicking stops, and I remember Kenyon is there, watching this unfold. Crap.

Tyler throws his arms to the side. "Surprise," he says, then he steps toward me and kneels.

He's actually getting down on one knee to ask me to prom. I couldn't have scripted this better if I tried. I'm practically bubbling over with excitement. This is really happening.

"Quincy Walker, will you go to prom with me?"

Distantly, I hear a chair push across the floor. From the corner of my eye, I see Kenyon walk past us on the way to the door.

Tyler's still on his knee, looking up at me expectantly. This has been the perfect promposal, which is why what comes out of my mouth next surprises all three of us.

"No."

Tyler looks stunned. Kenyon freezes in the doorway.

"What?" Tyler says softly.

"I said no." I take a step back from Tyler. I can't believe I'm doing this, turning him down. But it feels right.

He gets to his feet. "I thought you wanted me to ask you," he says. "All those things you said that night—"

"I did," I say simply, cutting him off. "I wanted you to ask me to prom. So badly. But I wanted to go to prom with you because you *wanted* to ask me. Not because I'm a last resort."

"You're not—"

I laugh. "Prom's in four days, Tyler! Who waits till four days before prom unless it's a last resort?" My eyes dart to Kenyon, and I recognize the irony of having asked him only two nights ago. He doesn't seem upset, though. Instead, he stares at me and Tyler wide-eyed, like he can't quite believe what he's witnessing.

Tyler flinches at my words. "I didn't think . . . are you already going with someone?"

Heat rushes to my cheeks, but I refuse to let embarrassment take over. I don't need a pity date, and I don't need to spend my night with someone who only wants to take me because he doesn't have anyone else.

"No, I'm not," I tell him.

"So why—?"

"Because I'm better than this." With that, I step around him and walk toward the door. Kenyon's still standing there, and when I pass him, he gives me a small nod. For the first time, I truly understand what he's been going through. This feeling of being second-best, stuck in the wings to wait for someone to decide they want you—it sucks. And I promise I'll never let him feel that way again.

chapter
THIRTY-NINE

"AM I SELFISH?"

Nana pauses her fork in midair. "Excuse me?"

"Am I selfish?" I repeat. I've been thinking about it a lot the past few days, going over my fights with Naoise, Clark, and Kenyon, and one thing keeps coming to the front: they all said I only think about myself. I've always been driven and determined, going for what I want, but now I'm wondering if my determination is nothing more than a cover for pure selfishness.

"Do *you* think you're selfish?" A classic Nana non-answer. She's excellent at turning things back to me.

I sigh. "I don't know. Maybe? I keep screwing things up."

"But you're fixing them too, Quincy." She looks over her glasses—thick, turquoise frames today—at me. "A selfish person wouldn't do that."

"I guess." I shrug, dropping my eyes to my lap.

Nana sighs deeply and asks, "Did you know I didn't want your daddy to marry your mama?"

My head snaps up to meet her gaze. She couldn't have surprised me more if she tried. "What?"

She shrugs. "I didn't figure your mama ever told you. She was too nice. But it's true. When Rob brought her home, I instantly disliked her. I tried to convince him she wasn't good for him." She laughs. "Of course, that probably drove him even closer to her."

"But I thought you always liked Mom." I'm sure my face is showing her how shocked I am by this confession.

"Oh, I did, eventually. Your mama was very likeable."

The server sets a plate of cheesecake in front of me. I pick up my fork and poke at it. "So why didn't you like her at first?"

"She was an actor," Nana says simply.

"But *you're* an actor!"

"And I wasn't always a great mother. You know I had an alcohol problem when your daddy was young. I was flighty and unreliable. Hell, I don't even know who your granddaddy is." She shrugs again. "I was so scared your mama would be like me, and I didn't want that for my Rob."

"Well, you're not like that anymore," I say. "You changed."

"I had to. One night, when your daddy was about six, it was made clear that if I didn't change my life, I'd lose him. I went to my first AA meeting the next day."

I've heard most of this backstory already. Nana's never tried to hide her past from me. She says we can't learn from her mistakes if she pretends she never made any. The part about her not liking Mom is news, though.

"Okay," I say. "Why are you telling me this now?"

"You are not like me," she says, staring hard at me. "I was selfish, and it nearly destroyed me and everyone around me. You're more like your mama."

Tears spring to my eyes, and I dab them quickly with my napkin. "I dunno."

"Oh, you're not *perfect*." She laughs, deep and husky. "You make mistakes, but you've got a big heart, my girl. You'll make things right."

I sure hope so. With Nana's help, I've fixed the prom debacle, if not my friendship with Naoise yet. I only hope I can manage to repair the damage I've done to my relationship with Kenyon.

"When did you change your mind about Mama?"

Nana signals to our server that we're ready for the check. "Sometime around your parents' fourth date," she says. "I was out with a girlfriend, and I happened to see Rob and Desiree sitting at a little café on the riverfront. Your daddy was showing her something in a book, but she wasn't looking at the pages."

Nana's eyes have a far-off look, and a smile slips onto her face. "Your mama was looking right at your daddy with so much adoration that I knew I had nothing to worry about."

A tear escapes my eye and drops onto my cheek. Before I can blot it with the napkin, Nana reaches across the table and wipes it with her thumb.

"Your mama loved more fiercely than anyone I've ever known," she says. "She loved your daddy like that, and she loved you kids like that. Her love was all-consuming."

I'm crying in earnest now, earning some looks from the people around the restaurant, but I don't care.

"I miss her so much," I say.

"I know. But you are so much like her. You have the same spunk and drive, and you have the same heart."

I wipe my cheek on the shoulder of my dress, leaving behind a wet spot. "I don't know about that."

"You do," she insists. "That's why you feel things so deeply."

"You make her sound so brave," I say. "I'm not like that."

"You can be. Stop trying to protect your heart. You can love as fiercely as your mama if you let yourself."

Suddenly, I know what I need to do. Jumping from the table, I nearly knock my chair to the floor, righting it before it tips too far. I circle the table and give Nana a tight hug.

"Thank you so much," I say through the tears that are still falling. "I'll meet you outside, okay?"

Not even to the door of the restaurant, I pull my phone out and start a new group text. I scroll through my contacts to find Marcus, Ezra, Kira, Hadley, and Donovan, then I start typing.

ME: Hey y'all. I need your help. Can we meet at Hadley's Sunday afternoon?

I hit send and hug my phone to my chest. This had better work.

chapter
FORTY

"YOU'RE GONNA BE LATE IF YOU DON'T HURRY," DAD CALLS from the living room. Prom starts in half an hour, and I'm currently standing in the bathroom, staring at myself in the mirror. Shyla brought my completed dress by last night, and I can't get over how wonderful it is. Naoise is seriously talented. I texted her a thank you, but she hasn't replied.

Dad's right—I'm going to be late if I don't leave soon. I can't believe that, after all the stress of trying to make this a perfect prom moment, I'm going stag. Even more unbelievable is that I'm not upset about it. This feels right. I'd rather go alone than with someone who didn't really want to ask me.

Besides, my friends will be there. They'll all have dates, but I'll have fun with them anyway.

"Quin, come on!" Clark yells from the next room.

It's time.

Dad's out of his chair leaning on the crutches with a camera held to his face when I get to the living room. I hear the click of the shutter as he takes picture after picture.

"Oh, Quincy, you look just like your mama." Nana has a hand clutched to her chest, a soft fist resting below her throat, and I see a shimmer in her eyes as she watches me. The prickle of my own tears starts behind my eyes, but I force it back. I'm not going to cry on prom night.

"You look really great," Clark says, and I turn to him. When I see what he's wearing, I gasp.

My brother is in a fitted suit with a crisp white shirt unbuttoned at the neck. The dark blue of the jacket and pants makes his eyes blaze.

"Why are you so fancy?"

Clark crosses the room in three long steps and offers me his arm. "M'lady."

I look from my brother to where Dad and Nana are standing. "What's going on?"

"Well, we can't have you going to the prom alone," Nana says. "That'd be improper."

I snort in a very un-ladylike way. "Right. Because you've always worried about what proper young ladies do."

"Go on"—Nana gestures to my brother, who's still holding out his arm to me—"Clark will be your date."

"Oh, no," I say, but I loop my arm through Clark's anyway, if only because I can't stand him waiting for me to do so any longer. "I can't go to prom with my brother." I may *actually* die of humiliation. I can handle going alone, but not this.

"And your gay brother at that," Clark says. "What will people think?"

My head snaps to him so fast that I feel a twinge of pain in my neck. "What?"

"You were right," he says, patting my hand where it rests on his forearm. "I needed to tell Dad."

I study my brother's face and see that it's relaxed. He's comfortable in this house with us, maybe for the first time in years. We still have a long way to go to piece our family back together, but we'll get there.

"I'm glad," I say. "But I really *cannot* let you take me to the prom."

The camera clicks again from across the room, and Clark and I both turn toward it. Without a word, we lean together and smile, letting Dad capture a picture of the two of us. He checks the image on the back of the screen and gives us a thumbs-up before lowering himself into his chair. I try not to worry about how slow his movements are. The doctors say he'll be fine, and I need to trust that.

"Let me take you to dinner at least," Clark says. "You shouldn't go to your senior prom without a good dinner first."

"Prom starts in like twenty minutes," I protest.

"Oh, go on," Nana says. "You'll be fashionably late."

I look around the room, my eyes falling on Dad, Clark, and Nana. Our family may be broken, pieces forever missing, but it's perfect for me. My chest fills with the warmth of how lucky I am.

"Okay," I say, turning to my brother. "Let's do this."

When Clark pulls the car into the parking lot, I laugh, even as a pang of regret twists deep in me.

He cuts the engine. "What's so funny?"

"Nothing," I say. "This restaurant . . . it has memories."

He gives me a strange look but doesn't push. We're at Pier 23, where Kenyon took me for our first date. It seems like forever ago.

It's fitting that Clark and I would be here tonight. This restaurant was where everything started to change for me. Now, as my brother holds open the door, I hope that this night can be the beginning of something new for us as a family as well.

We make small talk for a few minutes as we wait for our server to take our orders. Then Clark says, "Why don't you have a date for prom again?"

"Ouch," I mumble, staring at the table. "Way to rub it in."

"That's not what I mean," he says. "I'm surprised, that's all. I thought someone would ask you."

I look up at him, and his face is so open and genuine that I feel a bit bad for thinking he'd been teasing me.

"I was asked, actually," I say. "But . . ."

I tell him about my promposal, and he listens so intently that, before I can stop myself, I've spilled the whole story to him—about my longtime crush on Tyler, the Operation Mystery Kisser debacle, my dates with Kenyon and how I messed that all up. The waiter comes and goes as I talk, and Clark nibbles on our pita chip and artichoke dip appetizer.

I look around the restaurant at the eclectic mix of tables and chairs. "This is where Kenyon and I went for our first date," I say.

"I have a confession," Clark says after a minute. I nod for him to continue. "I talked to your friend Shyla last night."

"You did?"

"Yeah. I ran into her when she was leaving the house."

"Okay?" It's not like Clark and Shyla have never talked before. She and Naoise used to sleep over all the time when he still lived at home, but this still comes as a surprise to me.

"She told me about your fight with Naoise."

"Oh." I'd hoped that Nana's amazing prom venue would have fixed things between us, but I'm realizing now that the problems between me and Neesh run deeper than that. She's right; I have been selfish.

Clark fishes out his phone from the inner pocket of his suit jacket and swipes his thumb across the screen. As he taps something into the phone, he says, "Did you know Eric's mom is a designer?"

"I had no idea."

He nods. "She's not a huge name or anything, but she does celebs for premieres sometimes. She gets a lot more studio work as a costume designer than anything. But what she loves to do most"—he spins his phone around and sets it screen-up on the table, sliding it across to me—"is mentor others."

My hands shake as I pick up the phone, and it takes me a full minute to piece together what I'm looking at: a website for something called *Dress Your Heart*.

"What is this?"

"A new show they're developing. A competition for young Southern fashion designers. They'll be filming the first season in August."

"Kinda like *Project Runway*?" I ask.

"Kind of," Clark says. "Eric's mom is the mentor—like the Tim Gunn role. Each week they'll provide classes for aspiring designers to learn new techniques, and then at the end of the week, the designers will get a challenge that tests what they learned. Judges vote based on how well they execute the design, but they'll also have viewer voting."

I scroll through the website, trying to piece together what he's telling me. This would be perfect for Naoise.

"If they're filming in a couple months, they've already picked the contestants, right?"

Clark beams at me and shakes his head. "They don't pick until the end of June."

There's still time for Naoise to try out. I text the website address to myself so I don't lose it before passing the phone back to my brother.

"I hope Neesh has enough time to get a portfolio pulled together," I say. She still has the designs she submitted to Lipscomb, which I think should work. I only hope she'll talk to me long enough for me to tell her about this.

"You haven't heard the best part yet," Clark says.

"What's that?"

"Contestants don't submit themselves. They have to be *nominated* by somebody else."

I dig my phone from the small, sparkly clutch Nana lent me and pull the website up. It takes only a moment to find what I'm looking for, and when I open the submissions tab, I read, "To nominate a contestant, please submit an essay, no longer than 500 words, on why you think they should be chosen for *Dress Your Heart*. Include up to five images of a single piece of your nominee's work for the judges to consider."

Setting the phone on the table, I look down at the dress I'm wearing. It's exquisite. I can feel a smile pulling at my face as the idea forms in my mind. I already know what I'm going to write in my essay. If Naoise doesn't land a spot on that show, I'll lose all faith in the judges. They'd be foolish not to take her.

"Thanks," I tell Clark. "This is great."

He smiles. This dinner has made me realize that we're both such different people from who we were a few years ago, and I like getting to know who he is now.

We pay the bill, and Clark waits for me as I fold the collection of cloth napkins I'd been using to protect my dress. When I stand, he offers his arm for the second time tonight, and I take it without hesitation.

"All right, princess," he says. "Let's get you to the prom."

FORTY-ONE

AIRLIE GARDENS IS A MAGICAL PLACE. NANA WOULDN'T let me join her and the crew she enlisted to set things up this morning. She said she wanted it to be a surprise for me as well, and as I walk the path to the party tent ahead of me, I'm glad she did.

Long strings of café lights hang in lazy curves under the tent and around the open dance floor. All around me, trees are wrapped in thousands of tiny white twinkle lights. Music already pours from the speakers, and a DJ stands behind a long table under a second, smaller tent. On the dance floor, girls' dresses catch the light as they twist and spin with their dates. From back here, they look like they're floating.

The whole thing is like something out of a movie, and I laugh when I realize it basically *is*.

I find Hadley and Tanner first. She looks amazing in her long, figure-hugging black dress. She's wearing black gloves up past her elbows and a sparkly cap-sleeve bolero to cover her shoulders. Her hair is twisted into a sleek updo with a small tiara nestled into it.

When Hadley sees me, she breaks away from Tanner and skip-runs across the floor, pulling me into a crushing hug. "You're here!"

"You look incredible," I say. "Like Holly Golightly."

"You don't think it's too much?" Hadley pulls back and pats her tiara self-consciously.

"Definitely not," I say.

We walk together to Tanner. Thankfully, a fast song starts up, and the three of us dance together for a few songs. When the DJ shifts gears and the music slows, Hadley claims she needs to pee and pushes me toward Tanner.

We both know she's trying to keep me from feeling left out, so we dance together. As we sway silently, I look at the couples around us.

It doesn't take long for me to spot Shyla and Donovan. Shyla radiates in her lehenga, and Donovan looks at her in a way that almost makes me feel like I'm intruding by watching them.

Naoise and Marcus are a few couples past them, talking and laughing as they dance. I'm glad they found each other. It'll be good for her to have a friend when she goes to Nashville next year. She looks happy, and the tightness in my chest loosens a bit. It might not be the prom she wanted, but at least it appears she's having fun.

The song is winding down when Tanner spins me around, and suddenly I'm staring right at Kenyon. Our eyes connect, and a jolt shoots through my core. He's holding Alicia close, one hand on the small of her back as they dance. Her temple rests gently on his cheek. I stare at him, a hard lump rising in my throat. I try to swallow it down.

Then Tanner spins again, and the connection is broken. He twirls me out to the end of his reach, then pulls me back in, fast. The song ends just as I crash into his chest, and we both explode in laughter.

"Thanks for the dance," I say, still laughing. He gives me a high five and pulls Hadley—who rejoined us—against his chest.

I try to peek around them without being obvious, but I can't find Kenyon. Maybe it's for the best.

It's another upbeat song and we dance for a bit longer before I spot Naoise standing by the refreshments, pouring punch into a plastic cup. Her dress is beautiful, everything I'd expect from her and more. The skirt is floor-length and flowy, a dusty plum at the hips fading into subtle peach at the bottom. I don't know what kind of fabric she used, but it looks like soft wisps of clouds flowing around her legs. The bodice is a complicated puzzle of straps and gathered fabric woven and twisted around itself. It hugs close to her frame and shows teasing peeks of her skin. Her hair falls softly over her shoulders, and I can see from here that her makeup is minimal and dewy.

She looks like a goddess.

Nodding toward her, I tell Hadley I'm going to grab a drink. Her eyes widen, and she pulls me into a quick hug. "Good luck," she says into my hair before letting me go and sending me across the dance floor.

"Hey," I say softly as I step up to the punch table.

Naoise looks at me. Marcus is a few feet away, eating a cupcake and laughing with another guy I recognize from the New Hanover High basketball team.

"Hi," she says stiffly.

"How's it going?" I ask. "Are you having fun?"

She nods, peering past me toward the dance floor. "I am. It's a nice night."

I hate the formality between us. We're standing right next to each other, but the distance I feel is like a canyon. I think I'd rather see her yell at me again than treat me like an acquaintance.

"I'm so sorry," I say, taking a half-step closer to her. "You were right. I was being awful and selfish, and I should have listened—"

Naoise still won't look at me, but suddenly her face lights up and she waves over my shoulder. "I gotta go," she tells me.

"But . . ."

"Have fun tonight," she says and breezes past me toward whoever caught her attention. I turn to watch as she goes, my gaze falling to her shoes. She's wearing the same glittery Keds I have on. We bought them together months ago, hers white and mine pink. She's mad at me now, but seeing those shoes gives me hope that we'll be able to work things out eventually. Finding a new prom venue didn't fix things between us, but maybe time will.

Suddenly, Donovan and Shyla are at my side. They act casual, like they simply want to say hi, but one look at Shyla's face tells me she saw what happened between me and her sister. I beg her with my eyes to not bring it up.

"I'm parched," she says dramatically as she pours herself a cup of punch. "Can you take Lord of the Dance off my hands for a minute?" She nods toward Donovan, who laughs and reaches out to pinch her side playfully.

"Punch, punch, punch!" she yells. She's holding the cup away from her lehenga, and I watch as the red liquid sloshes dangerously close to the cup's edge. I take a step back, hoping my dress is out of range if it spills.

Shyla finds a seat at a table, and Donovan leads me out to the dance floor. He really is a great dancer, and I feel a bit like a toddler flailing my limbs in comparison. We dance hard, until we're both sweating and laughing, and then we go back to Shyla.

"Pictures!" she says when we get there. She hops up from her seat and grabs Donovan's hand, pulling him toward the fountain where the photographer is setting up.

"Y'all have fun," I say.

Shyla grabs my wrist with her free hand. "You're coming with us."

I try to protest, but she pulls me behind her anyway. She insists on pictures with all three of us, then one with me and her and one with her and Donovan. Finally, I pose for a picture by myself. I feel my cheeks heat up as the other students in line watch me standing there by myself, but I don't care.

This is my prom, and I want the memories.

chapter
FORTY-TWO

THE NIGHT PASSES QUICKER THAN SEEMS POSSIBLE. Despite being alone, I'm never in want of a dance partner for long. Everyone dances in groups for fast songs, and I drift from group to group, dancing with more people than I can count.

When slow songs start, there's always someone willing to pass off their date for one dance while they run to the restroom or to grab refreshments. I dance with guys from all my classes, as well as with a few from other schools who I've never met before. About halfway through the night, I see Ezra on the other side of the dance floor, spinning Kira wildly around, both laughing, and I'm overwhelmingly happy to see them together.

I wonder briefly if any of the guys I dance with is the one from Nana's party—if we missed someone who was there that night. Had I kissed one of these guys, a kiss that changed everything? Now I know that, even if I had, I don't care anymore. That kiss is no more than a memory, a story I'll tell in the future. Nothing else.

I don't see Tyler all night, and I feel a twinge of guilt that he decided not to come. I didn't want him to miss his senior prom, but it's not my job to make sure he's happy. Turning him down was the right thing to do. I spent too much time hoping for him to ask me out. He's the one who couldn't see what was right in front of him until it was too late. I wish he were here tonight, but not for me.

I'm dancing all wild-like with a group of people from my English class, jumping up and down and flailing my arms, when the DJ announces there are only three songs left. The opening chords to a familiar slow song ring out into the air. A hand falls on my shoulder, soft, and I turn around.

"Oh," I say, my breath catching in my throat. "Hi."

Kenyon raises a hand to me. "Want to dance?"

I glance around him, scanning the crowd until I find Alicia. She's chatting with a group of friends, head thrown back in laughter. One of the other girls grabs her hand and twirls her onto the floor, where the two of them dance in an overexaggerated fashion. Kenyon clears his throat, and my attention snaps back to him. To us.

I step toward him, and I swear I'm floating. I can't feel my feet as they move across the floor. He wraps my hand in his and pulls it to his chest, where his heart beats hard beneath his white shirt. His top button is open, and a rich navy bow tie hangs loosely around his neck, the ends of it brushing against my knuckles. He's so handsome tonight that it almost hurts to look at him. His other hand wraps around my waist, resting on my lower back, and I reach mine to his upper arm, holding his shoulder.

Everyone else disappears, and it's just me and Kenyon, spinning in slow circles around the dance floor as a song plays for only us. My heart races, pounding against my rib cage so hard that I know he can feel it, as I still feel his. The hand on my back flexes, pulling me closer to him, and my eyes drift shut.

This feels so good. So perfect. So *right*. I let my hand slide over his shoulder and to the back of his neck. My fingers slip into his hair, and I twist a lock around them. His breath hitches.

When I open my eyes, he's staring at me with an intensity that makes me stumble, tripping over my own feet. Kenyon's arm tightens around me, keeping me balanced. He lets go of my hand, and I press it flat to his chest.

He cups my cheek, and I lean my face against his palm. Kenyon moves to brush my hair behind my ear then rests his hand against the side of my neck. He takes a deep breath, trembling, the warm air moving the baby hairs on my forehead as he exhales.

"Kenyon, I—"

The song is over, and he drops his hands from me and steps back. My skin is suddenly cold in the absence of his touch. He smiles sadly at me, then turns and walks away.

I leave the dance floor in a daze, not stopping until I'm back in the parking lot. I text my brother for a ride and start walking toward home.

chapter
FORTY-THREE

"REMEMBER, WHILE THIS MAY BE THE END OF ONE CHAPTER, it's the beginning of the rest of your life, and the people you choose to take with you will make all the difference."

Ezra's eyes meet mine for a moment as he's speaking before drifting behind me to where our parents sit, along with Nana, Clark, and Eric.

I was thrilled when Clark showed up at the house this morning with Eric at his side to attend my graduation ceremony. My brother looked lighter than he had in years, and I finally understood how heavily his secret had been weighing on him all this time.

Our fight that night in my bedroom seems to have been a turning point for us. Maybe we should have screamed at each other two years ago. It would have saved us a lot of time. Or maybe— and I suspect this is the case—we needed the time to pass before either of us was willing to deal with our separate issues.

Ezra returns to his seat, his salutatorian speech over, and the principal gestures for all of us to stand and line up to receive our diplomas.

I can't believe graduation is already here. Back in September, this day seemed more like a distant possibility than something that would happen. Even a couple months ago, it seemed too far away to think about. But now, here we are, high school behind us and our whole lives still to come.

Names are called alphabetically, so I'm toward the back of the line. I watch as my friends cross the stage to receive their diplomas, first Naoise and Shyla, then, a few minutes later, Hadley.

My nerves break free when Kenyon's name is called, coiling tight in my stomach as he crosses the stage and shakes hands with Mr. Russell.

Suddenly, I'm not sure if I'm ready for this afternoon.

Before graduation, Donovan met me with my hard drive in his hand.

"Is it done?" I asked him as he handed it over.

He nodded.

"And everything worked okay?"

"It's perfect. Better than before."

The Sunday after prom, we'd all met at Hadley's house, and I told them my plan. If I had any chance of making this work, we needed to shoot some new scenes as soon as possible. We didn't have the Blackmagic anymore, so I had to catch everything on my Canon, but the new material would be able to transition into the finished film. I gave Ezra and Kira their revised scripts, and we agreed to film the next day.

It became quickly apparent that I don't have Kenyon's eye for shots, but I did my best and was happy with the results. Ezra and Kira were more comfortable with each other now, their chemistry palpable. We were able to catch the new scenes in only a couple hours, and then I passed everything off to Donovan to work his magic.

The hard drive is stashed in my bag now, and my anxiety skyrockets when I think about the fact that I won't have time to view it before the screening this afternoon. I only hope that this works the way I want.

Before I know it, Mr. Russell calls my name, and I climb the short ramp to the stage. As I cross, I look out over the audience to see my family, standing and cheering. Dad lets out a loud "Whoop!" and Nana smacks his arm, laughing. Eric has an arm tight around Clark, and Lylah beams so much pride at me that my chest constricts. My mom might be gone, but I still have the next best thing. This mismatched group of people is the best family a girl like me could ask for.

chapter
FORTY-FOUR

"THANKS SO MUCH FOR COMING OUT, Y'ALL," I SAY TO THE group of people gathered in Hadley's home theater. "We couldn't have done this without all your help, and I can't possibly thank you enough for everything you've done to help us make *Maybe, Probably*."

The room is packed with more people than I thought would be here. I'd expected it to be mostly cast and crew, but as I look around, I see my entire family, along with Hadley's sister and her fiancé. Mr. Welles hovers in the back of the room, and a couple kids from school who heard about the screening are settling onto one of the couches. Samantha is even here, but without Oscar the parrot.

"All right. The party's starting in two hours, so without further ado, let's start this show!"

The gathered crowd claps, and we move to find our seats. Hadley's dad volunteered the barn and yard for our all-night graduation party, with deacons from his church chaperoning. Outside, they're rushing to get everything set up before the rest of the senior class arrives, but inside, the room falls silent in anticipation of what's coming. I make my way to the back of the room and nod to Marcus, who dims the lights and pushes play.

The projector comes to life, and someone at the front hoots when Ezra's face fills the screen. My heart is racing, beating painfully hard. Dad squeezes my hand, and I lean over to wrap an arm around his shoulder, holding him tight.

With each laugh the movie pulls from the crowd, I relax a bit more. It's good, I realize. Really, really good. This might have an actual shot at winning me that internship. I'd always hoped that would be the case, but it's not until now that I feel I have a real chance.

We're getting closer to the new scenes, and the blissful calm I've been feeling disappears in an instant. Kenyon's in the second row, sitting with Donovan and Shyla. I watch the light from the screen flicker off his profile, and suddenly I know I can't be in here when he sees what I've done. I thought I could handle it, but there's no way I can watch his reaction.

"I'll be back," I whisper to Dad. He's so absorbed in the movie that he barely grunts a response. My chest swells with pride. My documentary-loving father is captivated by my little romantic comedy.

Outside, it's a flurry of activity. Workers are setting up a giant inflatable slide next to the barn, and one of the deacons is directing a bunch of college-aged guys as they put together giant yard games: larger-than-life Jenga, bowling, and Yahtzee.

Apparently, the way to celebrate graduating high school is to go back to acting like third graders. My classmates are going to love it.

I make my way across the huge backyard to the giant tree where Hadley and I used to climb as kids. There are less than twenty minutes left in the movie. I can hide out here until it's done. With my back to the tree, I sit on the ground and watch as the all-night party is built around me.

I hear footsteps close behind me a few minutes later. I turn as the steps slow.

Kenyon stands there, hands deep in his pockets. I scramble to my feet and wipe grass and dirt off the back of my dress. What is he doing here? I was supposed to find him at the party later. I'm not ready for this.

"You're missing the end of your movie," he says.

"So are you." I want so badly to step closer, but I can't tell how he feels about me right now. "Anyway, it's *our* movie. All of ours."

He runs a hand through his hair, and a stray lock falls in front of one eye. "I thought you didn't like grand gestures," he says.

So, he *did* see the new scenes—Adalyn's grand romantic gesture, letting go of her stubbornness and pride to run back to Sebastian and tell him she loves him. I was starting to worry that he left before that scene.

I shrug, trying to play it casual, but my heart is in my throat, racing. This is it. He's here in front of me, and he's seen what I did. My grand gesture.

"You were right," I say. "It's better this way."

He stares at me, and I watch as a war of emotions crosses his face. He seems uncertain, like he's afraid to let go.

Then his eyes lock with mine, and he flashes a quick smile. In two steps, he's in front of me, hands on either side of my face, holding me like I'm the most precious thing he's ever touched.

He leans down, and my heart explodes.

When his lips touch mine, I rise onto my tiptoes, trying to get even closer. I wrap my arms around his neck, my hands meeting at the back of his head as I pull him to me.

Kenyon's arms circle my waist, and suddenly I'm in the air. He spins me in circles, both of us laughing in between kisses. When he sets me down, I'm dizzy from either the spinning or the kissing. Maybe a bit of both.

"I'm so sorry," I whisper.

He doesn't answer and instead presses his mouth to mine again, softly. He barely brushes his lips across mine, the soft touches he gives leaving blazing heat in their wake. When I can't take the teasing any longer, I grab a fistful of his shirt and pull him down to my level, kissing him for real.

I don't know how long we've been standing there, kissing under the trees, when someone starts cheering. Kenyon and I break apart and turn toward the house. Shyla and Donovan are standing at the edge of the lawn, holding hands and laughing. Behind them I see the rest of our friends and family pouring out the back door and onto the deck. I force myself to let go of Kenyon's shirt and take a step back. We're both breathing deep, ragged breaths, and all I want is to feel him again.

Nana steps to the front of the group, Eric helping her over the uneven terrain. "Don't you stop on our account!" she yells across the yard. "You go right on and kiss that boy."

The crowd laughs, and I turn to Kenyon. My heart soars when I see his easy smile and, right in front of my dad and brother and all our friends, I take Nana's advice.

I kiss the boy.

chapter
FORTY-FIVE

THE OLD TRUCK SITS OUT BEHIND THE GARAGE WHERE Dad parked it the week after the accident. The glass has been replaced and, from this angle, you'd never know anything ever happened.

I flip the keys around my finger, clasping them tight in my fist each time they make a revolution. My hands shake, and my breath with them. I've not been in this truck since that night more than four years ago; I've done my best to not even look at it. But it's time.

The driver's side door makes a familiar groan as I pull it open, a loud *pop* sounding when the old hinges reach their limit. I climb inside.

Memories flood over me: dozens of days spent riding shotgun while Mom sped along the back roads, windows down and both of us singing at the top of our lungs. This was the truck she came to Wilmington in after she'd gotten her first bit part in a movie, breaking away from the parents who didn't support her dreams and making a life of her own. Even when she could afford a new car, she refused to sell this truck.

I sit for a few minutes, head back against the seat, eyes closed, letting the memories overwhelm me. I can feel her so close to me in this truck that I regret avoiding it for all this time.

The engine takes some coaxing before it sputters to life, its deep rumble soothing me. It coughs twice, but keeps running, ready to be driven again, finally.

Kenyon's waiting on his front porch when I pull up to the curb. I watch as he waves to his mom, who's working in the flower bed under the dining room window, then tosses a football to his little brother as he jogs across the yard. My chest warms with the same glow I get every time I see him. I hope with everything I have that the glow never goes away.

"Hey," I say when he climbs in. I lean across the long bench seat for a quick kiss before he buckles his seatbelt. "Did you talk to your dad?"

"Just got off the phone with him. He knows the date now— he'll be back at the end of October."

"That's excellent!"

He grabs my hand and rubs soft circles on my palm with his index finger. "I was thinking . . . maybe you could come to Colorado for Thanksgiving and meet him?"

"I'd love that." I've talked to Kenyon's dad on video chat a couple times this summer. He looks like his son, but instead of unruly, too-long hair, he has a short military crop, graying at the temples. I've enjoyed getting to know him the little bit I have so far, and I'm excited to finally meet him in person.

"So," Kenyon says as I pull the truck away from the curb, "where are we going?"

"You'll see." I give him a mischievous grin, and I wonder if he's also remembering our first date, when he said those same words to me before taking me to play mini golf.

The truck's stereo still doesn't work, so we ride in silence, the only sound the roar of the wind through the open windows. When we get close to where the accident happened, I reach for Kenyon's hand. He squeezes mine tight, grounding me. I wait for the familiar tingle of tears that will inevitably be shed, but it doesn't come. As we drive past, a calm washes over me instead—the warm hug of the mother who will always be with me.

I was afraid I wouldn't be able to find the right spot, but as soon as we round the last curve, I laugh at myself. There's no missing this place.

It's nothing more than an empty field, rolling hills dropping into the distance. Somewhere down in that valley, they hold the Bluegrass Festival every spring. Maybe I'll go one year.

I pull the truck off the road, bumping across the wild grass until I can turn us to face the right way. All the spare blankets and pillows I could find are stashed in plastic bins in the back, and I hop out of the cab to get them without a word.

"What are we doing?" Kenyon asks when he joins me around back. He sees the blankets and hops into the truck bed to help me lay them out.

The sky is starting to shift colors, the day drawing to an end, when we settle into the nest we've made. Kenyon leans against the cab, his arms around me, and I cuddle against his chest.

"I love you," he whispers into my hair.

Turning in his arms, I look up into the face I've gotten to know as well as my own over the past few months. His hair is still a bit too long, impossible to tame, a lock of it falling over his left eyebrow and in front of his eye. I reach up a hand to rest on his cheekbone.

When we kiss, my chest ignites with the light of a thousand fireflies. I twist to get better access, throwing one leg over his hips and straddling his lap. His hands run up my sides, raising goose bumps in their path despite the heat of the evening.

We kiss until we're both breathless, and I break away, resting my forehead on his as we try to regain control.

"I love you, too," I say. "So, so much."

He's leaving in the morning, heading for Colorado to start college. We won't see each other again until Thanksgiving break, and it takes everything I have not to focus on how far away that is.

The truth is, I don't know what will happen with us. Colorado is a long way from here, and college is a big deal for both of us. Maybe we'll be the couple that makes long-distance work, and our time apart will only bring us closer together. Maybe this night will end up being the last one we ever spend like this, wrapped up in each other.

I don't know, and possibly for the first time in my life, I'm okay not knowing what's coming next. Because I know that I love Kenyon right now, and I know that every time he kisses me, he makes the fireflies in my chest dance.

I never did find who was in that dark theater with me at Nana's party so long ago, but what I did find was so much better.

I may not know where this is going, but as I press my mouth to his again, I can't wait to find out.

ACKNOWLEDGMENTS

Every book has its own journey, and this book's journey was one I wasn't sure would ever happen. I owe endless gratitude to my extraordinary agent, Liza Fleissig, who was there every step of the way, tirelessly guiding me through countless false starts until we landed here. I don't know what I'd do without your boundless support and guidance. Seriously, a million thank yous can't quite cover it. You are the best.

To my uber-talented editor, Julie Matysik: thank you. For taking another chance on me, and for your marvelous work taking the mess of a book I gave to you and molding it into something we can be proud of. Thank you. (Again, because once is not enough. Neither is twice, but I only have so much room here.)

To the entire team at Running Press: thank you. My name is on the cover, but this book exists because of the awesome hard work of so many people: Amber Morris, Frances Soo Ping Chow, Becca Matheson, Duncan McHenry, Erica Lawrence, Kara Thornton, and Elizabeth Parks. I wish there were room on the cover for all of you. (The person holding this book is probably relieved it's not a billboard.)

Saskia Bueno, I literally squealed when I saw the first cover sketches. You managed to take a scene that existed only in my head and make it so much better than I ever imagined. How are you inside my brain? Thank you for giving me the cover of my dreams.

Huge thanks to Todd Cameron for your insight into all things broken legs, surgery, and hospitalization. If I messed it up, that's all on me, because your advice was invaluable. If I'm ever in need of an orthopedic surgeon, I know who I'm going to, but I hope to never have to see you professionally. Because . . . ouch.

Writer friends near and far, thank you so much for your support and encouragement. Mary, Jessica, Julie, Asher, and Sydney—my Montana Mythcreants—you were with me through the long slog of trying to find my next project. Thanks for listening to dozens of ideas that never got written and cheering me on as I finally wrote this one. Robb, Jen, Carrie, and Kellie—you all kept me moving through edits. You have no idea how much I appreciate your encouragement when the work gets hard. I may only get to see your faces through little Zoom squares, but I look forward to it every week. GROUP 16 ROCKS!

Sarah J. Schmitt, Jennifer Bardsley, and Erica George: you all inspire me more than you can possibly know. I feel so incredibly lucky that we found each other. (Thanks—again—for that, Liza!) How did we survive without a group text for so long? Thank you all for the gentle nudges and stern gifs reminding me to get back to work. I needed that!

It's easy to feel alone when you're deep in the process of writing a book, and I am eternally grateful to David Kirkpatrick for the loving, supportive community you've built with Story Summit. When I needed a place to land, to find fellow creatives to share my struggles and successes with, Story Summit was there to catch me. Huge thanks also to Debra Engle and Amy Ferris for everything you do with the Story Summit Writer's School. I've found education, support, and wonderful friends through the program, and I can't sing its praises enough.

Finally—last but never, ever least—to my family: How'd I get so lucky to have you three? For my boys, Connor and Holden, who cheer when I'm on deadline and resort to pizza for dinner. Again. I'm glad you still think I'm cool. You won't forever, so I'm going to soak it all in while I can. And Kelvin, my best friend, who takes it in stride when I'm lost in my own world and neglect the house for weeks on end. I'd promise to become a better housekeeper, but we both know that's a lie. So I'll simply promise to keep loving you the best I can. Thank you, eternally, for helping me chase my dreams. I love you.

Also Available from Rachel Bateman
and Running Press Teens

Available in stores and online
wherever books are sold.